NOW AND FOREVER

"You *want* me to touch you?"

"No! Y-yes. I don't know."

Where was that darned pesky conscience when he needed it? Where were all his vows and good intentions, his noble purpose in holding himself aloof to avoid getting further entangled with her? But Matt heard no inner whispers of caution when he caught Kate against him, when his fingers made nimble work of the ribbons at her throat and his lips found the pulse beating there.

Why didn't she resist him, remind him this wasn't part of their deal? Instead, her mouth was so wonderfully responsive, and almost as demanding as his own.

Books by Donna Valentino

Conquered by His Kiss
Mirage
Prairie Knight
Queen of My Heart
Always in My Heart

Published by HarperPaperbacks

Always in My Heart

Donna Valentino

HarperPaperbacks
A Division of HarperCollinsPublishers

🏭 HarperPaperbacks
A Division of HarperCollins*Publishers*
10 East 53rd Street, New York, N.Y. 10022-5299

This is a work of fiction. The characters, incidents, and
dialogues are products of the author's imagination and are not to
be construed as real. Any resemblance to actual events or
persons, living or dead, is entirely coincidental.

ISBN 0-06-108480-8

HarperCollins®, 🏭 ®, HarperPaperbacks™, and
HarperMonogram® are trademarks of HarperCollins*Publishers*, Inc.

Cover illustration by Jim Griffin

First printing: April 1997

Printed in the United States of America

Visit HarperPaperbacks on the World Wide Web at
http://www.harpercollins.com/paperbacks

❖ 10 9 8 7 6 5 4 3 2 1

1

"No change since your fourteenth call, Mr. Kincaid. Nothing can land or take off until this fog lifts." The airport dispatcher's voice came through the telephone wires sounding so clipped and bitten that Matt knew she had to be speaking through clenched teeth. "You're, uh, welcome to call back for an update."

Matt growled a thank you as insincere as the dispatcher's invitation and slammed the receiver into place. The digital display on the bedside clock wavered and then settled into 8:37. Or maybe only 8:31. Impossible to tell, since the top segment on the far right digit had burned out and no longer glowed red. All the numbers except one and four looked like they'd been scalped.

The most important day of his life. The biggest deal of his career. The final stepping stone toward claiming his destiny and achieving his long-nurtured heart's desire. All put on hold because the tiny private airstrip in this barely inhabited part of Nebraska couldn't handle traffic in dense fog.

Harlow Hastings, who owned the business that Matt meant to buy, had suggested this obscure campground alongside Nebraska's Dismal River for their meeting. Both men wanted to avoid media coverage; this sparsely populated area didn't even boast a weekly advertising paper, and rarely rated a mention in big city newscasts. More importantly, Hastings intended to commence his retirement on the spot by pursuing his interest in frontier history. The legendary Colonel W. F. "Buffalo Bill" Cody had ranched this stretch of Nebraska for many years. Historians tended to concentrate their studies on Cody's Wild West Show and North Platte holdings. Hastings had always wanted to explore this less well-known area of Buffalo Bill's life.

The lawyers had argued against conducting such complicated, important business away from the office, but Matt had willingly agreed to the remote location. No matter how lucrative the deal, self-made men like Hastings sometimes suffered last-minute pangs of regret when they actually sat down to sign their company over to someone new. Matt hoped Hastings wouldn't feel the tug of remorse with Buffalo Bill history practically oozing through the windows.

He had even ordered his secretary to find some Buffalo Bill memorabilia as a gift for Hastings. She'd unearthed a personal diary kept by some obscure drifter who'd lived during Cody's heyday. The diary sat in Matt's briefcase, tastefully wrapped and ready for gifting.

And now there was nothing to do but wait, and hope nobody succumbed to a last-minute change of heart. As if the thought provoked the very thing he sought to avoid, Matt felt a faltering in his pulse, a screaming sense of urgency to run and escape before permanently lashing himself to an anchor that would hold his spirit down forever. The muscles in his arms and legs bunched, ready to fight and flee a fate that suddenly held no appeal.

Amend that. Matt whipped his wayward thoughts back under control, startled by the foreboding that gripped him. Hastings might waffle, but his own intentions were cast in stone.

His life would change after today. Perhaps his inner agitation stemmed from eagerness to get on with it. Yes, that explained why he'd been roaring at full speed since before dawn, racing time. He'd insisted upon piloting his own aircraft because today he'd wanted to soar to his triumph, alone. Flying solo, the way he had throughout the years.

His tiny Piper was no match for the sleek corporate Lear, so he'd started earlier than the others and a brisk tail wind had helped him make better time than expected. He'd landed at the private airstrip a good forty-five minutes before the others were expected.

Nobody predicted the smothering blanket of white mist that appeared just as Matt steered his rental car onto the road leading to the Dismal Lodge. Recalling the terror of those few seconds sent adrenaline surging through him. He'd been damned lucky—he'd wrestled the car to a halt just as its nose kissed the large landscape boulder looming near the Lodge entrance. If he'd been driving a little faster, if he hadn't possessed a pilot's respect for fog, he might've ended up with his life's blood dripping down that damned rock. And that certainly hadn't been the destiny he'd traveled all this way to meet.

Both the Lear jet carrying the Kincaid Group lawyers and Hastings' own private aircraft had been diverted north; the lodge clerk had handed Matt the bad news when he'd checked in. They could all have been signing papers in the alternate location right now if Matt had traveled with the group. Instead, he'd spent the morning watching television newscasts, and cursing the stammering meteorologists who waved their pointers across weather maps in a vain attempt to explain why they'd been caught off guard by the fog.

He checked his Rolex. 8:32. "Jesus H. Christ," he muttered. A jittery sensation of entrapment pulsed through him, refusing to abate. Hard exercise would dull the edginess. A quick trip to the motel gym would help pass the time.

He yanked open the nightstand drawer and pawed past the omnipresent Bible. He pulled out a sheaf of brochures extolling the Dismal Lodge's amenities. A quick glance over the material told him he would just have to suffer. The aptly named Dismal Lodge didn't even offer a gift shop, let alone an exercise room. The fog hung so thick he couldn't go outside for a run for fear he might blunder head-on into a tree. Or that damned boulder.

That boulder, boasted the brochure, was the Lodge's main claim to fame. The enormous chunk of granite had been moved at great effort and expense from where it had once marked the boundary of Buffalo Bill's Scout's Rest Ranch. Bullet gouges and blood streaks still marked the rock, evidence of Buffalo Bill's innumerable battles against Indians.

"Yeah, right." Matt stuffed the brochure back into the drawer. The absence of an exercise room didn't make it any easier to stand still. Ten paces took him the length of the room to the closet offset, next to the Pine-Sol scented bathroom. Ten paces brought him back. With his arms out at his sides, he squeezed between the bed and so-called conference table, placing the customized heel of one Gucci-clad foot right

at the discreetly brass-tipped toe of the other. Twelve mincing steps carried him wall to wall for the width.

The lodge's best room held about a dozen square feet more than the cells they'd called bedrooms at Tylerville Juvenile Hall.

"Jesus H. Christ," he swore again, annoyed at being plagued by his carefully buried memories, today of all days.

But perhaps he shouldn't be surprised that they struggled for one last gasp. Once he absorbed Hastings Industries into his holdings, nobody would dare whisper about his somewhat unsavory youth. Magazines would list him among the top five hundred or so richest people in the world. Men with blue-blooded surnames would smile rather than blanch when he sauntered into their country clubs.

He had intended to reward himself today by picking a wife from among those very blue bloods. Some decorative female, appreciative of the worldly things he could provide, and smart enough to look elsewhere to slake her emotional needs. He'd battered his own into oblivion and had no intentions of ever rousing them again.

He'd held interviews of a sort—extensive background checks, followed by passionless and oh-so-polite bedroom romps that had narrowed the field down to a Tiffany, a Heather, and even a Pinckney who would suit his purposes well enough. With wealth in his wallet and the right wife on his arm, nobody would ever again sneer at Matt Kincaid.

He wrenched the insulated curtain away from the window. Fog pressed against the glass, cottony-white and impenetrable. Blank nothingness. If a crack suddenly developed in the thermopane glass, the silent mist could steal into the room, holding him immobile, stifling his screams of protest.

He gave a short, disbelieving laugh. For a man who ordinarily frowned upon fantasy, he'd certainly managed to conjure one doozy of an hallucination. Someone would probably claim that his anxiety, the sensation that he was suffocating, meant he didn't really want to embrace the glittering future he so diligently strove to achieve. Well, he didn't need to listen to that kind of psychological bullshit, especially from himself. Especially not today. He meant to embrace his destiny. Today. He meant to choose a wife. Today.

He closed his eyes, trying to visualize a beautiful woman floating toward him in a frothy lace gown, whiter than fog, drifting through a forest of white carnations pinned to white dinner jackets, all surrounding him until he drowned in a sea of bland, icy indifference . . .

His eyes popped open. The air-conditioning prickled against his forehead. His breath came in quick, short gasps.

This fog is giving you the chance to reconsider your goals, Matt Kincaid.

That intrusive, unplanned thought had sounded so clearly that it seemed someone had whispered it right into his ear. Matt shook his head to clear it of ridiculous notions. He hadn't gotten this far by filling his head with nonsense. Numbers. Dollar signs. He knew just what he needed—his laptop computer to productively pass the time.

Matt settled into the vinyl chair and reached for his briefcase. Annoyance gave way to anticipation. He loved his laptop the way he admired all finely crafted things. This little beauty represented the latest advances in microtechnology. His advisers had urged him to keep the computer buttoned up tight so the competition couldn't get wind of the astounding advances it contained, but he hadn't been able to resist packing it into his briefcase that morning. The notebook computer weighed less than the wrist weights he wore while working out and fit snugly inside his briefcase, leaving plenty of room for files— and brown paper-wrapped parcels.

Matt frowned at the packet for a moment before realizing it was the antique diary he'd brought as a gift for Hastings.

He wanted no reminders of how this day *should* have gone, so he ignored the diary in favor of his laptop. But as he drew the computer from his briefcase, it somehow snagged the diary's wrapping, ripping a sizable chunk from the brown paper.

Matt's frown deepened. He'd have to mention the incident to his design engineers. Customers wouldn't risk exposing the important papers in their briefcases to a laptop with destructive edges. He scowled at the ruined wrapping hanging from the diary. He couldn't hand a gift to Hastings looking like that. He shredded the rest of the brown paper away, revealing the title that had been inexpertly hand-burned into the worn leather.

Buford Tarsy: Diary of a Man Who Spited Them All.

A man who spited them all. Matt felt a mild stirring of kinship. For the first time that day, a smile tugged at his lips. He clicked the laptop open, but his gaze drifted toward the diary. Shaking his head over his folly, he pushed the computer aside and picked up the diary.

He tilted the chair and leaned back, propping his long legs atop the shaky little conference table. He flipped open the diary. After skimming the last few pages and wincing at the excruciating detail Tarsy used to chronicle his final days, he turned to the front and began to read. Within moments, he found himself lost in the misspelled, poorly punctuated, century-old adventures of a sixty-something jack-of-all-trades.

A chair leg creaked, snapping his attention back to the present. He blinked; his laptop screen glared an ominous-looking shade of blue that wordlessly scolded him for wasting time reading the diary. A glance at his watch told him he'd wasted fifteen minutes reading. Fifteen minutes! With a muttered oath, he tossed the diary to the side and pulled the laptop into its place.

He decided to memo the design engineers about the sharp-edged computer casing while the paper-tearing incident was fresh in his mind. But instead of an executive reprimand, he typed: *Buford Tarsy: Diary of a Man Who Spited Them All.*

What the hell was wrong with him? He'd been acting out of character all day. *So what?* whispered a voice in his mind. This remote location, the concealing fog, promised anonymity. He could do anything he damn well wanted to do without worrying that someone might catch him having fun.

He wondered when the concept of having fun had become something to be ashamed of. Longer ago than he could recall. So long ago that he wasn't sure what a profit-driven business mogul was supposed to do for fun.

"I'm sitting here talking to myself while I type the title of a stupid diary onto the world's most sophisticated computer," he mumbled, feeling the hot stain of embarrassment creeping up his neck.

He silently cursed his lapse while he deleted the title into oblivion. His fingers thrummed idly on the keyboard, and before he realized what he was typing, B-T-D-O-A-M-W-S-T-A, the first letter from each word in the diary's title, glowed from the screen.

His finger hovered over the delete key, and he

found himself remembering one of the solitary games he'd played to pass time when confined to his Tylerville cell. Back then, time had been something to get through, not something to use. He wondered how many words he could make up if his Scrabble holder held the letters B-T-D-O-A-M-W-S-T-A.

DOT. Nah, he'd be here all night if he went for three-letter words.

BOAT.

MOAT. Foursies weren't any challenge either. He'd shoot for fivesies.

TOAST. BOAST.

Hmm.

Er, *WOAST,* as Elmer Fudd might say when describing what he'd had for dinner that night. That one probably wouldn't count.

WAST-D. Bogus for *wasted,* as in all this time he'd spent screwing around. Hell, he'd never been any good at Scrabble.

"Christ." He whispered the curse, scarcely able to believe his own behavior. He clicked a few keys and strung a few short words into one. T-O-M, B-A-T-S, W-A-D. Drivel. He employed the delete key and then punched out D-O-W-M-T-A-B-S-T-A. More drivel. It wasn't even close to a real word.

Maybe saying it aloud would shake him out of the mental fog. "DOWMTABSTA!" he thundered, loudly, out of anger, at the ridiculous word, the fog, the waiting.

The room started to vibrate.

Fingers of fog seeped from the corners of the room toward the conference table. Impossible—unless . . .

"Earthquake!" He dived past the closet offset and wedged himself into the bathroom doorway. He pulled his suit jacket up over his head and wrapped his arms around it for extra protection.

And then, despite the bulk of his arms and the jacket muffling his ears, he heard music. A glorious fanfare, a wondrous sound, as if master musicians from centuries past had miraculously joined together, creating this single perfect moment. The music held him, resonated within him. The air shivered. He was completely submerged in sound, and yet felt utterly serene.

Tears pricked his eyes when the music shimmered into silence.

The room no longer quaked. He lifted his head and shrugged his jacket back into place—and then he froze. A shuffling sound came from the conference table, where his prototype laptop sat.

Son of a *bitch!* All of those annoying warnings from his people against removing the computer from the high-security lab took on sudden relevance. He cursed silently, wondering if the day's bizarre happenings had been organized by a particularly creative corporate technology thief. If so, he ought to try hiring the guy. *After* he rescued his computer.

He shifted into a crouch and edged past the closet, praying the thief didn't suspect his presence. Surprise was Matt's only weapon—and he threw it away by gasping in disbelief at the sight that greeted his eyes.

An old man stood bent over the conference table. Scrawny, saggy arms protuded from a tanktop that had never known a sweat stain. He'd tugged his jogging shorts snug up to his armpits, but they flapped loosely at his bowed thighs. His tube socks rose from spanking new running shoes, past spindle-shanked calves, over the bulge of his skinny kneecaps. He cocked his head from the laptop to the diary and back again.

"Stand away from my computer," Matt ordered,

though the man looked more like a sunrise mall walker than a technology thief.

The old man rested a palsied hand atop the diary and sent Matt a huge, gap-toothed smile. "Howdy do."

"Spare me the pleasantries." Matt stepped up to confront the man. He kept to the balls of his feet and held his arms in a deceptive tang soo do position, although he felt a little silly maintaining his wary edge around such a frail, bewildered-looking geezer. "Who are you, and what are you doing in my hotel room?"

"Yew don't recognize me?"

"Of course not," Matt snapped—and then he experienced a pang of doubt. "That is, unless you're Harlow Hastings?"

"Naw." The old man picked up the diary and pressed it against his concave chest. He closed his eyes briefly, rapturous delight radiating from him. "It's me, Bufie. Buford Tarsy. The man who spited them all."

"Oh. Of course you are." Pity flooded through Matt, along with the verdict: *Alzheimer's.* The old fellow must have become confused during the eathquake and wandered in here. He could just as easily be calling himself MicroTactic SuperSub Notebook as Buford Tarsy. Matt pasted on an encouraging smile. "Why don't you sit down, Mister, er, Tarsy, and I'll call the front desk. They'll know where you belong."

"Oh, I'm in the right place." The old fellow tapped the diary, which rested against his heart. "We ain't got no time for settin' and callin' desks. We got work t' do."

"I see." Matt attempted to humor the old man. "What kind of work might that be?"

"Hell, yew summoned *me*. It ain't my place t' be tellin' yew what we oughta do, though I have a right good idea."

Matt felt a sudden appreciation for the people who

cared for confused souls. These few minutes with the so-called Mr. Tarsy were already straining the limits of his patience. "I didn't summon you."

"The hell yew didn't." The old man scowled and hopped from one foot to the other, showing all the agitation Matt had sought to avoid. "Heard yew myself. Been waitin' nigh onto a hunnerd years fer my chance, so it ain't like I was apt t' come runnin' fer the wrong secret word, now is it?"

"Secret word? What secret word?"

"I ain't allowed t' say it!"

The old man's voice quavered. His rheumy eyes bulged, his liver-spotted face took on high color. Matt made soothing motions with his hands and spoke very softly. "Calm down now, Mr. Tarsy. We'll figure out how you got here."

Tarsy's jaw clenched with stubbornness. "Ain't nuthin' t' figger. Yew came here t' meet yer destiny, but deep down yew ain't sure it'll git yew yer heart's desire. Yew called out one o' the Almighty's names three times. Yew said my secret word. Yew heard them trumpets and harps clangin' and caterwaulin'. Yew know what all thet means."

"No." Matt leaned against the wall, baffled into curiosity. "I have no idea what you think this means."

"Why, it means yew sprung yerself an angel, Matt Kincaid."

"Where?"

"Here." Tarsy wiggled his shoulders and craned his neck so he could look at them, as if he expected wings would unfurl from the motion. "Me. I'm sorter like an angel."

Matt snorted his derision.

"Me 'n' Gabriel's jist like this." Tarsy twisted two

fingers together and then gifted Matt with a modest smile. For a brief moment, it seemed as though Tarsy's bent, ancient form was gilded with golden light, that the lingering wisps of fog hovered like angel's wings behind him. The illusion vanished when Tarsy scratched his stomach with the diary and gave a mighty yawn. He swiveled the computer until it faced Matt. D-O-W-M-T-A-B-S-T-A glowed from the screen.

DOWMTABSTA. Matt *had* spoken that nonsense word aloud; he'd cussed aloud at least three times, too. Maybe three hundred times, given his foul mood. Tarsy had most likely been listening in the next room while Matt harangued the airport dispatcher, while he'd cursed the fog.

But where did Tarsy get that sentimental crap about Matt's coming here to meet his destiny and achieve his heart's desire?

He'd never hinted to his most trusted advisers, not by so much as a whisper, that this day held special, personal significance for him. Tarsy couldn't possibly know that closing the Hastings Industries deal would catapult Matt's company into the financial stratosphere. And as for the personal significance of the day, well, not even the three contenders knew for sure that Matt meant to choose one among them for a wife.

Then, too, Matt was pretty sure that he hadn't told the old fart his name, but somehow Tarsy had known it. A tingle of apprehension coursed along his spine.

Matt picked up the telephone, intending to call the front desk. No dial tone.

The line had gone dead.

Tarsy chuckled. "Matt Kincaid, Big 'Un sent me here t' make sure yew don't screw up yer destiny."

2

Tarsy finished guzzling his third Coke and cast a hopeful look toward Matt's can.

"Forget it. I've already finished it all. I've spent all my change and this dump's antique vending machine doesn't accept dollar bills."

Tarsy shrugged. "Don't matter. Tastes right good all chilled like that, but I have t' say it carried more of a wallop in my day. Feller could count on a wild time if he swallered a belly load of Coca-Cola."

"Mr. Tarsy, you've had enough sugar and caffeine to wake up a dead man—"

"Thet's what I been sayin'," Tarsy interrupted, looking smug. "And I told yew, I like it when yew call me Bufie. Always did."

Matt pressed his fingers into his forehead and rubbed. He'd spent the past hour attempting to reason with Tarsy, to no avail. If anything, the oldster had grown even more delusional. Short of dragging him kicking and screaming from the room, Matt didn't see how he'd ever get rid of him. "Look, why don't we go find this 'Big 'Un' you keep talking about?"

"Big 'Un don't want t' see the likes o' yew fer a good long time yet. Why don't *yew* listen t' what I'm tryin' t' tell yew?" Tarsy challenged.

"Because you don't make any sense. You are not the Buford Tarsy who wrote this diary."

"Am so."

"Look at yourself. You're dressed like you should be running in the Galleria Mall's 1997 Senior Citizen Relay Race. Wouldn't you be wearing cowboy clothes, like chaps and a ten-gallon hat, if you hailed from a hundred years ago?"

"Big 'Un saw t' my duds. Big 'Un always takes care o' details like clothes."

Matt's headache jolted right through his fingers. Gentle coercion wasn't working; maybe getting quickly to the heart of the matter would shake Tarsy from his delusions. "Okay, Bufie, how did you die? I'm warning you, I've already read the end of the diary, and whoever wrote it knew how he was going to go."

A hint of uncertainty crossed Tarsy's face. "Why, I don't rightly know the answer t' thet, Matt."

"Surely a ghost, or angel, or whatever you claim to be, would remember something as momentous as his own death."

"Not hardly. Big 'Un set it up deliberate so's a body don't remember. Thet way, bad 'uns cain't gloat if they got away too easy, and folks what had a terrible passin' ain't stuck with painful memories throughout eternity."

"Well, that's awfully considerate of Big 'Un." Though Matt spoke sarcastically, the notion held a rather comforting appeal.

"Considerate, nothin'. Big 'Un jist wanted t' avoid gittin' bored. Yew ever git stuck in a room fulla people complainin' about their medical miseries? Even Big 'Un can stomach only so much when it comes t' hearin' about bursted innards and rough birthin's."

"I take it you're referring to God when you say 'Big 'Un?'"

Tarsy shrugged. "Cain't rightly say thet, either. 'Big 'Un's' sorter my pet name fer the Almighty. Yew can call the Almighty God if'n yew want. The Almighty'll listen no matter what name a body calls out, no matter what all them so-called religious leaders try t' tell yew." He cast a loving eye skyward. "Folks're always surprised at how easygoin' and nice things is once they git away from here."

"Let's bypass the theological discussions. Let's talk about that word, DOWM—"

"Don't say it now!" Tarsy shrieked. "It ain't time! Yew'll send me away afore I finish my assignment!"

"Well, now that you know the secret word, you could just say it yourself and come right back."

"I already told yew I cain't say it." Tarsy shot him a look that told Matt he expected better sense from a goat. "Hell, if dead 'uns could work their own keys, they'd be flittin' back and forth like lightnin' bugs."

"You mean every dead person has his own key word?"

"Ain't always a word. Everyone leaves somethin' behind, somethin' thet holds the key t' let 'em return and have fun doin' a good deed every now and agin. Didn't know it when I started keepin' it, but my diary was my key. It's jist a matter of the person in need o' a little divine intervention happenin' upon the key at the right time in the right place. Like I said, it took nigh unto a hunnerd years fer yew t' stumble acrost mine."

"Then maybe the secret word should be a little easier to stumble across, wouldn't you say?"

"Hell, no! Imagine what'd happen if someone was t' have an easy secret word, mebbe *beer*. All's someone in the right frame o' mind would have t' do is yell 'Hey, barkeep, gimme a *beer*,' and that poor heavenly soul'd be jerked there. Then supposin' the mortal says, 'Where's my *beer*, barkeep?' and wham! there goes the poor heavenly soul back t' where he came afore he has the chance t' git anythin' done. It'd wear him to a frazzle in no time flat."

Matt found himself nodding, beginning to see the man's point, and then sagged back in his chair when he realized what he was doing. If he kept talking to Tarsy, his head would end up as addled as the old man's.

"Okay, Bufie, you win. If I pretend to believe everything you say, will you behave yourself and leave?"

"Cain't go 'til I carry out Big 'Un's orders."

"And Big 'Un ordered you to stop me from screwing up my destiny."

Tarsy nodded energetically, the white wisps of his hair fluffing around his head like goose down. "Now we're gittin' somewheres."

"Sorry to disappoint you and Big 'Un. You've wasted your little visit. I'm a careful man. Even if today's deal gets blown, I have another one lined up. I can't screw up getting rich, because I'm already there."

"Huh?"

"My destiny. Money and power. My heart's desire."

Tarsy merely blinked uncomprehendingly. "Huh?"

"Fortune and fame—my destiny."

"Well, hell." Tarsy scowled, his features darkening with disappointment. "Fortune and fame? Thet sure is a pisser. Big 'Un said this'd be a good assignment. I was hopin' fer somethin' involvin' stuff like true love and findin' a haven fer a questin' heart, seein' as how I'm such a romantical sorter feller."

Matt gritted his teeth. "You're not playing along. You promised to behave if I pretended to believe you."

Tarsy blushed. "Ye're right. I got no call t' complain t' yew on account o' my misunderstandin'. Fortune and fame it is. What'll it be then. Lottery? Easy to do, and don't take no explainin'."

Matt couldn't help smiling. "I'm afraid a lottery win wouldn't earn the proper respect in the social circles I'm aiming to reach."

"I got an idea thet's sorter providential, considerin' as how it was my diary what got us together." Matt lifted a questioning brow. "How's about one o' them *New York Times* best-seller books what takes the whole publishin' world by surprise?"

"Everyone knows I'd never waste time on something as uncertain as writing fiction, Bufie. They'd suspect something fishy."

"Oh." Tarsy gnawed at his lower lip, and then smiled. "How's about an Academy Award? We'll git yew a part 'n' a share o' the profits in one o' them sleepers what earns a couple hunnerd million dollars—"

"No, Bufie," Matt said gently. "Really. I don't need any help in fulfilling my destiny." He ignored Tarsy's warning hiss. "A man doesn't get where I am today without developing a plan and following it without deviation. I'm in perfect control of my life. I never screw up. I don't need any help, not even from Big 'Un."

Tarsy's eyes bulged. He clapped both hands over his mouth. Matt reached toward him, concerned. Then two seconds later, Tarsy burst into full-throated laughter. He braced his hands against his thighs, rocking back and forth while he wheezed his mirth.

"I don't see what's so funny," Matt said through a clenched jaw. Nobody had dared laugh at him to his face in a long time, but that did nothing to ease his loathing for being the butt of a joke.

"Naw, I guess yew don't." Tarsy choked out one final guffaw. "Hell, I thought yew'd cotton to me bein' sarcastic jabberin' about lotteries and suchlike. I'm *really* plannin' t' send yew back in time t' make the personal acquaintance o' Colonel W. F. Cody."

"Buffalo Bill." Matt hid the apprehension that snaked through him. The nonsense about traveling back through time didn't bother him at all compared to Tarsy's mention of Buffalo Bill. Tarsy—or whoever he was—smirked at him, looking quite pleased with himself. How could he possibly know that the lure of Buffalo Bill had determined that Matt would be in this place on this day? What the hell was going on here? "My destiny has nothing to do with Buffalo Bill."

"Ain't what Big 'Un told me. Big 'Un says yer destiny's tied up back there with ole Colonel Cody."

"Tarsy—"

"Aw, it'll be fun, Matt. The colonel's a helluva feller." Tarsy jerked a thumb toward the window, where fog seethed so thickly it blocked the sunlight. "Anyways, Big 'Un saw t' it thet you ain't got nothin' else t' do t'day."

Nothing in Matt's career had prepared him for dealing with a delusional old man who considered time travel a perfect diversion on a foggy day. But nobody outside of Matt's circle of trusted advisers knew why he'd traveled to Nebraska. Tarsy's honing in on the Buffalo Bill angle hinted at a high-level strategy leak and demanded pursuing. Maybe, by playing along in an adversarial manner, he could trick the old fart into revealing what he knew about the Harlow Hastings deal.

"I'm not at all interested in meeting Buffalo Bill. From what I've heard of the man, he almost single-handedly wiped out the American bison. He'd be vilified by the environmentalists if he were around today."

Tarsy shot him a look filled with scorn. "I got but one word t' say t' yew: cow farts."

"Cow farts is two words."

"Well, excuuuuuuse me."

"Men who claim they've been dead since the turn of the century shouldn't try to imitate Steve Martin."

"Jist 'cause I died don't mean I stopped payin' attention t' the world's goin's on, Mr. I-Never-Screw-Up. Fer instance, I know thet yer precious environmentalists is all worried about thet there ozone layer. Could be Will Cody saved the ozone by cuttin' down the numbers o' them fartin' varmints. And he made up fer all thet huntin' he did. He kept a private herd fer his Wild West Show, and without Cody's animals, they might never have had enough t' start breedin' buffalo in captivity."

Matt abandoned his corporate espionage theory. Tarsy was nuts, plain and simple—and he knew a hell of a lot more about Buffalo Bill than Matt did. Matt hated arguing from weakness, so he shifted the debate to safer ground.

"I thought the concept of time travel had been pretty much debunked. Something about there being too great a risk of disturbing the time-space continuum."

Tarsy chuckled. "Yew can carry on all yew like back there. Big 'Un ain't hardly gonna let some mortal screw up the overall plan. Ain't nothin' yew can mess up thet Big 'Un cain't fix. Folks from there won't remember yew oncet ye're back here, and anything you did thet shouldn't o' been done'll be set straight."

Matt glanced at his watch. Nearly noon. He'd explored his own paranoid concerns, and tried everything else from common sense to patronizing, and nothing had swayed Tarsy from his rambling nonsense. Time to put an end to this madness.

"Okay, Bufie, I'll have to admit that you've given me a few laughs. But I have things to do and I can't baby-sit you any longer. I'm sure someone's looking for you by now. So you have two choices. You can let me get rid of you by escorting you to the front desk."

"Thet's only one choice, Mr. I'm-In-Perfect-Control."

"The alternative should be obvious. *You* can get rid of *me.* I'd be happy to let you send me back in time to meet Buffalo Bill if it'll get you out of my hair."

For the first time, Tarsy seemed struck speechless. The blessed quiet didn't last for long. "Yew'd go jist like thet, without even askin' me how yew'd git yerself back?"

"Considering that I don't expect you to send me anywhere, it hardly seems likely that I'd need to know how to get back. The alternative I suggested was meant to convey sarcasm, Tarsy."

Matt expected Tarsy would react with wounded pride; instead, the old man beamed with satisfaction. "Don't matter none if ye're sarcastic, so long's yew agreed t' go of yer own free will." Tarsy stabbed a finger at the laptop screen. "Don't fergit that word."

"Not to worry. I have a photographic memory."

"Well, ain't thet nice. All's yew have t' do t' start yer adventure is t' say thet word. Then, if'n yew want t' come home, jist say thet word twicet, and Big 'Un'll zap yew right back. Unless . . ."

"Unless what?" Despite his impatience, Matt couldn't resist hearing the balance of Tarsy's fantasy.

"Unless yew git yerself caught up in some sorter emotional involvement thet changes another person's life. Then the word won't work fer yew."

"So I'd be stuck back in time with Buffalo Bill."

"Naw. Yew can git back. All's yew gotta do is git the person whose life yew changed t' say the secret word twicet. But seein' as how yew didn't ask thet person's permission t' change their life, yew cain't jist ask them right out t' say the secret word, neither."

"This doesn't seem fair, Bufie. You're allowed to *ask* me to say the word, but I have to *trick* someone into saying it."

"The rules is different fer me than they are fer yew."

Matt grinned; he'd played under that assumption for all his adult life. "I'm afraid I don't have time for all that. I have to be back here by the time the fog lifts."

"It don't have t' take too long, Matt. There's a hunnerd ways t' trick a body into sayin' somethin'. Fer instance, jist write the word twicet on a piece of paper and ask the person t' read it aloud. Works ever' time."

"It sounds like a lot of trouble."

"Big 'Un figures thet once yew've changed a person's life, yew oughta think long and hard about leavin' them behind. One o' the rules is no one can come back with yew. Yew'll wanna be careful about gettin' involved with someone and then askin' them t' send yew away."

"Quite thoughtful of Big 'Un."

"Big 'Un's known fer benevolence and suchlike. Yew might find cause t' appreciate that little delayin' tactic. Now, lemme see if I'm fergittin' anythin' else." His wrinkled face screwed with concentration. "Oh!

The temporary indisposition. It takes a while fer the body t' git its sea legs, so t' speak. Yew'll be sorter paralyzed fer a good spell."

"This little adventure sounds more enticing by the minute."

"Well, look on the bright side. It's sorter hard t' git caught up in a life-changin' emotional involvement when ye're paralyzed."

"I'm quite good at avoiding emotional involvements even when I'm not paralyzed, Bufie."

"I know, son." For a fleeting moment, Tarsy's eyes seemed to contain a universe of knowledge, all of it sad. For a fleeting moment, it seemed to Matt that this demented old man actually pitied him—*him!* Matt Kincaid, the virile young turk standing poised to meet his destiny.

Matt turned away and faced the fog.

"I gotta warn yew, Matt, thet emotions get tangled up awful easy, in ways a body seldom considers. And sometimes a person fights agin' it when he should be embracin' it with all his heart. I won't be allowed t' help yew—yew'll be on yer own. Remember ye're in danger of screwin' up yer true destiny. Yew be careful what yew decide t' do back there."

"I'm not going anywhere."

"Oh yeah? Jist say the word. I'll go back where I sprung from and the word'll send yew on yer way."

"I'm tired of humoring your senility, Tarsy."

"Jist say it."

"No."

"Chicken!"

Matt glanced over his shoulder to see Tarsy tuck his hands beneath his armpits. Tarsy flapped his elbows. "Bawk! Bawk! Bawk! Yeller-bellied chicken liver! Hey, ever'body, Matt Kincaid's a chicken liver!"

"Screw it," Matt ground out. "If it'll shut you up, then listen to this—DOWMTABSTA."

Before Matt could reflect on the senselessness of rising to Tarsy's baiting, the window he faced shimmered into nothingness.

"I told yew there was a hunnerd ways t' git a body t' say the secret word." Tarsy's self-satisfied voice floated from the heavens. "Good luck, Matt. Try t' have a little fun, but don't fergit the rules."

Fog swirled through the opening, relentlessly suffocating. It stole Matt's breath, muffled his protests, numbed all feeling. It sucked his very consciousness into its roiling void, sparing him time for one single thought: the smothering of all sensation didn't put an end to the soul's pain.

3

When he was just a kid, and hadn't understood what a waste of time it was, Matt had spent every spare dime going to the movies. He'd hoarded his lunch money if his current set of foster parents earned enough to keep him off the free-lunch program. He'd looked for loose change between the living room furniture cushions and sneaked into closets to check through the adults' pockets when lunch money wasn't available.

He'd always considered the hunger pangs and the risk of getting caught to be worth it. No matter how dumb, how predictable the movie plots might be, there was always a moment—longer, if he was lucky—when he found himself sucked out of his own existence.

One minute he'd be hunched in his seat, his empty stomach growling from the scent of the popcorn he couldn't afford, his too-short pants riding up against his shins. And then the movie would start and reality would retreat. He'd be in the middle of the scene, his very existence reduced to a distant memory while he lived and breathed in a world of dreams.

Sometimes, though, the moviemakers delved into the world of nightmares. Just like now. An embarrassing terror gripped him, held him immobile, while cottony fog dulled his hearing, blinded him. Matt hadn't felt so helpless since those long-ago days, when an adolescent boy feared make-believe monsters more than life's real dangers.

This fog had the unearthly ability to mask physical terrors and send him spiraling into the recesses inside himself where he'd buried the monsters that could really hurt him. Loneliness. Heartache. A gut-clawing fear that the inevitable abandonment would strike the minute he let down his guard and dared to trust, dared to believe in promises.

He tried to scream, but couldn't work his throat. He tried to run, and couldn't move at all. The fog rendered him totally vulnerable to any physical threat, but he feared the resurgence of those old, inner demons far more. He always had. With a sinking sense of inevitability, he realized he always would.

But he had developed, long ago, a strength of will that let him switch mental gears. With a mere shift in thought he could seal off his fears and concentrate upon something totally banal. He tried it again now. Good-bye vulnerability. Hello . . .

Godzilla vs. The Fog Monster.

No. It had been *Godzilla vs. The Smog Monster.*

Godzilla would've had a tougher fight on his hands if he'd taken on a Fog Monster. Anyone who experienced this suffocating agony would advise the bone-headed reptile to tuck his tail between his legs and surrender. No entity could possess a more frightening weapon than this complete and utter desolation.

His mental gymnastics were working, because the mist seemed to be fading.

And he could smell the fog. Not a putrid Fog Monsterish smell, but something hot and acrid, like the odor drifting from a pistol range. Gunpowder. Gunsmoke. *Gunsmoke. Godzilla and The Fog Monster vs. Matt Dillon.*

Wait a minute—his iron-willed control proved he was Matt Kincaid, not Matt Dillon. He wanted to shout his name aloud, but his lips wouldn't move. The damned fog had sealed them shut. Frozen his eyelids open, too, which meant he couldn't blink away the burning, gunpowder-scented fog. Couldn't move away from the rough lumps that dug into his back. Couldn't move anything. Couldn't even think straight. Didn't seem fair, that the fog would drain him of everything except the ability to feel pain.

Just wait until he got hold of that Buford Tarsy. Tarsy must've clunked him on the head and dragged him out here into the desert so Matt couldn't turn him over to his caretakers. Embarrassment heated him from head to toe. Thank God there'd been no witnesses to his humiliation at the old man's hands. He'd never live it down if *Forbes* magazine ran a report revealing that Matt Kincaid, businessman extraordinaire, had half believed Tarsy's crazy promises, or that he'd fallen for a sucker punch from a scrawny old codger who could barely keep up his shorts.

Matt's back shrieked in agony when he started a slow, inch-by-inch slide down whatever it was that gouged at him from behind. It felt like he'd been propped against a big rock, like the huge, knobby Buffalo Bill boulder outside the lodge, and that it was stripping the flesh from Matt's back to pay for his temporary occupancy of the bullet-pocked surface.

Buford Tarsy's senile meanderings echoed through his mind, promising to send Matt traveling back through time, the fun-filled adventure of a lifetime tempered by a few moments of inconvenience. *Takes a while fer the body t' git its sea legs . . . yew'll be sorter paralyzed fer a good spell . . .*

Nothing good about this spell, Bufie, Matt wanted to say.

A woman's scream pierced his pain, in concert with a thunderous blast that vibrated through the air. The scream, the blast, mingled and reverberated endlessly while Matt continued his inexorable slide down the rock face.

Everything he heard sounded distorted, as if submerged in water, or like a recording played at the wrong speed. From somewhere beyond the dissipating mist, a man's garbled voice cried, "No, Kate, stop!"

The lingering wisps of fog disappeared, revealing to his unblinking eyes a sight that would've left him speechless if his vocal cords hadn't already been numbed.

A slender woman stood a hundred feet in front of him, framed by a gloriously blue, cloudless sky. The fringes on her buckskin dress fluttered in the breeze. Her chocolate-brown hair shielded one eye and curled down over her shoulder.

Her other eye was aligned along the barrel of an antique rifle, and he caught the merest hint of smoky green framed by long, long lashes. Her cheek pressed tight against the rifle's wooden stock; its sights aimed straight at his heart.

One slim finger still curled around the trigger. Smoke billowed from the bore. Matt thought about flinching. He would've had time to duck the bullet, if he could've moved. Everything around him happened in such slow motion that he could actually see the bullet barreling its way toward him.

"No, Kate, no!" hollered the unseen man once more.

"Oh my God! I couldn't stop, Henry, it was too late! Where in the hell did he come from?"

The bullet spiraled toward him. Hell, if he was Superman, maybe even Clark Kent, he could just reach out and grab it . . . but he was Matt Kincaid, ordinary mortal. He couldn't even wake himself up to bring an end to this ridiculous hallucination.

Look on the bright side. It's sorter hard t' git caught up in a life-changin' emotional involvement when yer paralyzed.

Sort of hard to evade bullets, too, Bufie, Matt wanted to say. Fortuitously, being paralyzed made it sort of hard to stand erect. It seemed to take an eternity, and yet Matt collapsed more quickly than would have been possible if he'd been able to exert conscious control of his muscles. The bullet plowed into his upper shoulder a good six inches above his heart. Burned like hell. So did his back. He remembered reading in that damned brochure that the bullet gouges and blood streaks adorning the boulder had resulted from Buffalo Bill's Indian fights. Ha! He folded into a semi-upright heap at the base of the rock with his back wedged against the boulder, his legs twisted and sprawled out like an octopus, his head angled along his burning shoulder. Probably looked like an idiot. He hoped he wasn't drooling.

The woman's face turned pale, even though he was the one losing all the blood. She gripped her rifle at arm's length, staring at it with the horror-filled expression of someone who'd accidentally hoisted a rattlesnake. She made an inarticulate sound of revulsion, and then flung the museum-quality firearm away from her with a wrist motion any Frisbee fanatic would envy.

Her companion—Henry, she'd called him—ran into Matt's line of vision. Ugly son of a bitch with craggy, Charles Bronson-type features. He lifted Matt's hand and swore when he loosened his hold and Matt's hand flopped into the dust. He tipped up Matt's chin and poked a dirty finger toward his eye. "Aw, shit," he muttered when Matt failed to blink.

"Is he . . . Is he . . ."

With his head propped up, Matt could see that the woman had taken shelter behind Henry and peered around his bulk. Henry gave a noncommittal grunt, and she knelt to inspect Matt's wound. "Oh, thank the lord! I hit his shoulder, Henry. A bitty hole like this won't kill him."

"Tell that to the judge. Look at how he's laying there. He's a goner, Kate."

Nothing, nothing could be worse than to lie there paralyzed and hear himself declared dead.

"No!" Kate stuffed her fist against her lips. Matt yearned to cheer her denial, but not even a thready gasp passed his lips. "I don't believe it. I'll find his heartbeat."

Two seconds later, Matt learned that there were worse tortures than being thought dead.

She leaned over him. Kate. She didn't cringe from the blood he felt trickling over his skin. She eased his shirt buttons free and ran gentle fingers across his chest, her sun-warmed hair brushing against his nipples. Her scent wafted over him, filling all the emptiness the fog had created with the intoxicating freshness of sweet, clean woman. He felt subtle, *very* subtle stirrings swell within his loins. Ha! Not everything had been paralyzed. No business deal he'd ever negotiated matched that little surge of elation.

"Good heavens, Henry, I do believe this fellow shaves his chest! It feels a mite stubbly."

"You can't be fondling a stranger out in the open like that, Kate, 'specially a sissy with a shaved chest. Button him up."

"I'm checking for a heartbeat." She traced the ridge along Matt's collarbone, and then lower, until it seemed that she outlined each and every muscle from his neck to his belly. No doubt about it, an interested, speculative gleam lit those stormy green eyes. Matt silently applauded all the sweat-drenched hours he'd spent working out with his Soloflex.

"He's so . . . warm. I don't think he's dead."

Henry rested his hand on Kate's shoulder and put a stop to her delightful explorations. "It'd be better for you and this poor bastard if he was dead. Get away from him now. I'll go fetch your rifle."

"We can look for the rifle later."

"We need it *now*. We have to finish him off and get rid of the body before anyone finds out what you did."

Kate rose and stepped away from the wounded stranger. She caught Henry's hand in hers, a once-common gesture that she'd avoided lately. She knew her touch would keep him at her side, take his mind off looking for her rifle, while she strove to find the right words, words that would allow her foster brother to back off from his impossible declaration without losing face. Since Pa had died, Henry had taken to turning pricklier than a porcupine in the presence of other men, and Kate wasn't at all sure that she could stop him from blasting that poor stranger into the next world if she showed any real concern for him.

"Don't worry, Henry, I'm sure he's not suffering.

And anyway, it's not like he's a wounded horse we have to put out of its misery. He's just stunned. I'll bet he cracked his head against the boulder."

She squeezed Henry's hand and prayed he wouldn't notice how quickly and eagerly she ended the contact. She turned her attention back to the stranger.

He hadn't budged an inch. She knelt in the dirt alongside him and stared hard into his unblinking eyes, willing him to understand that she hadn't meant to shoot him, that she couldn't fuss over him without riling Henry. *I'm sorry,* she mouthed.

Her heart skittered a little when she fancied she saw understanding kindle in his remarkable eyes. Golden brown they were, and sparkly as a polished topaz. She'd never seen eyes like that on any man, or hair like his, either, come to think of it. It sprouted thick from his skull, rich and honey-brown, shimmering gold where the sun struck against it. Most of the men around North Platte unsuccessfully tried to fashion their straggly, sun-dried locks into an imitation of Colonel Cody's long luxuriant style. This man had the hair for it, but he wore it chopped off to just below the ears. It fell back from his face with all the layered perfection of feathers along a bird's wing, looking as if no amount of wind or exertion could displace a single strand.

"We got to get rid of him one way or another, Kate."

Henry's interruption jolted her out of her inappropriate fascination. "You don't just get rid of a man, Henry. I'm going to close his eyes so they don't dry out in this wind." She pressed her fingers over the stranger's eyelids until they fluttered down and she found herself once again mesmerized, this time by the way his golden brown lashes spiked low and lush against his skin.

"You wouldn't have to close a living man's eyes. He's dead."

"No. He can't be." Her denial stemmed less from a reluctance to believe that she'd killed him than from a sizzling internal awareness of the stranger's essential masculinity. A dead man wouldn't make her skin prickle, her pulse quicken, just from being close to him. Blast! All her life she'd guarded against acting silly over any man. Maybe it was a good thing that the first one who tickled her feminity into life couldn't even twitch a muscle.

She cupped his head and probed gently through his hair, searching for bumps, hoping to find something, anything, that would account for his eerie stillness. His head lolled and she shifted to provide extra support. His face settled right into the valley between her breasts, robbing her of all breath. At the same instant a heated whoosh drifted from his lips and snuck past her buttons, tickling skin that had no business letting itself get tickled.

"Oh, God," she groaned, cradling him in her arms. "He surely is alive."

"Stand back, Kate. I'll get rid of him for you."

She hadn't even noticed that Henry had plodded off and found her rifle. "I don't understand you, brother. We ought to be thanking our guardian angels that I didn't accidentally kill this man—"

"I'm not your brother," Henry interrupted.

She flinched. There was nothing she felt less like doing just then than arguing with Henry over the essential nature of their relationship, but she could not let him believe, even for a second, that she was relenting in that regard.

"Maybe you're not my flesh-and-blood brother, but we grew up together and you're my brother in my heart."

"Hearts don't count for nothing, Kate. Townsfolk don't think so, either, or they wouldn't be so nasty about you and me living together now that Pa's gone."

"They don't understand."

"Sure they do. They know you and me ain't blood kin."

"Getting married would only make things worse. They'd . . . they'd consider it unnatural." *As I do,* she added to herself. "Everyone knows Pa raised us as brother and sister."

"And now Pa's gone, and the folks in town see it my way. If they considered us brother and sister, they wouldn't be gossiping so hard. The talk'll get even worse once they hear what you done to this fellow."

She welcomed the shift back to the stranger lying so still and silent in her arms. The battle with Henry had been raging ever since her father died; it was apparent she wouldn't resolve it now. She'd try again, after seeing to the stranger.

"I shot him by accident! He just popped up out of nowhere. Nobody can fault me for it."

"Everyone in town knows you're a sure shot. They're eager enough as it is to believe the worst of you. Nobody will believe for a single minute that you didn't shoot him on purpose."

Kate's arms trembled, and she lowered the stranger's head back against the rock.

"What do you expect him to do if you let him walk away from here? He's not going to tip his hat and thank you for shooting him. My guess is he'll hear gossip in town about us, about what you inherited from Pa. After he realizes that his injury's gonna keep him laid up for a while, he'll sue for big money."

Kate stared down at the stranger's still face. He looked so noble and handsome, as if wrangling with lawyers and initiating a flurry of paperwork would never enter his mind. He also looked like the last person in the world who deserved to get shot and knocked unconscious for no reason. "That would be all right. I didn't mean to do it, but I hurt him. I should pay. I can afford it."

"Maybe so. But you can't afford to stir up more gossip, not when you have that audition lined up with Colonel Cody. I wouldn't be surprised if a dozen female sharpshooters show up asking for jobs now that Annie Oakley's up and left the Wild West Show. The colonel'll have his pick. He'd never choose *you* if he hears you have a habit of shooting innocent bystanders."

Kate sucked in her breath and clutched her hands together in her lap. Thousands of people, *tens* of thousands of people, attended the colonel's extravaganzas. She'd always been so confident of her marksmanship that she'd never spent one minute worrying over what she would do if a child or careless adult wandered past the ropes and out into the arena while she exhibited her shooting skills. Annie Oakley had never shot an innocent bystander. Kate's head commenced pounding, as if the dreams it contained struggled to remind her of their existence.

"I guess you ain't as serious as you claim, if you're willing to give up everything for some no-account who had no business sneaking onto our property while you were practicing."

A wicked voice inside her head whispered, *Listen to Henry. He's right.* Her instincts countered with another suggestion: Henry was trying to force her to give up her dream by suggesting she'd have to condone murder in order to achieve it.

Henry seemed to sense her indecision. He turned smooth and persuasive, earning little cheers from her inner wicked voice. "He could be a rustler. It'd serve him right if we shot him for trespassing and buried him out here. Nobody would know."

"I would know," she said. If only the stranger would move, or jolt upright, or just pop back to wherever he'd come from—but he just lay there.

She wished that she hadn't closed his eyes, because now he did look sort of like a corpse. It would've been easier to point out the flaws in Henry's reasoning if the stranger didn't appear quite so dead. Maybe she ought to lean over him, let his breath warm her unmentionable skin again to remind her of how very much alive he was. Her cheeks burned with mortification, she craved his warmth so.

Henry continued his relentless assault. "Since it's so important to keep this quiet, I'll bury him behind the boulder where the ground's sandy. Easy digging, and lots of little stones to cover the grave."

To prove his point, he drove his heel into the ground, plunging a good two inches into the soft sandy soil. "I'm not suggesting this course for my account, Kate. I'm just offering one possible way to cover up your mistake. Of course, I won't be able to help you like this once you run off. You might want to think about how you'll bury your next mistake all by your lonesome self."

Regardless of his motivation, Henry spoke the truth about this accident destroying her chance of replacing Annie Oakley in the Wild West Show. But it would be easy to hide her mistake and go on as if nothing had ever happened. It would be easy to turn away while Henry took care of everything—but maybe not quite so easy to live with herself later.

She closed her eyes, wondering if that made her look dead, like the stranger. She sure didn't feel dead. She tried to imagine walking along and having someone blast her head against a rock, and to lie there helpless as a butterfly in a cocoon while strangers discussed digging her grave deep in sandy soil. No wonder people worried so much about being buried alive. She cracked open one eyelid to study the stranger. Her skin commenced tingling at once at the remembered feel of his warm breath brushing against it. She couldn't let Henry do what he wanted. Impossible.

Her hand drifted to the stranger's chest. Warm, pliant skin covered uncompromising bands of underlying muscle. The body of a man accustomed to sustained, strenuous effort and yet the hand curled in his lap bore no calluses or ingrained dirt. Odd. She tried to imagine herself wrapping all that golden male splendor in horse blankets while Henry's shovel scraped against stone and sand, preparing his easy grave. Even more impossible.

"We can't kill him, Henry."

"Kate, just think about this for a minute —"

"I've done all the thinking I have to do. Pa would tell me a fancy career isn't worth spit if it comes at the expense of a man's life."

Victory flared in Henry's eyes. "Then you're going to give up on your crazy notions."

She kept her hand on the stranger's chest and a tiny tremor rewarded her. His heartbeat. The sensation bolstered her resolve and seemed to lend her extra strength. "I'm not giving up anything. I'll take my chances. I want you to go fetch a doctor."

"I'll fetch an undertaker. He's dead, Kate."

"He's not. He needs a doctor."

"You go fetch one." Henry's face took on its normal sullen expression. "Unless you're afraid to leave me here alone with him, *sister.*"

She bit her lip in time to stop from telling him that that was exactly what she feared. "Please, Henry. I'd . . . I'd be grateful."

The old Henry would have offered her a shy smile, ducked his homely face, and gone off filled with quiet joy at doing something to please her. This new, distressing Henry studied her with the anticipatory, proprietary interest of a well-fed puma studying a baby elk, marking its position for the next time hunger pangs struck the puma's belly.

"All right, I'll go for someone who'll set your mind at ease," he said at length. "But you and me have some talking to do when I get back."

"We've never been at a loss for words with each other, brother."

"No we haven't, and that's another mark in favor of what I mean to discuss with you." He nudged the stranger's leg with his worn dusty boot. "Could be that this fellow did me a favor by showing up the way he did. I'll stand by you, Kate, no matter what happens. The way a man stands by his woman, if you get my meaning."

She didn't respond. After a long moment, Henry sighed. She felt him touch her hair and knew that he'd picked up a long wavy strand and wound it around his finger. He gave it a tiny tug, a gesture he'd often used to tease her—but one that, at that moment, struck her more like someone tying her to a hitching post so she couldn't run away. She fought hard to avoid showing her revulsion when he ran his finger down her back.

"Hurry, Henry. He needs help."

Henry mounted his horse and clapped his battered hat onto his head. "I'll be back."

4

I'll be back . . .

Who the hell did this Henry think he was—Arnold Schwarzenegger? Maybe so, considering the Terminator-like attitude he'd betrayed. Or maybe Matt hadn't been so far off in comparing him to Charles Bronson. Henry certainly exhibited a death wish.

Matt's breath hitched in a strangled-sounding burble meant as a laugh. *Godzilla. Superman. Terminator. Death Wish.* Who would've believed it? Matt Kincaid, business wizard, lying in dirt and obsessing over characters from old movies, while country bumpkins argued the pros and cons of murdering him and hiding the evidence.

Well, he amended, at least Henry was a country bumpkin. Nothing bumpkinish about Kate, even if she did favor cowgirl dresses. The females he pursued typically fitted themselves out in designer silks; he'd never realized how cute women looked wearing western gear. No wonder he overheard so many of his male employees talking about frequenting the country-western nightclubs. He'd never been invited along. He particularly relished the way Kate's chest fringes danced in the afternoon breeze . . .

He could see. He'd opened his eyes on his own!

She noticed. She didn't seem to be worried about ruining her pantyhose as she fell to her knees beside him. She peered earnestly into his face. He could see the bare hint of freckles underlying her golden tan.

"Howdy," she whispered.

She was really into this country-western mode. It suited her. Matt resolved to throw around a few western phrases himself, if he ever regained the ability to speak. For now, he could do little more than think *yippee kay aye.*

He blinked.

This cheered her tremendously. A radiant smile lit her features and he blinked again, partly because he had to, and partly because he wanted to see again how a simple shifting of lips and eyes could transform her into a creature of such ethereal beauty. Her eyes tilted with pleasure and glittered like smoky green emeralds. A delicate hint of pink tinged her cheeks. Her lips, invitingly full and soft, bore no trace of lip-stick but beckoned with the allure of a lone wild-flower blooming amidst a field of sun-dappled snow. He remembered Henry's comments hinting that unsavory gossip swirled around her, and couldn't imagine anything that such an innocent beauty could do that would cause tongues to wag.

Matt reined his thoughts in tight. Ha! There was a good western metaphor to remind him how careful a man had to be when it came to consorting with women. Kate's innocent charm could lure any man into forgetting what was best for him. *Almost* any man—certainly not Matt Kincaid. She didn't tempt him at all. Especially after what Henry'd said about the people in town holding a low opinion of her. Matt understood the risks of dallying with a woman who could turn into a social liability. No, he wouldn't be indulging in any sort of relationship with her, but he might as well enjoy himself. Bufie had, after all, urged him to have fun.

Fun. *Whoo-ee.* Fat chance. The first time in years that he'd contemplated cutting loose, and he lay flat on his back, paralyzed and unable to do anything about it.

"Blink once for yes," Kate said. Matt complied. "Blink twice for no." When he accomplished that, she expressed more delight than his most manly physical exertion had ever elicited.

"Do you hail from around here?" He blinked twice. "How's about kin in the area? Any close relatives who ought to know what happened to you?" He blinked twice again.

"Um." She moistened her lips with a quick darting motion of her little pink tongue. "How's about a wife?"

He blinked twice.

Her flush deepened and faded in the space of a heartbeat. She absently patted at her hair and tucked a shimmering sable strand behind her ear. Her glance skipped away and settled back on him. "Well, that's good. Not that you don't have wife or kin, I mean, but that we can sort of talk to one another."

He blinked once, and wished that she would smile at him again.

Instead, she lifted his hands out of the dirt and set

them carefully along his thighs. Then she scooted around until she sat out of his range of vision. He blinked twice, *no*, and then twice again, and then couldn't blink at all when he felt her hand delve its way between his back and the boulder.

It startled him, that she would deliberately initiate close contact. She had, after all, already determined that he lived and that his faculties were returning. How odd, that a woman would touch him in his dusty, bloody state, without bemoaning the damage to her nail polish or the staining of her dress.

"It doesn't seem right to have your sore head resting against a rock. And I can't stretch you out on the ground. I'm not strong enough to lift you, and it could hurt you worse if your head flops around while I pull on your legs." She wriggled closer until the softness of her breast pressed against his biceps. She tugged, giving a surprised little oof as though his weight proved more stubborn than she'd expected, and then tugged again until his upper body shifted away from the rock to be pillowed against the most exquisite cushion he'd ever reclined upon.

He tried to imagine the reaction of the women on his short list of potential wives if they found themselves alone with an unknown man in Matt's condition. Tiffany would no doubt crumple into a gibbering heap of hysterical tears. Heather would probably say "Ewww," wrinkle her aristocratic little nose, and mince away as fast and as far as her high heels would take her. Pinckney might order her servants to clean up the mess and have his body shipped off to some nursing home, where people who were paid to do that sort of thing could look after him. No doubt about it, such a cool and efficient solution to a messy problem would give the edge to Pinckney in the Kincaid wife sweepstakes.

But Kate . . . Kate comforted him.

He suddenly forgot all about his wife sweepstakes.

"There." Kate's breath caressed his ear. Her slim form cradled him from behind; her arms hugged his sides while her hands met across his middle. "I'll just hold you like this for a little while."

Every ounce of animosity toward Buford Tarsy drained right out of Matt. Getting shot and finding himself paralyzed seemed like a small price to pay for Kate's unique brand of coddling.

"I'll have to ease on out when we hear Henry's horse," she said a long while later. He felt her shudder at the mention of Henry's return and wondered whether she was aware of how she betrayed her aversion. "It'd probably rile him to see us sitting close like this. He took it too much to heart when Pa told him to watch over me. Henry wants to do the right thing but isn't sure how to go about doing it. He's kind of eager and clumsy, like a half-trained sheepdog."

More like a Rottweiler with homicidal tendencies, Matt thought.

"I have this horrible feeling that Henry's got himself set on doing something stupid. I have to figure out a way to make him back off a little until he calms down."

She shifted behind him. Matt worried that his weight might be too much for her, but she merely settled him into an even more enjoyable position, pillowed against her shoulder while her hair drifted over them both. "Is this okay?" she asked. "I know I'm a mite on the bony side. Could be I'm no softer than that old rock."

Her matter-of-fact tone told Matt she wasn't fishing for compliments—a good thing, considering his inability to speak. But his body stepped in with all the flattering responses his lips weren't capable of making. She thought herself bony? Good lord, she felt so firm and taut against him, so warm and supple! Those mild stirrings he'd noted earlier escalated into something that might embarrass her if she chanced to glance below his beltline. His pulse picked up its sluggish pace, coursing hot and hard, and he actually ached with the urge to touch her.

"Oh, hallelujah!" she cried. "Look—your fingers are twitching!" She gave him a rapturous hug that prompted even more blood-pounding and stirring within him.

He glanced down to see his fingers. And then he nearly lost all the progress he'd made by forgetting to breathe.

His hands looked much the same as always: wide, well-manicured, a little rough around the knuckles. But they rested atop denim-clad thighs. His thighs? Couldn't be his thighs. He distinctly remembered dressing in his charcoal Armani suit that morning. That son of a bitch Tarsy must've switched pants on him after knocking him in the head. No—Tarsy had been wearing jogging shorts. He must've stolen the suit, and then dressed Matt in the casual clothes packed in his suitcase.

But Matt understood that making the right appearance overruled common sense when it came to fashion. His designer jeans cost more than most off-the-rack suits. He didn't own plain denims like these, with such primitive stitching and boxy fit.

He didn't own a shirt like the one tucked into his pants, either, would never have wasted a dime on a garment constructed from such an ill-woven, unidentifiable material. His foot jerked, drawing his disbelieving gaze down toward scuffed leather boots that wrinkled around his ankles with evidence of long, hard use. Good lord, he was dressed like a cowboy fresh from the range!

Like someone set to make the personal acquaintance of Buffalo Bill Cody.

Big 'Un always takes care of details like clothes, Tarsy had said.

Impossible. There had to be a rational explanation.

Matt's head clamored with flashing images he'd been too dazed to analyze. Kate, decked out in fringed buckskin, firing an antique rifle. Henry, taking off on a horse instead of a quad-runner or motorcycle, hunting down a doctor instead of calling one over a cellular phone. They'd been babbling something about the Wild West Show, about Annie Oakley; they'd calmly discussed Matt's murder and burial as a matter easily hidden, as if they lived in the free-wheeling 1880s instead of the Big-Brother-is-watching era of the late 1990s.

Matt darted a frantic look around for something familiar, anything that would anchor him firmly in his own time. The rock they were propped against—it had to be that large landscape boulder, the one that had nearly killed him, outside the Dismal Lodge. But the lodge was nowhere in sight. No buildings, no airplanes droning high overhead, no muted roar from far-off highway traffic.

He took five breaths, not as deep as he would've liked, because his chest muscles weren't working all that well. Then he took five more.

The rush of oxygen cleared his head of the ridiculous notion that Tarsy had somehow pulled off his promise to send him back in time. He sucked in more air. It smelled almost too damned good, too rich in oxygen, the way air must have felt a hundred years ago. *Amend that.* He knew he had to stop thinking those kinds of thoughts, if he meant to banish his doubts.

His labored breathing must have alarmed Kate. She gently eased herself away from him until he rested once more against the rock. Matt decided he hated that rock.

"Are you all right, stranger?"

He forgot all about the once-for-yes, twice-for-no blinking signal. She looked so heartbreakingly lovely with her hair mussed from where she'd rested her head against his. No avariciousness, no speculation marked her features, only a genuine concern for him as a man, a selfless caring that he could never recall being directed his way. How could he have lived for thirty-two years without knowing a woman could look at a man in this way? His heart lurched, and something warm and fine flickered through him, a strange sensation, as though hopes that had been asleep for a very long time had stirred back into awareness.

"Kate," he croaked, and it felt fitting, that her name should be the first word to pass his lips since finding himself in this fix.

Sheer joy illuminated her, as if his rasping, barely intelligible grunt sounded sweeter to her ears than hearing Mel Gibson recite a Shakespearean sonnet for her alone.

Her unwarranted delight, and his own yearning to bask in it, started warning bells clanging in his mind. His self-preservation instincts came into play. Kate— no, better to think of her as *this woman*—had every reason to divert him with pretty smiles and pretended sincerity. She'd shot him, paralyzed him, and even though he felt the strength seeping back into his limbs, it could be some time before he determined whether or not he'd been permanently incapacitated.

"What's your name, stranger?"

"M-m-m . . ." He gasped for breath. "Matt."

"Matt? Short for Matthew?"

"Just . . . just Matt."

She broke into a wide smile upon learning his given name. "Our names give us something in common."

He doubted that. Not many people got christened by a wino who'd found a wailing newborn rolled up in a Kincaid & Co. bath mat. A county caseworker had told Matt all about his origins once, remarking that he'd been lucky that a sharp-eyed nurse had tacked an extra letter 't' onto his first name before recording his birth certificate. The one-blink-for-yes, two-blinks-for-no communication system couldn't convey all that information.

His silence didn't seem to bother Kate. "I'm just Kate. Folks're always thinking it's short for Katherine, but they're wrong. How about your last name?"

He tried, but couldn't squeeze *Kincaid* out of his throat. And, warned his instincts, maybe that wasn't such a bad thing.

He remembered more snippets of her conversation with Henry, the worry over inheritances and lawsuits. That typical, twentieth-century conversation revolving around the protection of assets in a litigation-prone era cheered him. So much for indulging the thought that he'd traveled more than a hundred years into the past! Surely Americans hadn't been so litigious during the 1880s.

But what would happen when they learned that Kate had shot Matt Kincaid, one of the country's most successful businessmen? Any remorse she felt could well vanish before the prospect of filing a countersuit against one of the richest men in the world. Any half-decent lawyer could make a case that he'd brought the incident on himself. Matt would rather cave in to an out-of-court settlement than listen to her lie on the witness stand, watching her expression harden into greedy self-righteousness without the slightest hint of warmth.

"Kate." He choked her name once again, dismayed at the difficulty of forming the single syllable, at the desolation washing away the odd sense of homecoming he'd found in Kate's arms. It seemed almost sacrilegious to find himself weighing his legal options rather than luxuriating in Kate's simple ministrations.

But then, he should be used to it. His careful relationships were always conducted with the utmost care. No man in his position dared risk a sexual harassment charge, a breach of promise suit. Even the bride he meant to choose when this weird nightmare ended would not be permitted to announce their merger to her friends until a prenuptial arrangement had been hammered out.

That was the trouble with women like Kate. She appeared so sweet and innocent that a man could be lulled into forgetting to protect himself.

Somehow, she sensed his new wariness. Her smile wavered. She tipped her head to the side, and her lips parted, but anything she meant to say or ask died unsaid when the pounding of hoofbeats intruded.

"Henry's back," she announced. She swiveled to watch her cohort's approach. Matt found he could turn his head ever so slightly, so he was able to see a cloud of dust that followed closely on Henry's heels. The cloud sorted itself out into a sorry-looking

wagon, pulled by a mangy mule, and driven by someone who looked very, very familiar.

The newcomer's wispy white hair floated around
his head like the blossom on an overblown dandelion.
His charcoal black jacket hung from skinny shoulders
and his trousers flapped loosely against scrawny legs.

Buford Tarsy. And that outfit he was wearing
matched the color of Matt's missing thousand-dollar
suit.

Tarsy sat straight and proud atop his wagon bench,
looking a good fifteen years younger, proving the old
adage that clothes make the man.

Relief left Matt giddy. He would have laughed at
himself, except he couldn't summon the strength. It
didn't matter. The rock at his back, Tarsy in his face,
proved he hadn't gone anywhere, let alone traveling
through time. He grudgingly gave the old man credit
for possessing a fine set of balls, for showing up to
accept responsibility for all that he'd done. Matt
couldn't wait to hear Tarsy's meandering explanation
for knocking him out cold and switching clothes. He
wondered how the old fart had managed to come up
with a mule-drawn wagon.

His fears, so vibrant a moment before, now struck
him with their utter absurdity. Thank God he had
been struck speechless! Kate and Henry would have
howled with laughter if Matt had dared whisper his
belief that saying a stupid, made-up word had
whisked him back through time. Now that he'd
regained the limited ability to speak, he ought to say
the word again, just to prove Tarsy had lied about
everything.

Yes, saying the word would dispel the last lingering traces of doubt. Tarsy had promised that saying it
twice would return Matt to his own time, providing

he hadn't done anything to change another person's life. Fat chance of that, when he couldn't lift a finger or utter more than single-syllable words. He could say that damned word a thousand times and still find himself lying next to Kate.

Or, if Tarsy had spoken the truth, repeating the word would fling him back to 1997, leaving Kate no more substantial than a half-remembered dream. The notion left him feeling sick with dread, while a sharp pain coursed through his right side, up high, near his heart. Probably from the damned gunshot wound.

Matt Kincaid wasn't afraid of anything. He'd proved it time and again throughout his life. "DOWMTAB-STA," he whispered, twice, and clenched his teeth, just in case the swirling fog decided to return and sweep him back into his hotel room.

Nothing happened. His heart pounded a joyous dance. Not because Kate bent over him, concern creasing her brow, but because it proved he hadn't traveled through time.

"What did you say?" Kate angled her head toward his lips.

"DOWM . . . TAB . . . STA." Damn, the weakness was returning. He had to catch his breath between each syllable.

She pulled back and treated him to a look of wide-eyed consternation. She reached toward him and then jerked her hand back, and then swallowed bravely and reached for him again. She gave him a quick pat on the shoulder. "Whatever you say, Matt."

He didn't care for her sudden wariness. Perhaps in his eagerness to show off his newly regained ability to speak, he hadn't made things as clear to her as they were to him.

"Still . . . still here," he rasped. "Nineteen . . . ninety-seven."

She tilted her head and a small frown puckered her forehead. Her hair cascaded into a silken pool along her shoulder. She looked like she couldn't decide whether he was stating the year, or quoting the price of the latest infomercial gadget.

He had to make her understand, even if talking set his progress back. He summoned his rapidly retreating reserves of strength. "Buffalo Bill . . . long dead. The air . . . I . . . I don't smell any . . . cow farts."

She rose and backed away slowly without taking her eyes from him until she was well beyond his reach. "You keep quiet and try to rest now," she said, and then she whirled about and began running to meet the approaching men. She formed a sort of megaphone with her hands.

"Hurry on up with that doctor, Henry! This fellow's gone stark raving mad!"

5

Well, Kate thought, she'd dipped herself into a fine pickle.

It had twisted her all up inside to hear the stranger's voice. Matt's voice. The way he'd murmured her name, stretching it out in a lingering verbal caress so that plain-old Kate sounded fine and classy, better even than a real fancy name like Ophelia or Marvella.

For a minute, when he'd said that one strange word, DOWM-something, she'd thought he might be a foreigner. A Frenchman, maybe, since she'd heard they had a knack for mesmerizing the ladies, but then he'd gone and ruined that notion by talking in perfect English about Colonel Cody being dead and . . . and *cow farts!* Good lord, her heart still hadn't regained its normal place, Matt had sent it plunging so low.

Of course, she couldn't hold it against him, because he had no way of knowing how thoroughly her dreams were wrapped up with Colonel Cody's continued good health. But it had seemed like a sacrilege to hear the rest of his nonsensical raving coming from Matt's firm, chiseled lips. It saddened her beyond reason to realize he must be nothing more than an addle-pated crazy man who'd stumbled across her path at the worst possible time.

What had she expected—that Matt had appeared by magic just when she needed someone to help her smooth over some rough spots in her life? She wrapped her arms around her middle as a tiny shiver coursed through her despite the unusually warm Indian summer sun.

Henry pulled up his horse and waited for her to come to him. It would be a victory of sorts for him if she approached him like a supplicant. Her feet dragged, but she had no choice. She had to coax Henry into helping her.

He studied Matt for a long moment, and then dismounted and stared down at Kate with smug assurance. "How do you know he's gone crazy? He ain't moved a muscle. Your mind's the only thing playing tricks on you, Kate."

"A man doesn't have to flail around to prove he's lost his mind." She recognized his companion and tamped down a twinge of annoyance. "And what on earth is Buford Tarsy doing here? You were supposed to fetch a doctor."

Henry's jaw tightened. "Bufie's reliable."

Kate knew her pa had enjoyed Bufie's company. The two of them had held memberships in several North Platte subscription societies. Bufie had been an occasional visitor to the ranch. He and Pa had spent most of those visits out in the barn, sampling her father's private whiskey store. Pa had never vouched one way or the other for Bufie's reliability. Kate had always considered the old man something of an opportunist.

She kept her opinion to herself as Buford tugged his mule to a halt and joined them. He made a self-conscious effort to slick down his wispy hair and brush some of the dust from his suit. When he turned toward Kate, she noticed that he'd fixed a doleful expression on his face that was completely at odds with the avid gleam in his eyes.

"So sorry fer yer grief, Katie. At times like this, it's quickest—I mean easiest on the bereaved if'n we—"

"Bufie belongs to that society that verifies the dead. I told you I'd bring someone to set your mind at ease. He knows a right nice funeral service." Henry didn't meet Kate's eyes. He strode purposefully toward Matt.

"Henry, stop!" She croaked the command through a throat gone tight at the certainty that Henry meant harm. She knew she could not permit her foster brother to spend even a half-minute alone with Matt. Henry's strong hands could bring down a near-grown steer. Henry's hands could just as easily close around Matt's throat; Henry's not inconsiderable weight could press against that barely moving chest and crush out the tiny spark of life before she or Bufie caught up with him.

And it would be her fault, all her fault. Even if Henry did the deed with his own hands, Matt's blood would be on hers. And Henry would forever have a weapon to hold over her head.

Henry halted, and cast her a look over his shoulder that silently dared her to voice her new distrust of his motives, and she knew her fears were grounded in reality. "He's not dead," she whispered, while a sense of betrayal such as she had never known rocked her to her core.

"Well, I guess that's why Henry brought me here. Figgerin' out if folks is dead is sorter one o' my sidelines." Bufie, oblivious to Kate's distress, patted his vest and dug inside a pocket. He pulled out a handful of cardboard rectangles and thumbed through them before choosing one. "Here's my carte de visite."

He pressed the card into Kate's hand. Unable to look anymore at Henry, she glanced down at the photographic image and saw Bufie standing alongside a closed coffin, wearing the same dusty black suit and with that same doleful look pasted on his face. She puzzled out the caption: Buford Tarsy, President, SPPBBA.

"Them letters stand fer 'Society fer the Prevention o' People Bein' Buried Alive,'" Bufie whispered respectfully. "Photographer says all them words won't fit on the carte, so I have t' explain the letters every time."

"I don't understand."

"Henry warned me thet yer so wild with grief over accidentally killin' this fellow thet yew won't admit he's a goner. If'n it'll ease yer mind, Katie, I'll rig one o' them Bateson Revival Devices inside his buryin' box so's he can ring a bell if'n he ain't really departed this vale o' tears."

"He's not dead," Kate reiterated. She lifted her chin and let her will silently clash with Henry's. "I'm not letting you get away with this, Henry. He was talking to me, not making much sense I'll admit, but talking. You can either go back and fetch the doctor, or I'll go into town myself and tell everyone what happened here today. *Everything* that happened here today. So you see, it won't matter if you hide the evidence."

"Evidence?" Bufie's interest sharpened perceptibly. "Say, Henry—this sounds a mite more serious than yew led me t' believe."

"Aw, hell." Henry glowered at Bufie, looking as if he mightily regretted bringing the old codger on the scene. He crossed his arms and shifted his stance, and then shook his head. "If Kate's so determined to destroy everything she worked for, I won't stand in her way. You just forget about this and go on back to town, Bufie."

Bufie had been following their conversation with so much head-swiveling that his hair had come unslicked. He darted out his tongue for a quick swipe over his lower lip. "Yew promised me a jug o' corn fer preachin' a funeral."

"Kate says he ain't dead. No funeral, no liquor."

"Well, thet sure is a pisser." Bufie scowled, and then brightened immediately. He began patting at his vest and pulled out his fistful of cardboard again. "Say, I got an idea! Why don't yew let me have a per-fessional gander at the feller. Could be he's only tem-porarily paralyzed. I might have a little elixir thet'll git him back on his feet."

He snatched his carte de visite from Kate's numb fingers and replaced it with another. She stared down at the new one for a few moments, working out the words. Buford Tarsy, Patent Medicine Specialist, read the caption beneath a photograph of Bufie wearing the same suit, trying his best to look wise and learned as he posed next to a table crammed with small dark bottles and stoppered vials. Bufie fished what looked like one of those very bottles from another pocket in his vest.

"I might try forcin' a little o' this down his throat." He cast Henry a sideways glance. "O' course, this bein' a sovereign remedy 'n' all, I'd expect t' be paid the same fer a dose as I'd git fer, say, conductin' a funeral."

Kate seized upon the idea. She thought she might do anything at that moment to distract her from Henry's perfidy. Also, she wanted more than anything to kneel once more by Matt's side, reassure herself with the spark of life glowing in his wondrous eyes, and maybe even thrill at the sound of her name coming from his lips. "I'll stand you to a jug of corn, Bufie. Let's try."

Matt watched them approach and felt his confidence plummet when he realized Tarsy wasn't wearing the stolen Armani, merely an ill-made frock coat and pants of a similar charcoal hue. Tarsy's swagger, and a firmer elasticity to his skin, made him look years younger than he had in the motel room.

Tarsy bent over him and studied him without the slightest flicker of recognition.

"My oh my, this case looks like a bad 'un. Mmm, mmm, mmm." Tarsy muttered doubtfully while studying Kate from the corner of his eye. She seemed unaware of the old man's assessment, and Matt wanted to call out to her, to warn her not to fall for any of Tarsy's tricks.

"Kate." He managed only her name.

As before, she took on a glowing radiance and it did not go unnoticed by Tarsy, who pursed his lips thoughtfully. "Curin' him could be a mite tougher than I bargained fer."

"*Two* jugs of corn, Bufie, if you unparalyze him, or bring him back to his senses." Kate made the promise as she dropped to her knees alongside Matt. He felt her fingers cool against the skin of his neck, felt them skim swiftly over his chest, as though she were embarrassed to be touching his bare skin but wanted to reassure herself that he still breathed.

He tried, as hard as he could, to draw a deep breath for her, and wished he could laugh at the irony. He'd literally showered women with diamonds and furs, and yet he knew with gut-deep certainty that no costly gift could please Kate so much as one hearty, rib-stretching breath. The realization sent an odd flutter through him, as if her gentle touch had somehow brushed against his heart.

Tarsy hooked his finger in the corner of Matt's mouth and tugged, and then poured a vile-tasting substance into the pocket between Matt's cheek and teeth. Tarsy clamped his hand over Matt's mouth, sealing it against Matt's inclination to spit it right back out. "There. Thet oughta bring a rise outta him if'n there's anythin' left t' rise."

The potion trickled down the back of Matt's throat. His nose and eyes began watering while the inside of his mouth and the lining of his throat burned as though he'd swallowed liquid fire. He recognized the taste from his long-ago college days when constant scrounging for tuition hadn't left much money to spend on alcohol. White lightning. Pure, unadulterated moonshine.

Kate watched with her hands clapped over her mouth. Her eyes watered, too, and her throat worked as if she'd swallowed a hefty dose of Tarsy's so-called cure herself.

Tarsy poured another measure. This one didn't blister Matt's throat or sting his nasal passages quite so much. He swallowed it, and the next dose went down even easier. After another mouthful, his toes started tingling.

"He ain't getting any better." Henry made the blunt announcement as he joined them. "You might as well just give up, Bufie, and be on your way."

"She promised me two jugs o' corn."

"After you promised to cure him." Henry jutted his jaw toward Matt. "If you ask me, he looks worse than he did before you started messing with him. His mouth's gone all slack and his eyes look like they can't focus on anything."

Matt didn't care for the image that created. He tried hard to smile, but wasn't really surprised when he didn't succeed. He smiled so seldom that those muscles had probably atrophied well before he'd gotten paralyzed. He focused all his energy on Kate, but looking at her only robbed him of caring about his own appearance. He was far more interested in the way the sun teased golden shimmers from her dark hair, and how gloriously green her eyes looked surrounded by the backdrop of dusty brown desert.

"It don't seem fair thet yew hauled me clear out here 'n' now I hafta go back with nothin'," Tarsy groused. "I stood ready t' preach a funeral. I dosed him with my remedy. It ain't my fault he didn't take t' either thing."

"No, this is all my fault," Kate rested a hand against Tarsy's shoulder. "Henry shouldn't have brought you here. There was nothing you could do. I guess . . . I guess nobody can help us now."

Tarsy straightened his shoulders, like a medieval knight accepting a challenge flung by his ladylove. "Could be I got another idee, Katie. Gimme back my patent medicine carte de visite." Kate handed Tarsy a cardboard rectangle that looked suspiciously like a black-and-white baseball card, which Tarsy stuffed into his vest. He rummaged through his pockets for a moment and then pulled out another rectangle that looked exactly the same and pressed that one into Kate's hand. "Go on, read the caption."

"It's a good likeness of you, Bufie." Kate studied the card with the intensity of an amateur astronomer given the rare treat of peering through the Hubble telescope. After a long moment, she looked over the cardboard at Tarsy. "Looks like you were wearing that very suit when you posed for it."

"Yup, it's my best 'un. I made sure t' change int' it after Henry came bustin' int' town lookin' fer my help." He scowled at Henry, and then turned a smile on Kate. "Go on, honey. Read thet caption out loud."

A line furrowed her brow as she studied the photograph. "That's a nice Bible you're holding," she said at length. "I haven't seen a crucifix so fine outside of chapel."

Tarsy preened modestly.

"And that expression on your face—why, I declare you look so kind and sincere!"

"Us reverends have t' be that way," said Tarsy.

"You ain't no real reverend," Henry growled.

"Am so."

"He sure is, it says so right here." Kate shoved the cardboard close to Henry's face. "The Rev . . . Rev . . ." She bit her lip and swallowed, as if saying the next words tested her bravery. "*The Reverend Buford Tarsy.* Isn't that what it says, Bufie?"

Matt understood her hesitancy in reading out the caption. He'd have choked over it himself.

"Got my mail order license straight from the Church o' the Righteous Redeemer."

"You're a fraud!" Henry said.

Bufie made a great, Christian-like show of twisting his neck to present his other cheek toward Henry. "I don't make much of a fuss about how important I am, seein' as some folks might consider bein' a ordained minister at odds with some o' my other sidelines. But thet's what I am. And bein' as I'm so sensitive t' the needs o' my flock, I kin recognize ye're in trouble, Katie."

"I am." Her lashes fluttered low.

"Kate," Henry warned her. "Watch what you say now."

She darted him a quick look and flushed, and then words came from her in such a rush that she didn't take a single breath, almost as though she feared she wouldn't finish unless she kept up her momentum. "I shot him, Bufie. It was an accident, and probably his own fault, but nobody will ever believe it. Colonel Cody probably won't let me audition for the Wild West Show if he hears about it, and Henry's afraid that maybe the stranger will haul me in front of a judge once he gets his strength back."

Tarsy chuckled. "Is thet all? Hell, I already figgered out a solution t' yer problems."

Henry reddened until his face resembled a cartoon thermometer ready to explode. "I've heard about all I need to hear. You two can stay here all day jabbering until you think you've solved everything, but you'll figure out soon enough that my way's the only way. I'll give you a couple of minutes to think about it while I have a look at my gelding's hoof. You call out for me once you come to your senses." He stalked away.

Kate caught her breath as if she'd been kicked. They all watched Henry until he crouched beside his horse and began poking at the animal's hoof.

Tarsy gripped Kate's hand and placed it on top of Matt's. He lowered his voice to a conspiratorial whisper. "There really is an easy way out o' this, Katie. All we got t'do is hold us a little weddin' ceremony. Lemme hitch yew 'n' this feller t'gether as man and wife."

6

Marry Matt.

Bufie's outrageous suggestion circled repeatedly through Kate's mind the way a hawk's whistle echoed round canyon walls. And just as the hawk's piercing cry declared its absolute soaring freedom, so would marrying Matt pronounce Kate's release from an intolerable situation.

If she married Matt, Henry would have to abandon his romantic notions. If she married Matt, she would be somebody's wife, and immune to the gossip and finger-pointing that condemned her and her foster brother for continuing to share the same roof without benefit of blood ties.

If she married Matt— No, there wasn't any point in even considering it. She was twenty-six years old, for heaven's sake! Her one and only romance had blossomed and died so long ago that she never even thought about it anymore. She was well set in her spinsterish ways.

"We'd better come up with another plan, Bufie. I'm not very good wife material."

"Who ever told yew a dang-fool thing like thet, Katie?"

She waved vaguely in the general direction of North Platte, where any number of women had taken delight in giggling over her feminine shortcomings. "Oh, I can shoot and repair guns, but I can't fix a decent dinner. I'm more comfortable cradling my Colt against my hip than a baby."

"Yer pa raised yew jist right. A man could use a straight-shootin', gun-fixin' wife out on this here frontier," Bufie said.

"Well, that's another thing. I'm not planning to stay on this frontier. You know I'm hoping to get hired by the Colonel. No man wants to marry a woman who'll be traipsing all over the world."

"Yew might have somethin' there. Sorry as I am t' say it, this feller's traipsin' days might be done."

And it's all your fault. Bufie didn't say the words, but Kate's mind did a fine job of filling them in.

"He's going to be all right, I just know it. But I . . . I guess I am rather obligated to care for him until he regains his health." She knew she sounded ungracious, but the words came hard. "That doesn't mean I have to marry him, though."

"Well, Katie, yew tended yer pa whilst he was dyin'. Are yew sure ye're up t' takin' on them private sortser tasks without the benefit o' vows t' pertect yer reputation?"

Oh lord, she hadn't considered the propriety of caring for the wounded man! The town's tongues wagged hard enough as it was just because she refused to evict Henry from the home where he'd been welcomed as part of her family for so many years. Sheltering another man under her roof, particularly a man so helpless that she would be responsible for attending his most personal needs, would indeed blacken her reputation beyond repair.

"Much 's I hate t' go along with thet Henry, I hafta admit he might have a point about this feller tryin' t' sue you. All the more reason fer yew 'n' him t' git hitched. Seems t' me I heard it said thet husbands 'n' wives cain't testify agin each other."

Kate pressed her lips together against the very unladylike urge to curse. Loud and long. And she knew exactly what she wanted to curse: Time, with a capital T. It almost seemed that Time had taken on a life of its own, that it had turned into a malicious imp determined to bring all the problems in her life to a head just when she was on the verge of making her dreams come true.

The more she thought on it, the better Bufie's idea sounded. She'd make a terrible wife, but then Matt didn't appear like he'd be a rip-snorter of a husband just then, either. Maybe the two of them would be perfect for each other. He couldn't make any conjugal demands upon her, wouldn't complain about her cooking, and she could tuck him into bed or sort of prop him up in a chair while she practiced her marksmanship.

She and Henry could regain the easy, companionable relationship she treasured, the only familial bond she had left on this earth. They had been close before Henry's sense of obligation and some incomprehensible male compulsion had twisted his feelings toward her.

Once things were back to normal and Matt was back on his feet, she'd set him free in exchange for his promise not to sue her. In fact, if she married him that very minute, she might accomplish everything before her audition with Colonel Cody. Why, she could gain her satisfaction over that blasted Time! Bufie's suggestion resolved every one of her immediate problems.

"I do," she blurted while waves of relief made her dizzy.

"I'm glad yew like my idee, Katie, but mebbe yew oughta give me a chance t' recite the weddin' ceremony. And mebbe we oughta ask this feller if he don't mind obligin' us with his name."

"Oh!" Good heavens, she didn't know a single thing about the man she meant to marry except for his given name. "It's Matt," said Kate. "Not Matthew—just Matt."

"Well, what about the rest? I cain't hardly pronounce yew Missus Matt, kin I? 'Sides, 'Kate Matt' ain't got no pleasant ring t' it atall."

She glanced down at Matt and immediately lost her confidence in the plan. His physical impact rocked her; it seemed impossible for someone who sprawled that motionlessly to exude so much power. How on earth would she tuck him into a bed without crawling in next to him to savor the feel of his heart beating next to hers, to press her toes against the heat she could feel wafting from him through the already warm desert air? How could she spoon the abysmal results of her cooking past that mouth without worrying whether the taste and texture pleased him, whether the food heartened him and gave him strength to overcome the injuries she'd caused?

The hint of a smile curved Matt's lips, and his golden-brown eyes glittered at her from behind his half-closed eyelids. She knew he'd heard everything she and Bufie had said, and wondered if he was amused by their audacity. A man like him didn't simply lie there and let himself be married to a sharpshooter just so she could discourage her foster brother's intentions, just so she could land herself a good job.

Matt had already told her—blinked at her, rather—that he didn't have a wife, but he looked well past the age when men settled down. It just went to prove that he was picky about who he chose as his wife, because she had no doubt that an endless procession of ladies vied for the position. If he had this much of an effect on her while he was paralyzed, imagine how women reacted to his walking, talking self! Why, they probably swarmed over him like ants attacking a honeybun.

"Is there someone else you're sweet on?" she asked, miserably certain of what his answer would be.

"N-n-n . . ." His response ended in a thready gasp.

"Sounded like a 'no' t' me," said Bufie. "I think he needs a little more o' my special remedy." He bent over Matt. Kate heard a glug-glug sound as Bufie tilted his small bottle, and when Bufie straightened, Matt looked somehow happier, if a bit dazed and watery around the eyes.

"Tell me straight out," Bufie demanded of Matt. "Do yew have any objections t' marryin' this gal?"

Matt wheezed.

"He didn't say no," said Bufie, looking inordinately pleased. "Looks like the weddin's on and I'm gonna git my two jugs o' corn."

Matt's eyes met hers. All the glittering amusement had fled, leaving only panic. She remembered all the taunts she'd endured while growing up and found herself more interested in honing her marksmanship than playing with dolls: *Boys aren't interested in girls who don't act like ladies.* Matt's apparent distress proved the point.

"I think he lost his voice."

"Well, I hafta admit, Katie, thet my remedy sometimes has thet effect on a body."

"Maybe we should wait until the effect wears off."

Bufie scowled.

Matt wheezed again. His eyes darted from Kate to Bufie and back again, while his lips formed a word Kate couldn't decipher. His fingers twitched and then curled. Bufie pointed toward them excitedly. "Say, mebbe he kin write us his answer." He produced a pencil stub from his coat pocket and pulled from her hand the carte de visite that Kate was still holding.

"Now, don't you go pressin' so hard on thet pencil thet you make marks clear through t' the other side," Bufie cautioned as he formed Matt's fingers around the pencil and slid the carte de visite, backside up, under Matt's fist. "I ain't got but three o' these reverend cartes left."

There seemed little chance of Matt's writing damaging the face of the carte. He lost his hold on the pencil in the middle of his first shaky stroke. Kate plucked it from the ground and rubbed the dust off against her skirt. She kept her hand over Matt's to lend support while he laboriously traced his letters, and tried to ignore how large and warm his hand felt beneath hers.

D-O-W-M-T-A-B-S-T-A.

His hand quivered to a halt, and he looked at her in a mute appeal.

"I . . . I don't know what you're trying to say," she whispered.

He began the process all over again, and she mentally sounded each letter as he created it. She tried blending them together, praying that somehow they would begin to form a word that she recognized. Not

for the first time, she regretted her early departure
from formal schooling, before she'd mastered the full
set of *McGuffey's Readers*. What with Bufie's assorted
cartes de visite and Matt's scribbling, she hadn't been
asked to read so much in one day since leaving Miss
Baxter's schoolroom.

She took the carte from Matt when his hand stilled
and another breathy sigh hissed from him. The letters
wobbled and slanted, but she could make them out.
DOWMTABSTA. DOWMTABSTA. Was that how he
spelled the gibberish word he'd said to her earlier?
She couldn't bring herself to say the word aloud once,
let alone twice, for fear she'd sound foolish. She
thrust the carte toward Bufie.

"This doesn't make any sense to me."

Bufie held the carte at arm's length and squinted.
"Must be important, on account of he writ it out
twicet. DOWMTABSTA, DOWMTABSTA."

Matt's eyes dimmed with disappointment.
Obviously, Kate thought, Bufie hadn't said the word
right, even though he'd pronounced it exactly the way
Matt had earlier, and the way Kate herself would have
said it. She was fervently glad she'd avoided embarrassing herself.

"He could've jist writ 'hell no' 'stead of all that
scrawlin', if he didn't want t' marry yew, Katie. I suspect thet since we was askin' about his full handle,
mebbe thet's his surname."

"Maybe it's senseless drivel to go along with what
you two have been spouting for the past fifteen minutes." Henry had evidently tired of waiting for her to
come to her senses. He stormed back into their little
group, his feet raising miniature clouds of dust. "Let
me see what you're yapping about." He snatched the
carte from Bufie and mouthed the words before

saying them. "DOWMTABSTA, DOWMTABSTA. What the hell is that supposed to mean?"

"I guess it's my new last name, Henry." Kate spoke quietly. She stared down at Matt, wishing for a minute that he was whole and well and could lend her a bit of strength at that moment. "I'm going to marry him."

Her words seemed to hang in the air long after the stirred-up dust settled back to the ground.

"No. I won't permit it." Henry gripped her shoulder and pulled her away from Matt's side.

There was nothing Henry could have said or done to solidify her intention more.

"I don't need your permission." Kate shook off his hold and stood. She met her foster brother's gaze unflinchingly, even though she wanted nothing more than to subside into a huddle of tears at what she read in his eyes. Her hope that they might regain their old, easy friendship died then and there. Henry stared at her with so much hunger that she knew he'd like to swallow her whole. His fingers curved as if he'd been practicing for the right moment, when he could wrap them around her wrists and never let her go.

"He can't have you. You're mine."

She understood then that he'd meant all along to force himself upon her, to make her his wife, even though the very thought made her shudder with revulsion. Matt's sudden appearance had simply provoked Henry into betraying his determination quicker than he'd intended. And maybe Time hadn't been impish after all in sending Matt her way, for she would've latched onto anyone—even Bufie Tarsy—rather than enter into an unnatural relationship with her foster brother.

She drew a shaky breath and stared down at Matt,

her unexpected savior. Flat on his back and helpless as an upended turtle, he looked as horrified as it was possible for a mostly paralyzed man to look. She had to marry him now whether he wanted her or not— and he obviously didn't want her. She vowed that she would somehow make up for all the trouble she'd caused him.

"Go on, Bufie," she said. "Start the ceremony."

"Dearly beloved," Bufie droned at once. "Uh, we're sorter gathered here—"

"I won't allow this!" Henry shouted.

"*Stop it, Henry.* Just stop it, before you make it impossible for us to even speak to each other."

Henry paled and backed away, looking as stunned by her fierceness as she was. He stared at her with a hunger, with a despair, that made her want to cry for everything that was lost between them. He whirled and ran to his horse, leaped onto its back and goaded it into a gallop.

She stood there while Bufie struggled to complete his ceremony, making no response when he muttered regrets over leaving his wedding tracts in his room and apologized for the many lapses in his memory. And when he asked her somewhat doubtfully if she would indeed take Matt Dowmtabsta as her lawful wedded husband, she said, "I do."

Her new husband stared at her unblinkingly, evidently so drained by agitation that he'd lost his limited ability to speak. Soon utter exhaustion settled upon him, until his eyelids fluttered closed.

Some wedding, she thought. Years ago, when she was just a girl, she'd allowed herself to dream she might find a man who could love her and marry her despite her unfeminine ways. She'd imagined that she'd miraculously be transformed into a perfect lady on her wedding day, all alabaster-skinned, with her unruly hair arranged in glorious curls, and her too-tall frame looking small and delicate in a gown fit for a princess.

She'd never envisioned standing on a desolate Nebraska plain listening to Bufie Tarsy stumble over phrases that lapsed now and then into what sounded suspiciously like a funeral service. Nor had she imagined that she'd have to bag a husband with a shot that would've toppled an elk in order to hold him still long enough to marry her.

But there she stood, with her knees skinned from kneeling in the dirt, with sweat pasting her hair to her neck, promising to love, honor, and obey a man who couldn't squeeze two words past his lips, taking on a new name she was afraid to pronounce.

She wondered how many of Matt's marital dreams she'd slain that day, wondered if he was the sort of man who might have looked forward to standing in a fancy church, watching his pretty, feminine bride glide gracefully down the aisle trailing yards of pristine white satin and lace. She doubted he'd ever considered hitching himself to a sunburned, buckskin-fringed old maid who smelled of spent gunpowder.

"Yew kin kiss the bride." Bufie finished with a courtly bow that brought him nose to nose with Matt. He backed up hastily when Matt's eyelids popped open to reveal a furious glare. "Er, mebbe yew'd best tend t' the kissin' part, Katie."

Kate bent and brushed a kiss against Matt's forehead. "I'm so sorry," she whispered against his skin. "So very sorry."

7

Something shriller and more deafening than a firehouse siren blasted against Matt's ear, jolting him awake.

Sunlight flooded the room, temporarily blinding his just-opened eyes. By reflex, he roared his best tang soo do threat to confound the unseen enemy while he clumsily lurched to his knees. The noise pounded him again, pinpointing the position of its source. Matt swiveled in that direction, grimly determined to give as good as he got.

His eyes adjusted to the light and he found himself ready to unleash his deadliest black-belt blow upon a wary-eyed, black-and-brown rooster clinging to the sill of an unscreened window.

The bird, not intimidated at all, puffed out its neck feathers and shimmied its wings, and then belted him with another eardrum-shattering shriek.

Let him crow, let him crow, let him crow. Matt

almost sang out the words in tune with the old Christmas-time refrain. It felt better than Christmas morning as he stared down at his upraised hands in wonderment. He could move!

He tested himself by swiveling his head, shifting his knees, flexing from the hips. Instant agony. His skull felt as if one more cock-a-doodle-doo would crack it wide open; his muscles screamed in protest. He relished every twinge. He curved his hands into claws and plunged them into his hair, and then began a systematic rubbing over every square inch of himself that he could reach. He wanted to weep from the relief. He'd never realized how itches could torment a clean human body, until he'd been paralyzed.

Abruptly, his hands stilled. He'd just been rather rudely awakened from sleep. Could it be . . . could it be that he'd *dreamed* all that stuff about traveling through time, being paralyzed and getting shot . . . being practically pickled in moonshine and forced into marriage with a cowgirl?

Absurd. More likely he'd succeeded in finding a place to work out, punished his body with too much hard exercise, and sought anesthesia in a bar. His muscles ached, especially his left shoulder. He glanced down and realized he was naked from the waist up, the way he often dressed for workouts, except that he usually wore sweats instead of boxy denims. Yes, a good solid workout had to be responsible for his discomfort. His temporary confusion, the lingering notion that he'd somehow earned those aches and pains while being jounced into near-toothlessness in the back of Buford Tarsy's buckboard, had to be the remnants of a whiskey-inspired dream.

Then he studied his surroundings. He knelt in a bed, upon a thin mattress that sagged so much that he doubted any boxspring supported it. His knees pressed through the mattress and made little pockets, almost as though only the webs of a net trapped each knee and stopped him from crashing to the floor. A worn, faded quilt drooped over his thighs. It must have been tucked over him and gotten dislodged when he'd jolted upright at the rooster's crow.

Everything in the room looked to have been built by a barely competent carpenter using nothing but planks. The headboard consisted of four planks. A plank door. Plank floors, with a small braided rug providing the only bit of color against the unremitting grayish brown. Plank walls, sporting a crooked row of wooden knobs that might be meant to hold hats or coats. A dresser of sorts had been fashioned with a plank surface, and two sideways planks formed the front of each drawer. Small squares of wood served as handles. A cracked china cup decorated with hand-painted roses adorned the dresser along with a rectangular wood-framed mirror.

He'd toured finer accommodations in the homeless shelters that were always begging for more of his money. The thought cheered him. He seemed to remember something about Kate being left well-off by her father, and this place certainly didn't look like guest quarters in a wealthy woman's home.

The rooster cocked its red eye toward him, and that gave Matt another idea. His pounding headache rivaled his raging thirst, and those discomforts coupled with the hazy state of his thoughts, could mean his eyes were just as bloodshot as that old rooster's. Maybe his hazy memory of belting down moonshine meant he'd gone on one hell of a drinking binge back there at the Dismal Lodge, and they'd brought him to this place to sleep it off.

It was a great theory. A terrific theory, providing he ignored the little voice in his head that whispered, *Oh yeah? You know you never drink yourself silly. What happened to your regular exercise clothes? What about the way your forehead still tingles where Kate kissed you, and your ears burn from hearing her say how sorry she was to marry you?*

Damn moonshine. All of these hazy half-memories were white lightning-zapped perversions of reality. No way a totally unsuitable woman like Kate would feel obligated to apologize for marrying Matt Kincaid, whom any number of trendy magazines had dubbed one of the world's most eligible bachelors. Marriage had been on his mind, so he'd had a nightmare about getting married. That's all it was. A good, old-fashioned nightmare, with enough residue lingering around to remind him how important it was to choose the right woman.

He made a sound of disgust and shook his head, ignoring the pain each movement sent throbbing through him. He had to get a grip on himself, stop mixing up fantasy with reality. There was no such thing as time travel, no goofy words he had to trick people into saying, no woman like Kate-with-no-last-name, who'd cradled him in her arms without knowing or caring whether he was a burger-flipper or a triple-digit millionaire. None of it was real. And that was a great theory, a terrific theory, so there was no reason why accepting it should leave him feeling as though something important had been snatched away just as he was about to grab on to it.

He took a deep breath to clear his mind, and gasped aloud at the agony shafting through his left shoulder. He grimaced and reached with his right hand to massage the ache and found a wad of cloth binding his shoulder.

He craned his neck and peered down at the obstruction. A large reddish-brown stain blossomed against frayed yellowed strips that looked like they'd been torn from an old sheet. Dried blood. Son of a bitch! He *had* been shot!

His head jerked up at the sound of a female outcry.

Kate stood in the doorway, staring at him with open-mouthed disbelief. She held a tray, which slowly tilted downward until its contents—a roll of bandaging, a knife, a pewter mug filled with steaming water, and a pair of scissors—slid off and clattered to the floor.

Kate had abandoned her cute buckskin fringes for a prim white blouse that buttoned up to her chin and a dark blue skirt that cinched her narrow waist and fell in soft folds clear to the floor. She'd gathered her hair into a loose puffy upsweep, with the bulk of its length wound into a little ball perched at the back of her head. She was decked out exactly like Tiffany, or Heather, or Pinckney—he couldn't remember which—when he'd escorted one of them to a fundraiser with a Victorian afternoon tea theme.

"Good morning," Matt said.

His cautious greeting caused Kate to drop her tray, too. It crashed so resoundingly that the rooster squawked and fluttered away in a panic.

"You . . . you're up," she said.

"Hard to sleep with that feathered alarm clock screeching in my ear."

Her brow creased with puzzlement. "Oh! You mean Jasper. That darned rooster's bound for the stew pot, if you want to know the truth. Why, dawn broke hours ago without him paying any attention at all, and . . . and . . . oh, good lord, you're up. I prayed and prayed all night, and oh, my stars, just look at you."

Her voice broke with a little sob, and her eyes, behind a suspiciously watery sheen, held something of amazement, more than a hint of relief, and a sudden embarrassment as if she felt guilty for liking what she saw kneeling bare-chested on her bed.

Something primal and deep reacted to her furtive admiration and made Matt straighten his shoulders even as his spirits slumped. Her presence proved that she was no mere figment of his imagination. Her reaction to finding him upright indicated that she'd expected to find him lying helpless, flat on his back, paralyzed. The crude surroundings, her attire, her comments about knocking off her rooster for dinner belonged to another era.

For a minute, he felt paralyzed anew by the realization that he hadn't dreamed anything. And then his common sense kicked in. Men in his position ran the risk of being kidnapped and held for ransom. His security people had developed a code that would let it appear he was carrying out a terrorist's orders while secretly communicating vital information to the people who were looking for him. Maybe he ought to try speaking in code now. Cameras could be pointed through those gaps in the plank walls. Tape recorders could be taking down every word he said.

Or maybe this was all an elaborate hoax to trick him into acting like a lunatic. He could see the headlines in the tabloids: *Business Whiz Can't Remember What Year It Is; Wall Street Sent Reeling.*

He shuddered, thinking that he'd grown more paranoid than his security staff. There had to be another explanation—but what? Cowgirls didn't gun down men like Matt Kincaid and hold them hostage in plank-walled rooms. Not in 1997.

That didn't necessarily mean he'd traveled backward

through time. A few well-chosen questions ought to dispel that nonsensical worry without branding him a lunatic.

"I seem to have one hell of a hangover. Do you have any ibuprofen?"

"Ibuprofen?" Kate's brow furrowed.

"Ibuprofen works best for me, but I'll settle for acetaminophen."

"I don't have *one* minnow fin, let alone a whole set of them."

It took him a moment to decipher her meaning, and then he gave a short laugh. "No, Kate, not 'a set of minnow fin'—acetaminophen, the non-aspirin pain reliever." She continued to treat him to a blank stare. "Like, well, like Tylenol." He grimaced as he said it. Kincaid Group owned a pharmaceutical company that produced generic medications, and he hated like hell to plug the name-brand competitors, even under these circumstances.

"You sure use a lot of strange words." She said it defensively, as if daring him to mock her for not understanding.

He eased himself off the bed and stood upright for what felt like the first time in a hundred years.

"You've never heard of Tylenol."

"No." She backed up a step, but he didn't think he'd frightened her by saying Tylenol, although his PR team would love it if it were true. "I've never heard of ibuprofen, or aceta . . . acetaminna something, or . . . or that other word you said yesterday, either."

He knew exactly what word he'd said the day before: DOWMTABSTA.

He reached toward the dresser for balance when utter certainty descended upon him. Against all odds, he'd been flung into another century. Everything,

everything Buford Tarsy had told him in the Dismal Lodge was true. He'd traveled through time because he'd said that stupid word. He'd somehow gotten himself emotionally entangled with one of the three people he'd met. The only way out of this nightmare was to get that person to repeat that damned secret word twice.

Both Tarsy and Henry had repeated it aloud without whisking him back to 1997, so that meant he'd somehow managed to change Kate's life. Kate was the only one who could set him free—and she acted as if she'd rather chew nails than say DOWMTABSTA.

His natural inclination was to bark an order, intimidate her into saying the word, but Tarsy had warned Matt that he couldn't come right out and ask her to say it, or the word wouldn't work.

"I said a word that confused you?" he asked with false casualness. "I wonder what it was?"

"DOWM—" she began. Matt's surge of elation was quickly dampened when she tightened her lips before the full word escaped. "I guess I don't rightly recall what you said."

She lied; she betrayed it with a sudden blush and a remorseful widening of her eyes. She looked so stricken by her minor prevarication that Matt wanted to pull her into his arms, hug her, tell her it didn't matter. But of course it mattered. He had better things to do with his life than hang around in the nineteenth century reassuring Kate.

She held you by the rock when you were hurt and confused. She promised you everything would be all right, whispered an inner voice.

He tamped down that memory. He needed to focus all his brain power to work out a way to trick her into saying the word, something that shouldn't be too difficult for a man who'd outwitted the finest business minds in the country. He'd tackled far tougher opponents than an Annie Oakley wannabe.

He winced at the cold-blooded cruelty of that thought. It embarrassed him, even though he hadn't articulated the insult, because he knew instinctively that Kate would never mock his dreams that way.

He wondered when in the hell he'd developed a conscience about such things. Thank God it had never plagued him during his own time, when a sudden pang of remorse could have fouled up more than one important deal. He stifled it with a low angry growl.

"Does the wound pain you, Matt?"

Kate crossed the room to stand in front of him. She reached toward his bandage, and then quickly lowered her hand. She twisted it into the folds of her skirt and darted him a glance filled with equal measures of guilt and chagrin.

"I meant to tend you, but I dropped all the necessaries. I've become a little clumsy lately."

She waved toward the spilled goods, a graceful gesture that contradicted her claim of clumsiness. He swallowed the urge to demand that she retract her comment. Every inch of her, from her hair to the polished black shoes peeping from beneath her skirt, looked smooth and shining and perfectly put together. There was no reason why she should think herself clumsy, and even less reason why he should hate hearing her ridicule herself.

"Do you always do that?" he asked.

"Not always, but Henry's remarked on it lately. I told you, recently I've gotten a little clum—"

"I'm not talking about dropping trays, Kate. I want to know if you always put yourself down."

She tilted her head and blinked at him, looking completely amazed by his concern. He'd pretty much amazed himself, as well. He swallowed, trying to quell the sudden tripping of his heart. He'd amaze himself right into a heart attack if he didn't stop this uncharacteristic concern for another person's feelings. It didn't matter squat to him if Kate needed a good dose of reassurance. People had to learn to look within themselves for strength. They'd only get disappointed and hurt if they depended on others. Kate ought to have learned that lesson by now. He decided to give her a refresher course.

He narrowed his gaze upon her, an old trick they didn't teach in Management 101, that forced subordinates to pay attention, and found himself momentarily diverted by her eyes. Smoky green, long lashes, beautiful without the false enhancements of powdered shadow or eyeliner or mascara . . . instead of the stern lesson he'd meant to preach, he found himself providing her with excuses for her weakness.

"Clumsiness had nothing to do with dropping that tray. You were expecting to find me flat on my back. I took you by surprise."

"I'll say you did. You still do."

He didn't know what startled her more: his absolving her of guilt for spilling the tray, or her sudden awareness of her proximity to his naked chest. She stiffened, appearing to lean back without moving an inch. She kept her eyes riveted on the spot where his skin met the bandage, as if she were intent upon counting every torn fiber that curled along the frayed boundary.

For a long moment, only the rhythm of their breathing broke the silence, Kate's light and erratic, his own harsh but otherwise controlled. And then he began noticing other sounds, soft and soothing things like birdsong trilling outside, and the whisper of dry leaves scooting over the ground. Such gentle sounds never intruded past the sealed windows of a Chicago high-rise. Or an LA condo. Or a New York apartment.

His breath stirred the few stray strands that had escaped the knot at the top of Kate's head. Her forehead came level with his chin, making her just the right height for talking to and kissing—not that he intended to do much of the former, or any at all of the latter.

He was accustomed to women who dieted and worked out incessantly, driven by the dictates of fashion. Heather, Tiffany, and Pinckney would envy Kate's taut fitness and demand to know how she achieved it without the benefit of exercise equipment. With her natural fine-boned delicacy, Kate looked more alluring in her sober attire than any supermodel who draped herself in the latest designer fashion. She carried herself and moved with the unconscious grace of someone perfectly comfortable with her body, as though she neither demanded more from it than it could attain or expected less from it than it was capable of achieving.

He'd been gulping a lot of deep breaths since meeting her, hoping to clear his head. He drew another one now and succeeded only in inhaling an intoxicating combination of soap, woman, and an elusive floral essence he couldn't identify.

"God, you smell good."

She pressed a finger against her lace-trimmed collar, and he imagined her dabbing a touch of scent onto the tender skin at the base of her throat just before she buttoned her blouse.

"It's lily of the valley. My mother taught me how to make a tincture of it when I was just a little girl. It was her favorite scent, too. I have a nice flower patch over at the house."

"You don't live here?"

"No, Henry and I live over in the ranch house. You're in our bunkhouse. I asked Bufie to drop us off here last night."

He recalled moaning half-conscious, inarticulate protests from the back of the wagon while she and Bufie had argued over what to do with him. "I remember you telling him that there wasn't enough moonlight to let him guide his mule around the gopher holes."

"Exactly."

But not quite exactly, and with the blush that crested her cheeks and the tip of her nose, she practically signaled that concern for Bufie's wagon wheels hadn't been her sole reason for keeping Matt away from her house. Matt dredged the murky recesses of his mind for a few more snippets of memory. He recalled how Bufie and Kate's discussion had revolved around Henry and how things might work out more smoothly if Matt didn't move into the main house straightaway.

"Did Henry come home last night?"

"Yes."

Matt phrased the next question very carefully. "Does he know you slept alone . . . on your wedding night?"

She hesitated, long enough for him to dare hope that she might be seeking the words to tell him that they weren't married at all, that everything that had happened over the past twenty-four hours was either a hoax or a delusion on his part.

"Yes," she whispered again, deflating his hopes. "It seemed to cheer him up considerably."

Anger seared through him, as explosive as it was unexpected. Matt Kincaid simply did not permit anger to rule him. And yet he found himself clenching his teeth to avoid bellowing his outrage—over what? Surely not because Kate's words conjured the image of a smirking Henry thumbing his nose in the direction of the bunkhouse while he locked Matt outside for the night.

Perhaps the rage stemmed from the unfairness of being ripped away from everything he'd earned. Yes, that was it. He wanted his old life back! He wanted everything, and he wanted it *now*. He didn't have time for this jaunt to the past, and he'd go stark raving mad if he had to spend another minute listening to that damned little inner voice. Even now, in the midst of his white-hot rage, it taunted him. *I'll just bet Henry was tickled pink to know she slept by herself last night.*

"Matt? Please . . . you're holding me a little too tight."

Dazed, he glanced down and realized he gripped Kate by the shoulders. "Oh, God, I'm sorry." He relaxed his hold, but found himself oddly reluctant to drop his hands.

She shrugged him off, and then cleared her throat for a shaky laugh. "I don't bruise easily. I'll be fine."

"Listen, Kate. We have to talk."

"I know. But let's talk later, okay? I have to look after your injury, which means I'll have to boil water all over again." She whirled away from him and then dropped to her knees and began gathering the scattered supplies, keeping up a steady stream of low mutters, taking herself to task for dropping everything.

Matt decided Henry probably had much to do with undermining Kate's self-esteem. Restoring her confidence would be a project any turn-around specialist would relish. It would be a delightful task to play Professor Higgins to this fair lady, so delightful that hanging around to help her could get *his* emotions tangled up. *Whoa, boy,* he cautioned himself. No more tiptoeing around—he had to get out of this time and place.

He crouched beside her. He caught her hand just as it lifted the pewter mug, and then he used his other hand to tip her chin so she would be forced to look at him.

"We just need to set a few things straight now. We can save all the details for later."

She stared wide-eyed at him, and then gave a tentative nod.

"I have to know—have you fallen in love with me?"

"Fallen in love with *you?* Ha!" She drew back and treated him to a glance of withering scorn. "I wish I'd never laid eyes on you, if you want to know the truth."

"But—" He bit his lip to keep from protesting. Kate *had* to be the one who'd gotten emotionally involved with him, or else the secret word would have worked once either Bufie or Henry had said it. "Believe me, the feeling is mutual. I wish I could leave this place right now."

"You can't," she blurted quickly. "I . . . I need you, Matt."

I need you, Matt. He couldn't remember anyone ever saying those words to him outside of the demands of business. He felt a dizzying wonderment for a moment, and a foolish smile tugged at his lips, until he remembered exactly why she needed him: to keep gossip down, and to discourage Henry.

And he had no choice but to stick around Kate until he could trick her into saying the secret word.

"I need you, too." The admission grated harsh against his ears.

"You do?" She blinked at him, and relaxed beneath his grip, losing some of her starchy defensiveness.

"I need . . . transportation . . . back to my . . . back to where I live." God, he sounded like a stammering fool, but admitting the full truth could lead her to lock him up in an insane asylum.

"I can lend you the money for a train ticket." She glanced at his wounded shoulder and then quickly away. "You don't even have to pay me back. I owe you that much."

"No! You're the only one who can help me." God, how could he talk his way out of this without sounding like an idiot? He decided to lie, and found he couldn't while he held her hand. He reluctantly abandoned his grip and then leaned away from her. "I . . . my memory's a little hazy, Kate. I'm not feeling up to going off by myself just yet."

"I knew you hit your head against that rock." She looked so miserable that he regretted his lie, but he couldn't risk failure by easing her mind.

"That's right. I hit my head and developed amnesia. Partial amnesia," he amended. "I'd like to stick around here until I get all my thoughts in order."

"If you stay on the ranch, you won't be able to tell anyone that I shot you."

"That's right. You see, I'd have to give details, and just now my memory's a blank."

"About everything? You don't remember where you live, or what you're doing here?"

"I don't want you asking me any personal questions. I'd only get frustrated, since I can't tell you the answers."

Her eyes widened with sympathy, as if she cared more about his lost memory than the damage he could cause by reporting her. She reached toward him, but he flinched away from her touch. He couldn't permit her to develop any soft feelings for him. Whether she admitted it or not, she had to have fallen in love with him. He had to get her to say the secret word twice so he could get the hell back to his own time.

"And I won't tell anyone that you shot me," he said.

"Thank you."

But he didn't want Kate's gratitude. He wanted . . . he wanted . . . he didn't know what the hell he wanted.

No, that wasn't true. He wanted to get back to 1997. The last thing he needed was a temporary wife who read more into his polite remarks than he intended. Kate needed protecting all right—from all those emotions that glowed from her gorgeous eyes. She had to toughen herself up.

But then she wouldn't be the same Kate anymore.

Well, what did he care? He'd be out of here before much longer. It wouldn't matter to him if she dissolved in a flood of emotion.

"My shoulder hurts. Take care of it." He barked the order like a drill sergeant trying to intimidate a raw recruit.

"That's what I aim to do." She spoke with a quiet dignity that shamed him. She lowered her voice until he could barely hear her. "I swear, I liked you a lot better when you couldn't move or speak."

He'd liked himself better then, too, he realized with a pang. Then, he'd been awestruck and grateful, content with her attention.

She rose, and kicked at the roll of bandaging that had turned soggy from absorbing much of the spilled liquid. "It'll take me a little while to get fresh supplies from the house. I'll be back in about—"

"I'm going with you."

She set her lips in a mulish line, and he knew she would rather invite a rabid grizzly bear into her home.

"It seems that we need each other just now, Kate. I'm not completely convinced that we're legally married—"

"Bufie's a reverend. He has a license."

"That may be, but he didn't get my name right."

Her interest sharpened. "Oh, how do you pronounce it, then?"

"Kincaid." He gave himself a mental kick as soon as he'd said it, for he'd lost an opportunity to make her say the word.

"Kincaid? But we thought it was Dowm . . ."

"Yes?" He urged her to say it.

"Matt Kincaid, huh? That makes me Kate Kincaid. It sounds a sight better than Kate Dowm . . ."

Matt gritted his teeth in frustration when she bit off the end of the word. It was apparent that it was going to take a good deal of trickery to get her to set him free, and he wouldn't make much progress if he was stuck here in the bunkhouse while she lived with Henry in the main house.

"There are other things that have to happen before a marriage is legal, Kate."

"Like what?"

She stared at him with such sweet innocence that he wished he could show her instead of tell her. "A marriage has to be consummated, or else it can be annulled. Henry will figure out soon enough that we're man and wife in name only if I sleep out here while you go back to the house every night. If he started blabbing about our sleeping arrangements, everybody in town would know we're not really married, and this whole scheme would have been for nothing."

She paled. "Then I guess we'll have to . . . sleep in the same room. Together."

A slight tremor shook her and shot to his loins as if they'd both been connected to a 220-volt power line. It sparked a craving within him to feel her tremble from passion rather than trepidation. His fingers curled at his sides, aching to curve around her instead of empty air, tingling with the need to loosen the top buttons of her collar so he could bury his face against the velvety hollow at the base of her throat and drown himself in the scent of lily of the valley.

"Sure, babe, we can sleep together if you want." Without thinking, he reverted to the low, husky predator's voice he normally reserved for sophisti-cated flirtation.

Kate's put-down technique might not work well in a New York City nightclub, but it served to squelch Matt's surging libido.

"I have to be honest with you," she said. "You didn't look like you were capable of . . . well, consummating. That played a big part in my decision to marry you."

He almost laughed. While he'd been worrying about her growing too susceptible to his charms, she'd been totally immune. Yes, it was almost worth laughing over, except for the niggling sense of hurt that she didn't find him attractive.

"Don't worry, I was only kidding. Actually, I was thinking you might have an extra sofa we could drag into your bedroom. I don't mind sacking out on a sofa for a little while. This is only a temporary arrangement, after all."

"Right. It's only for a couple of weeks."

Or less if he could help it. He thought he'd go nuts in a couple of *hours*.

"Right. It's only for a little while."

"Right." She paused, her brow furrowed in thought. "The problem is, we have but one sofa, and Henry would be sure to notice if we moved it out of the parlor. It wouldn't fit in my bedroom anyway."

The tip of her tongue edged past her lips while she pondered the puzzle. It left her lips moist, entirely kissable, and Matt spoke without weighing his words.

"Then I guess we'll just have to sleep together."

"No!" She pressed her fingers against her high-buttoned collar. "Henry works hard. He falls asleep early. I can leave our, I mean *my* bedroom, and slip into Pa's old room once he starts snoring. He snores something awful, but at least we'll know the coast is clear. I can be in the kitchen before Henry wakes up."

"I should be the one sneaking around, Kate. It doesn't seem fair to uproot you from your room."

"Oh lord, things have changed so much around here lately that I'll hardly notice one more difference," she said, waving off his concern. "Besides, I'll have to get used to sleeping in different beds. Once I start traveling with the Wild West Show, I'll be bunking down in hotels all around the world."

She was the type of woman a man wanted to keep at home, safe, away from other men's attentions. Matt felt a brief kinship with Henry. He could understand why Henry pretended to encourage her while secretly sabotaging her. If Kate belonged to Matt, he wouldn't want her gallivanting all over the world while he pined at home. He tightened his jaw before he could put those thoughts into words.

"Your plan should work, Kate. We won't have to sleep together."

He didn't much care for the cautious hope that sprang to her face. A woman who's just been told that one of *People* magazine's Sexiest Men Alive doesn't intend to make love to her ought to show a little disappointment.

But he couldn't touch her in that way, not even to give her a little taste of what she would be missing. He didn't know much about this time period, but he would bet that birth control wasn't perfected. The last thing he needed was to get her pregnant.

"I couldn't move my things into Pa's room, though." She still concentrated on working out the kinks in their plan while his thoughts had moved on to more pleasurable matters. Reluctantly, he turned away from the notion of having fun.

"No. Henry would be sure to notice."

"We'd have to pretend to go to bed together. I don't know much about a man's . . . I mean, I wouldn't want to do anything that would provoke your . . . I mean, I've heard that men . . ." She blushed and paled and blushed again. She clutched her hands together and the pressure pushed her breasts tight against the pristine white cotton of her blouse.

Matt swallowed the urge to tell her she didn't have to deliberately do anything to prompt his lusts—her unconscious movements did that well enough without any provocation. "Don't worry, Kate. I promise I wouldn't touch you if you were the last woman on earth."

She stared at him, all misty-eyed and blinking gratitude. "Why, I do believe that's one of the nicest things anyone's ever said to me, Matt Kincaid."

8

No man had ever stepped inside Kate's room. Oh, her pa had looked in a few times during that dark time after her mother died and Kate cried out from nightmares and grief, but that didn't count. Her grief had settled into a hard little nub permanently lodged near her heart. But the nightmares had embarrassed her, and she'd outgrown them quickly once she realized how much Pa and Henry depended on her to be strong.

When she and Henry were growing up, they'd sometimes played in her room because the space between her dresser and the window made a good pretend fort.

No grown man had ever crossed her threshold with the intention of sleeping within, until she led a half-naked Matt Kincaid to her room.

"This is—" she paused, while her mind added, *where you'll sleep.* "This is my room."

Matt nodded, and then looked over her belongings, treating each object to an intense analysis, almost as if he meant to burn the images into his mind. He expressed neither disappointment nor approval of what he saw, which heightened her nervousness. She tried making a joke of his scrutiny.

"You're studying my things so hard, I'll bet you could list each item by height and weight."

"By prospective value, too," he said, with no trace of humor.

"Do you immediately judge everything you see?"

"Of course. How else would I know whether or not it could be useful to me?" His glance drifted toward Miss Ada, Kate's treasured childhood doll, who sat in her usual place of honor against the pillow at the head of the bed.

Through Matt's eyes, Kate suddenly noticed how Miss Ada's porcelain skin had taken on a yellowish tinge, how the ruffles on the sateen gown her mama had made had faded except for the creases of the deepest folds.

"Not everything a person treasures has to be useful," Kate said in defense of her doll.

Matt did not answer, but he didn't seem convinced. She probably should feel embarrassed, a grown woman with a doll. Instead, she felt a stab of pity for Matt, that he'd never valued anything enough to cherish it after its original purpose had passed. When Kate got to missing her mother and father, she need only clutch Miss Ada to her bosom to be reminded how her pa had saved his money to buy that doll for her, how her mama had spent days stitching Miss Ada's special dress. Based on Matt's quick dismissal of her doll, Kate doubted that he'd ever been given a gift fashioned from love.

She shivered at the realization that he'd undoubtedly already turned his cold, impersonal calculation upon her. He'd grudgingly admitted that he needed her, so she supposed that placed her in the useful category. For now.

She vowed to be more careful when speaking to him. More careful when looking at him, too, because the sight of his bare, sculpted torso seemed to drive all sensible thought from her head. Her fingers tightened in the folds of the shirt she'd snatched from Henry's room. The sooner stout homespun covered Matt Kincaid's chest, the better, for her peace of mind.

"I washed your shirt this morning," she told Matt. "You can hardly see the bloodstains at all, but it's too shredded up to wear. I'll try mending it this evening."

Matt rubbed the bandage covering his left shoulder. "Shredded? You only shot me once."

She flinched at the reminder. "Well, lucky for you—lucky for all of us—the bullet went straight through."

"Ah. Entrance *and* exit wounds." He nodded.

"The back of the shirt got torn up some, too, when you slid down the boulder."

"That sounds like a lot of damage. From what I saw of that shirt, it isn't worth all the effort."

He spoke as if he had no more familiarity with his shirt than those few brief moments he'd spent staring down at himself while propped against the rock. And she'd never heard a more ridiculous comment than his saying his shirt wasn't worth fixing. Thrifty women sometimes patched their men's shirts so often that the original cloth was all but buried beneath the patches. Maybe Matt's assessment of her had already convinced him she wasn't good wife material, even temporarily.

"I don't mind mending it for you," she said. "I like sewing."

"Let me guess—Annie Oakley likes sewing, too."

She didn't care for the derisive edge to his voice, almost as if he scorned Annie's widely revered skill with a needle. "They say that all the top European designers are copying Annie's outfits." She was tempted to launch into a passionate defense of her heroine, but decided against it. Instead she bit her tongue and shoved Henry's shirt into Matt's stomach, taking a little satisfaction in his tiny oof of surprise. "Here, you can try on this shirt of Henry's. He's a large man, but I don't know if it'll fit you."

Sure enough, when Matt began pulling it on, the shoulders got stuck somehow around his upper arms. "Too tight," he pronounced as he shrugged it off. To her dismay he began yanking a sleeve, intent upon tearing it off. She'd never met a person so contemptuous of good clothing.

"Stop that! It took me hours to get that sleeve set in just right. You of all people ought to know how hard it is to get nice clothes."

"What's that supposed to mean?" He glared at her, but at least he stopped mangling Henry's shirt.

"It must be difficult for you to find clothes that fit." She gestured toward his naked torso. "What with you being built so funny and all."

"You think I'm built *funny?*" He stared down at the broad naked expanse of his chest and then scowled at her.

Mortified, Kate felt helpless to explain. It wasn't that Matt *looked* funny; if anything, the way he looked did funny things to her.

She'd never seen a man shaped like him, as broad as a blacksmith across the shoulders, slim as a boy around the waist, thighs as powerful as a professional bronco buster's. A woman couldn't live on a ranch for as long as she had without knowing the strength inherent in a man's body, but the male muscles she'd glimpsed usually didn't pop into noticeability until one of the ranch hands did something that required exertion, like branding a calf or tossing a bale of hay.

Matt simply stood there, doing nothing but look insulted, and she could see each and every muscle— from the sideways ones ridging his belly to the big powerful slabs banding his breast and arms—as clearly as if someone had outlined them with grease-paint. Everything about him fit together, from his long, unbowed legs to the shape of his head, and only the bandage marking where she'd shot him marred his perfection.

"I guess I shouldn't have said that," she muttered.

She might have launched into a full-fledged apology. She might even have gone so far as to admit how much she enjoyed looking at him, if he hadn't quirked his eyebrow and shot her a smug look that told her he couldn't wait to hear her tell him how perfect he was.

She swallowed her apologies. "I expect I could hack the sleeves from one of Henry's older shirts, if you think that would make it fit you."

She'd disappointed him, and maybe surprised him, as well, for she sensed a brief air of vulnerability, which he smothered at once. The contradiction struck her. A man who looked like Matt Kincaid shouldn't need verbal reassurances. Someone so outwardly confident should not be afraid to let any of his feelings show.

"You don't have to ruin one of Henry's shirts. I can buy—" He darted a hand into his britches pocket, and then turned so pale that she worried a spider had gotten in there and bitten his finger. "No, I can't," he said in a quavery kind of voice unlike his usual self-assured tones. "I can't buy a shirt. I don't have any money."

Henry would love to hear this.

"Most folks are cash-poor out here on the frontier," Kate said. "It's nothing to be ashamed of."

"I'm not poor!"

From the fierce way he snarled the denial, one would think she'd disparaged his manhood! "I told you before that I'll give you money. It's the least I can do. Just don't say anything to Henry."

"I don't accept handouts." Matt crossed his arms over his chest, which inflated the muscles around his upper arms to fascinating proportions. This further evidence of his physical power didn't scare her, though—she was too busy feeling confused, that she should find herself so physically attracted to a man with the personality of a treed cougar.

"There's plenty of work around here, if it'd make you feel better to work for pay." She crossed to the window and looked out over the ranch. "Horses, cows, chickens, pigs. Most hands are usually partial to working with one kind of animal over the others."

"I don't like animals."

"Oh." That was troubling; hands who didn't like animals tended to be mean-spirited and impatient, which fit right into the flashes of temper Matt had shown. "Well, there's always harness that needs mending, and it seems we no sooner get one section of the barn repaired than another starts falling apart all over again."

"I don't know anything about harness, and I've never hammered a nail."

For a man who claimed he didn't accept handouts,

he sure seemed picky about the jobs he'd tackle. She tried again.

"Henry's always complaining that he can't find enough hands to ride the fences. I'm sure he'd be glad of the help."

"If you mean riding a horse, forget it. I don't know how."

She stole a glance at him, wondering what on earth produced such a prodigious set of muscles upon a man who didn't appear to do any work of a manly nature. She couldn't think of any reason why he couldn't ride, or handle the most basic homesteading chores. "Well, what can you do, then? Are you a miner? A railroad worker? A bricklayer?"

He shook his head, dismissing every one of her guesses. "I'm a businessman, Kate. I work with my brains, not my body."

Kate swallowed. Except for Colonel Cody, North Platte businessmen did ordinary things, like ranching, or storekeeping. Of course, every town had its share of the unsavory sort who owned the saloons and gaming halls.

Matt had to be one of the other kinds of businessmen she'd heard about. Faceless, wealthy men who lived in far-off fancy towns, who bought up property sight unseen, who bribed the railroad, who foreclosed mortgages on hard-working farmers. She'd always imagined them to be bald and fat, puffing smelly cigars while they counted their stacks of greenbacks, not all golden and perfect like Matt.

"You must be from the East."

He parted his lips as if he meant to tell her where he hailed from, and then clamped them shut as if he'd reconsidered what he'd been about to say. "Not exactly. I pretty much divide my time among New York, Chicago, and L.A.—Los Angeles, I guess you'd call it."

"That's . . . that's a lot of traveling."

He shrugged, as if crisscrossing the continent was an inconsequential matter.

"Maybe you don't dislike animals, Matt. Maybe you're just not used to taking care of them, if you don't stay put in one place."

"An old cat hangs around the yard in L.A. I put out food sometimes."

"See that!" She imagined Matt saving a portion of his dinner beef and setting it outside for an old cat. "You must like cats, at least."

"No."

"Well, what do you do when she jumps onto your lap?"

"It . . . she doesn't."

"Maybe she's afraid to trust you, if you keep leaving her."

"Then she's smart."

His comment sounded like a warning, reminding her that he intended to leave her before too long. Well, he needn't bother warning her, she wouldn't be doing any cuddling on his lap.

And good lord, you would think he feared using up his lifetime supply of words from the way he rationed them. She'd never met anyone so blasted hard to talk to. She ought to leave him with nothing but his surly self for company while she found a shirt for him to wear. She edged toward the door, and then found herself blurting information sure to bore a coast-to-coast businessman.

"I've never been outside Nebraska, except for when I was a little girl. I was born in Kansas, and we only lived there a few years before moving here, so Nebraska's all I remember."

"So this has been your home for our entire life."

Once again, his attention swept over her room. All his smug derision deserted him, to be replaced by a wistfulness, as if he would happily have traded all his traveling for her stick-in-the-mud existence. With Matt studying her room and looking somewhat envious, she realized for the first time how difficult it would be to leave everything she'd known and loved for all her life.

"I don't know much about traveling," she said.

"You'll learn fast enough when you join the Wild West Show."

It was a brief comment, so short that he didn't even have to draw breath before making it, and yet it was more profound than any long-winded speech she'd ever heard.

When you join the Wild West Show, Matt had said. Not *if you get hired,* or *on the off-chance Colonel Cody takes you on,* but *when you join.* It felt so good to hear someone besides herself express confidence in her abilities. Nobody had truly believed in her since her pa had died.

Henry continued to encourage her, but she sensed an element of indulgence in his approval. As if she was an everyday cow pony who occasionally exhibited an extra burst of speed, but one Henry never expected to win the big race without getting exceptionally lucky. Matt, now, with a few words, made it sound as if the realization of her dream rested in her own two hands. As if she alone controlled her destiny, and nothing could stand in her way.

"You know what it's like, don't you?" she marveled. She knew as soon as she'd said the words that they were true. Everything about him, from the proud tilt of his head to the determined glint in those remarkable topaz-colored eyes, practically screamed that here was a man who knew what it meant to want something so much it made you ache; a man who understood that no sacrifice was too great, if you could just somehow make your dream come true. Matt Kincaid knew exactly what he wanted from life, and he meant to get it.

Except for yesterday, when he'd had a gunshot wound and an unwanted wife foisted on him.

"Enough about me," he said abruptly, though she felt sure she hadn't made any of her observations out loud. "Tell me how you spend your days."

His voice was like liquid honey, warm and rich and so intoxicating that she wouldn't mind feeling it pour over her forever. She wished she could tell him she spent her days embroidering pillow slips, working needlepoint, or arranging flowers, or any of a hundred ladylike activities instead of admitting the truth.

"I spend a few hours making repairs in the gun shop, and then I practice my marksmanship—or at least that's what I mostly did until my pa died."

She waited for him to steal a glance at her hands to see whether they bore the stains of gunpowder and grease. Waited to see his firm lips tilt in an infinitesimal sneer, for his expression to betray a brief flicker of derision.

"And now that he's gone?" he prompted.

"Well, I . . ." Good lord, his calm acceptance of her unladylike activities had her so flustered she could barely squeak out a list of her everyday chores. "I have to spend more time in the gun shop, on account of now I'm North Platte's only gunsmith."

His head snapped up, turning as alert as a hound testing the breeze for a whiff of an elusive rabbit. "You don't sound very enthusiastic about your gunsmithing."

"I guess I don't like it very much."

Good lord, how had that popped out of her mouth? She'd never admitted her dissatisfaction with her job to a soul.

"Is that why you want to run off with the Wild West Show?"

"Of course not!" She wished that he'd turn surly and close-mouthed again, because his keen perception and quick tongue breached her defenses with laughable ease. "I always wanted to be a gunsmith, and it turns out I'm pretty good at it. Pa expected me to carry on after he died. I know it eased his mind some to think that the townsfolk could count on me. But I've been dreaming for years of joining the Wild West Show."

"So you're giving up one dream to pursue another."

She scowled at him. Blast him and his prying! If she were truthful with herself, she would have to admit that there was a little hint of relief deep in her soul to know that leaving North Platte meant she could abandon her gunsmithing with no loss of face. She'd more or less forced her pa to allow her to learn his trade, and then had so reveled in his approval that she'd continued working in the gun shop long after its attraction dimmed.

"It's no use hanging onto a dream when it doesn't pan out. Some dreams just turn out better than others. Some don't turn out at all."

He whitened. "Only if you're careless about pursuing them."

His attitude puzzled her. She'd never met anyone so dead serious about dreams. "Gosh, Matt, lots of people find out they're not as happy as they thought they'd be once their dreams come true." It seemed he paled even more, and she could see his jaw tighten, a sure indication that he meant to argue with her. "But I guess you wouldn't know about that. I guess all your dreams turn out perfect."

A sudden yearning flitted over his features, a pain that spoke of familiarity with reaching for something that always eluded his grasp. And then that brief vulnerability was gone.

"I don't have dreams. I set goals. And yes, they all turn out exactly as planned, because I don't let soft-hearted notions intrude on what I want to do."

"Soft-hearted?"

"It's soft-hearted to work at a job you don't like, just to serve people who hold a low opinion of you."

She quivered while a deep ache suffused her. Put in his terms, her plugging away at a job that had gone boring did seem rather naive. Still, it irked her to have him act like such a smug know-it-all. "Well, if you have to be soft-hearted to dream, then I'll admit to it. I'd rather dream than set goals any day. Besides, you can't let the way people treat you steer you away from what's right."

"I'd say you haven't been hurt badly enough, if you buy into that ridiculous idea," Matt said.

"I don't have time to worry about their opinions anyway. I'm too busy with the household chores. I do the cooking even though I'm not much good at it, or else we'd have to eat beans and bacon all the time with the cowboys."

"Why don't you have a maid or someone to help around the house?"

"We lost our housekeeper when Pa died," she said quietly. "Mary Margaret's folks refused to let her stay on because they said it wasn't proper for me and Henry to live together."

"There must be other housekeepers who aren't so narrow-minded."

He obviously didn't understand a thing about North Platte society. "Henry's trying to find someone. In the meantime, I do all the housework."

"What about your practicing?" Matt eerily verbalized the question that drummed endlessly through her while she swept and baked and scrubbed and sewed.

"I can't complain about that."

"Why not?"

"Well . . . it'd be selfish."

"According to brother dearest, I assume?"

Though she knew that outwardly affectionate term applied to Henry, it didn't sound so nice, the way Matt colored the endearment with a little sneer.

She felt obligated to defend Henry's parsimony. "I spend a lot of money on bullets and glass balls. I use them for targets."

"Why don't you shoot cans? I would think they'd be free even in these days."

"Annie Oakley used glass balls in her act."

"Ah. That explains it."

"My pa always put his money into improving the stock and this homestead. We have the best of everything, but we never kept much ready cash. His funeral about wiped us out. Henry says we can't afford to hire any more men to take Pa's place just now. He's been doing all Pa's chores himself, except for the gunsmithing. I don't know what I'd do without Henry, because I'd never be able to run this place by myself."

She would swear Matt looked a little embarrassed. And then he went and asked the same question all over again. "What about your practicing?"

"I try to get a little in every day."

"Enough to keep you sharp enough to impress Colonel Cody?"

"I . . . I don't know." She gulped and glanced at Matt's bandaged shoulder, evidence of her poor aim, and felt the embarrassment of shooting him stain her face.

"Then I have a solution to one of our problems. I'll take over the cooking so you can have more time to practice."

"What?"

"I'm a terrific cook. I'm a whiz at pastas, and I make a mean Cajun-style ratatouille."

He was back to spouting unusual words. Even worse, his eyes twinkled, his lips curved in a smile, and a lock of his hair flopped down over his forehead. She wished he'd revert to his scowling, sneering, animal-hating self, because this suddenly engaging Matt Kincaid tempted her to smile back at him and reach out to tuck his hair back into place. She had the dreadful feeling that once she touched him, she might never be able to stop.

"Go on," Matt said. "Find a shirt for me, and then point me toward the kitchen. I'll fix dinner while you get some practice in."

She blinked against the sudden moisture that threatened to spurt from her eyes. Matt would be sure to notice, and she didn't want him to think she was the sort of woman prone to bursting into tears for no good reason.

"Thank you," she whispered. "It . . . it really means a lot to me."

9

She was like a caged bird set free, Matt thought, giddy with excitement over her unexpected freedom. She guided him on a whirlwind tour of the small five-room ranch house, pausing in Henry's room long enough to choose another shirt from his dresser drawer. She tore off the sleeves herself while making a vague promise to fix Matt's shirt that night, or make him a completely new one of his own, soon, very soon.

In between, she touched him a hundred times— quick, featherlight strokes so tentative he sometimes wondered if he imagined them. Perhaps the insubstantial nature of them made them endurable. Matt usually couldn't abide touchy-feely females, yet he found himself positively enjoying Kate's will-o'-the- wisp caresses.

She fluttered from object to object in the kitchen, pointing out a water pump he had no clue how to operate, a hulking black-and-chrome stove that had no more in common with his Jenn-Aire than Tarsy's buckboard had with Matt's Lamborghini.

Grave doubts settled in regarding his offer to cook. "Uh, Kate, I've never worked on a stove like this."

"That's what comes from having so many places to live that you can't put a nice stove in your kitchen. I swear, Matt, you won't have a bit of trouble. My pa bought it right before he died, so it's the latest model—it's just a little fancier." She reached toward him again, and snatched her hand away just when her finger brushed his skin. "Oh, I can't tell you how anxious I am to get out there!"

She didn't have to tell him. Her eyes sparkled with anticipation, continually darting toward the rifle hung on a rack next to the door, and her smile rewarded him again and again with the luscious tilt of her lips. His doubts about cooking shifted into something darker, directed inward. It took him a moment to recognize it: guilt.

Kate's smile would evaporate in an instant if she knew the truth. She'd spoken to him with such candor, enabling Matt to zero in on all her vulnerabilities, all her delusions. It had been laughably easy to recognize that her shithead of a foster brother meant to maneuver her into staying on the ranch with him. Henry was outwardly supportive, and yet he denied her the time she needed to practice, chipped away at her confidence until she thought herself nothing more than a clumsy, bony, poor excuse of a housekeeper.

The rare flashes of spirit she showed told Matt she hadn't always been so insecure, but he knew from personal experience how the death of a parent, the threatened loss of the only family a person knew, could make that person desperate enough to hang on to whatever crumbs were left regardless of the cost to his or her self-esteem.

I'll cook so you can practice, he had offered, knowing it would buy her gratitude. And yet he found no satisfaction when she practically gushed all over him, only a curious emptiness, as if something within him craved that those smiles and tentative touches could come to him unsullied by his manipulation.

She picked up her rifle and cradled it against her breast. "I'm not even going to change my clothes. And I won't waste time by going all the way to my practice rock—I'll just go down near the bunkhouse. I don't want to lose a minute of daylight."

He turned away from her brimming excitement.

He sensed her hesitate, and knew his return to aloofness puzzled her. *Now you're looking at the real me, Kate,* he wanted to say. He should admit that the smiling, sympathetic facade he'd shown had merely served to worm his way under her skin, so that she'd feel indebted to him. All so he could trick her into saying a stupid word and send him back to his own place and time, where women's smiles lacked sincerity and women's hands never touched him with the trembling wonder of one lonely soul reaching out to another.

He heard the door whine open and then thump closed, and he stood facing the wall until he'd mastered the urge to call out and tell her to wait, that he wanted to go with her.

This was what he'd been angling after, to find himself alone in her house.

He drew a deep breath. The air's purity struck him. No acrid tang of pollution, no heaviness in the lungs.

He gave a short laugh. Breathing hundred-year-ago air might be responsible for his uncharacteristic lapses of conscience. There'd been a *Star Trek* episode where Spock had reverted to a passionate, loving man completely unlike his usual unemotional self after traveling back through time. Matt Kincaid and Mr. Spock, two of a kind. Matt veed his right eyebrow and sent the split-fingered "live long and prosper" sign in the direction Kate had taken. And then he put his logical mind to work.

He'd promised to cook dinner, so he decided to check out the small pantry. Bags of flour and rice rested on the floor. Onions had been braided together and hung from a rafter. No garlic. Rows of jars held vegetables. Some he could recognize, like green beans, while others bore no resemblance to anything he'd ever seen.

He wondered where people kept eggs in this prerefrigeration era, and found a half-dozen nested in a bucket tucked back in a dark corner and covered with a damp piece of sacking. The eggs looked clean enough, but then salmonella bacteria was invisible.

Or did he have to worry about salmonella in the 1880s? Probably not. Bufie had advised that Big 'Un would fix any mistakes Matt made, and Matt felt pretty sure that he hadn't been sent back through time in order to kill Kate and Henry with food poisoning. He lifted another damp cloth from a plate to find a mound of whitish clay. He took a cautious sniff. Cheese of some sort.

Well, he could always fall back on the bachelor's standby of an omelette. Kate hadn't seemed very impressed at the mention of Cajun-style ratatouille, anyway.

Now, to find some paper and a pencil.

Although Buford Tarsy had promised that there were a hundred ways to trick a person into saying the secret word, Matt found himself unable to come up

with anything better than the old codger's suggestion
of writing the word out twice and leaving it around,
hoping Kate would find it and read it aloud.

It was pretty lame as far as plans went, and seemed
lamer still when a thorough search of the kitchen net-
ted him a pencil stub but failed to turn up a single sheet
of paper. Nothing in Kate's room, or Henry's, or the
bedroom that had belonged to Kate's father, either. He
remembered all the times he'd cursed the mounds of
paper awaiting his attention, the dreams he'd nurtured
of cashing in on the technology that would bring about
a paperless society. Faced with no writing materials, he
recalled that cavemen had lived in the ultimate paperless society and had had to resort to coloring on rocks.
He might end up following their example.

"Here we go," he muttered when he finally spotted
a folded newspaper atop a table in the parlor, the
Tribune. He shook it open; it lacked the heft and crisp
snap of his *Wall Street Journal.* He winced at the
dateline beneath the banner: October 28, 1888. No
arguing with that. The top headline was: Col' Cody
Due Home Soon.

Sitting down on the surprisingly slippery sofa, he
carefully tore the blank margins away from the
newsprint. He cross-ripped the long strips into slips
an inch or two long. On each slip he printed the
words: DOWMTABSTA, DOWMTABSTA. Each repetition raised his blood pressure a notch when he
thought about how he should be signing contracts
with Harlow Hastings instead of writing nonsense,
but he plugged away at it until he had several dozen
of the notes prepared.

He went through the house again, tucking the notes
into drawers, under cushions, between the spokes of
the kitchen chair where Kate said she always sat. He

eased through the door and stole across the yard to the outhouse, where he tucked a couple of strips into the pages of the Sears catalog sitting on a shelf.

He saved her room—their room—for last.

He slid one into the drawer that he hoped held her underwear. He refused to take a peek to verify its contents. He might have sunk low enough to lead on an innocent like Kate, but he wouldn't stoop to pawing through her underwear. He slipped a note under the bed's only pillow and considered what to do with the few strips of paper he had remaining. He frowned. He should have saved a bunch of the notes to pin onto her dresses.

As it turned out, she didn't have many dresses. One of the dresser drawers held three white blouses, the others some voluminous, lace-edged things that he thought might be petticoats. A skirt similar to the one she wore, except wine-colored instead of blue, hung from a peg on the back of the door. There wasn't any closet in the room. A length of coarse muslin had been draped over a few garments hung from pegs pounded into the wall. The muslin protected what had to be her best dress, made of yards and yards of some sort of slithery, rustling dark-blue cloth, as well as her fringed buckskin outfit, and a faded calico gown.

He grasped the calico gown near its waistline and crumpled the material into his fist. The movement released the scent of lily of the valley and a tantalizing hint of Kate's unique essence. The dress felt soft and almost insubstantial from too many washings; it couldn't possibly hold together much longer. A dress in such poor condition wouldn't even be accepted by a homeless shelter and should have been consigned to the garbage ages ago, but she'd hung it and covered it as carefully as a bride preserving a Dior original wedding gown.

A Wild West Show poster had been nailed to one wall, where anyone lying on the bed could drink in the image of Annie Oakley—"Little Sure Shot" according to the poster—wowing the crowds. It was the room's only decoration, except for the worn-out doll propped against the pillow.

The strictly functional furnishings shone with the patina of countless dustings and waxings. Kate considered herself wealthy, sheltered in this house that rated just a notch above a shack, surrounded by possessions that probably wouldn't be worth anything in a hundred years, even though they'd technically be called antiques. She considered herself lucky, she said, to have so much.

Maybe she was. The barely adequate house, the skimpy furnishings, the pathetic decorations, all managed somehow to feel like a home.

Matt blinked and realized he still bunched the calico in his fist. He let it fall back into place, and wondered at the ache that inexplicably tightened his throat.

The dress swished against the wall, and roused an answering rustle from its dark-blue peg mate. The soft sounds made him realize that it was awfully quiet, considering that Kate was supposed to be practicing her marksmanship right outside.

He returned to the kitchen, and stepped through the door to the small stoop. A few chickens scratching in the dirt squawked their alarm and raced about two feet farther away from him before berating each other with a chorus of puzzled clucks, apparently forgetting what had frightened them.

The bunkhouse stood a few hundred feet to the left, a barn about the same distance to the right. Kate stood under a tree at the far edge of the bunkhouse, aiming her weapon away from the barn toward a rail holding a few glass bottles, but Matt couldn't hear the sharp crack of a rifle retort, didn't see any puffs of smoke billowing from the barrel.

She wouldn't know if he stole a little closer and watched her practice for a few minutes. The hard-packed dirt muffled his footsteps, except for the faint creaking of boot leather. The chickens ignored him. He couldn't seem to stop himself from drawing in great drafts of the air, but he didn't think the sound of his breathing would carry above the overhead bird-song and the distant lowing of cows.

He darted beyond the edge of the bunkhouse. It wouldn't do, he thought, for Kate to think he had any real interest in her skill. He didn't. It was the curse of being a financial genius, that a man found himself for-ever bored by activities that consumed other people. Give him a good annual report to settle down with, or an investment proposal for new software developed by some nerd computer hacker to consider—those were productive and enjoyable ways to pass time. Watching a girl shoot glass bottles into shards—no way. Five minutes, tops, and he'd be bored silly.

And yet he found himself peeping around the bunkhouse corner with all the suppressed excitement of a child sneaking out of bed on Christmas Eve in hopes of catching Santa Claus at work.

He held his breath, waiting for her to shoot. Held it as long as he could, and still she didn't fire. He leaned sideways for a better look. A few leaves still clung to the branch she stood beneath. It quivered in the breeze, branch and dead leaves casting scattered shadows that made Kate appear to tremble.

She lowered the rifle.

Matt stepped completely free of his hiding place.

Kate's shoulders rose and fell from taking a deep breath. She hoisted the rifle again to her right shoulder, and angled her head toward it. Her hair on that side had come loose of its upsweep, as if she'd caught it too many times against the rifle stock.

But Matt hadn't heard a single shot, he would swear on it.

She lifted her head away from the rifle, again without shooting, and this time there was no confusing the tremor quaking through her with some trick of the sun. Her long trembling moan expressed an aching confusion that made him want to rush to her side and hold her, just hold her.

"Kate?" he called. And then, remembering what had happened the last time he'd surprised her while she was holding a firearm, he ducked back behind the bunkhouse wall.

Moments passed without a bullet whizzing past his hiding place. He edged one eye past the corner, and then surged toward her, swallowing a curse, when he realized she hadn't moved, hadn't reacted at all to hearing him call her name.

"Kate, what is it?" he asked when he came up behind her, though a sick feeling in his gut told him he knew the answer. From his greater height it was easy to see over her shoulder. She had the rifle pocketed against herself in a professional-looking manner. The weapon's long bore pointed toward the glass bottles she'd arranged as targets, but there was no way she could have hit them—the barrel jerked with every tremor racking through her.

"I can't do it, Matt." Her whisper ended in a harsh sob. "Every time I aim, I remember shooting you. I can't pull the trigger."

10

Emotions get tangled up *awful easy, in ways a body seldom considers. . . .*

Bufie's warning echoed in Matt's head while he cursed his blind arrogance. Kate's losing her confidence was an emotional entanglement Matt had never considered.

He felt like a thief. Worse—like a murderer. A murderer who secretly mourned the vitality that he'd stolen. The sweet, exuberant Kate who'd raced from the house, thrilled to be given a few moments alone for practicing, had been replaced by a pale wraith, as though the death of her dreams had killed the spark that made Kate Monroe unique among all women.

He'd been so sure that he'd gotten stuck in 1888 because Kate had developed an instant infatuation for him. And yet he'd been secretive, manipulative, and flat-out dishonest with her, not at all the sort of man that a candid, honorable woman like Kate would find irresistible. Shame rocketed through him at the realization of his arrogance. What had he thought—that she'd fallen under his spell because he'd given her an eyeful of his superbly toned pecs?

Why not? Women always hovered around him, though he'd never offered any of them more than his carefully polished exterior. That, and a taste of what his money could buy. He'd never been interested in delving beyond a woman's protective facade, either, and certainly never worried over coming up short when it came to meeting anyone's emotional needs.

He considered himself such an expert at judging character and motivation that he fancied he could size someone up in under a minute. It jolted him to realize how wrong he'd been about Kate. Could it be that he'd equally misjudged other people?

How easily he'd considered deserting Kate when he'd thought only her heart was at risk. Hearts, he knew, were meant to be broken, and, he knew, they always mended.

Dreams . . . dreams never died, even if, as it sometimes happened, the dreamer lacked the talent, the skill, or the fortitude to make them come true. Dreams forever haunted a person's soul.

The weight of responsibility settled over him. He had to go back into the house and gather up all the notes he'd hidden. He could not risk having Kate saying the secret word and sending him back to his own time, not if it meant making his dreams come true at the cost of hers. He could not abandon Kate now.

He remembered the headline he'd read in the *Tribune:* Col' Cody Due Home Soon.

Soon could mean anything from a few days to a few weeks—and Kate had been counting on an audition with Buffalo Bill when he came home to North

Platte. Now, thanks to Matt Kincaid, she couldn't perform at all, let alone impress one of the world's all-time great showmen.

"Don't worry," he said. "It's only temporary."

"How do you know?" A bit of color had crept back into her skin, but she still didn't look quite herself. She licked her lower lip, waiting for him to promise her everything would be all right. He felt nearly crushed by the urge to pull her into his arms and kiss her fear away, to tell her everything would be fine just because he wanted it to be.

When he spoke, his voice sounded unusually rough. "Considering what happened by the rock, it's not surprising that you developed a short-term phobia. I'm sure there are psychological techniques we could employ to work through this identity crisis."

"Matt," she began, and paused while a crease furrowed her brow. "Matt, I sure do enjoy hearing you talk, but I sometimes have the darnedest time figuring out what you're saying."

Small wonder—he'd sounded pedantic and insufferable to himself, and he wasn't even sure he'd gotten all the terms right. His tongue had turned so glib over the years that he scarcely had to devote any thought to dazzling and baffling others into silence.

Somewhere along the line, he'd forgotten how to say simple, heartfelt things, like: *I can't stand seeing you looking so lost and hopeless, Kate.*

Well, perhaps he hadn't technically forgotten how to say such things, not if he was able to *think* about saying them. He couldn't choke the phrase past his throat, though, even though he knew Kate needed to hear some reassuring words just then. Despising himself for a coward, he settled for a breezy, undemanding reassurance.

"What I mean is, I think we can figure out a way to help you work through your fear."

"Together?"

"Well sure, together."

Her question, his promise, hung in the air while they eyed each other with the nervous mistrust of two starving deer inching toward a bale of hay dropped from a rescue helicopter.

"What do we do first, Matt?"

What a question. Kate stared at him with breathless hope, waiting for him to cure her. It was too late to wish he'd memorized the text of a psychology book or two instead of *Winning Through Intimidation* and *In Search of Excellence*.

"You have to confront your phobia head-on. A phobia's the thing you're most afraid of," he added, when it seemed she didn't understand.

She nodded solemnly then, her eyes darkening with comprehension. "I'm looking straight at you."

"You're afraid to shoot, Kate. You're not afraid of me."

"I'm not so sure about that."

"I haven't done anything to frighten you." No, he'd merely screwed up her life. "You must know I'd never hurt you, Kate." He'd never hurt a woman—not physically, at least.

"Maybe I'm not explaining myself clearly." She swiveled away from him and lifted her rifle into shooting position. "See, I'm looking down the sights, and I'm just fine. But the minute I hook my finger around the trigger. . . "

Her voice drifted away. He didn't need a verbal explanation, not when the rifle began jerking around as if it were being controlled by an invisible puppeteer who had an aversion to guns.

She lowered the weapon, and when she glanced up at him, it seemed that he looked upon the face of a total stranger. It took him a moment to realize what had wrought such a change: she'd lost the inner hope, the air of anticipation, that normally animated her. All the hurt, all the pain Matt had endured throughout his life paled before the depth of Kate's despair.

"I'm afraid of hurting *you*," she whispered. "As soon as I fix to shoot, why, your face pops up in my mind and I get so scared I want to drop my rifle."

"You're afraid of hurting anyone. It's not just me." But as he automatically tried to distance himself from the responsibility her declaration forced upon him, there was something inside him that thrilled to hear that specific concern for *him* prompted her fear.

She shook her head. "I don't see Henry's face, which is too bad, because I've been thinking for a while now that it might smarten him up a little if I winged him. I don't see Mrs. Merriweather's face, which is also too bad, because I might feel better personally if I shot her, even though it would make things in town worse instead of better."

"Mrs. Merriweather?" He pounced on the stranger's name as a diversion.

"Mrs. Augusta Merriweather. I . . . I always call her 'Disgusta' in my mind."

"Did you ever slip up and call her that to her face?" He had to hide a smile, because he couldn't help contrasting Kate's harmless, unspoken insult against the vituperative slights he knew Heather, Tiffany, or Pinckney could hurl at will.

"No, but I live in such mortal fear of it that I make sure to always address her as Mrs. Merriweather, even though she says we're close enough to use given names. Every time she calls me 'Kate, my dear,' her

nose twitches and her lips pucker up like she's suck-
ing on a lemon."

"Your secret's safe with me." He made a zippering
motion over his mouth.

Her mouth wobbled a little and she flushed, as
though pleased that he'd fallen in with her, but
embarrassed that she'd admitted to such a grievous
fault in her nature.

Her reaction helped him reshape his plan of attack.
He would switch into his joking, teasing mode,
because she seemed to snap out of her funk when he
found a way to make her smile. A lighthearted
approach seemed like a good idea overall, better than
continuing to probe, to explore his interest in her, in
her way of life.

He supposed it was a lack of distractions that made
her so irresistibly interesting, because under normal
conditions Matt Kincaid would never be so consumed
with curiosity about a simple, homespun woman who
dabbed her pulse points with homemade lily-of-the-
valley perfume.

Joking and teasing with Kate, he felt a lightening of
his spirit. Bufie had, after all, encouraged him to have
fun.

"And what did that gol-danged Disgusta do to
merit such a horrible name?"

He must have gotten the cowboy slang right
because she didn't remark on it. "Well, she was
always criticizing my pa, saying he was selfish trying
to raise a little girl without a woman's influence. My
pa didn't have a selfish bone in his body and he was
so kindhearted that he didn't tell her to mind her own
business when she appointed herself my unofficial
chaperon. She makes notes of everything I do wrong,
and gives them to me so I can study them and

improve myself. And she was always after my father for letting me help him in the gun shop."

"Why?"

"Well, because it's not ladylike." The glance she sent him told him he should have figured that much out for himself. "Mrs. Merriweather knows my mother wouldn't have stood for it while she was alive. Mama always said that Pa really hankered after a son, and she wasn't about to let him turn me into the boy he really wanted."

He saw, in the darkening of her smoky green eyes, that Kate had long harbored the same suspicion herself. He imagined her as a little girl eager to gain her father's approval. How old had she been, he wondered, when she took up the unfeminine pursuit of target shooting? Did her interest in marksmanship predate Henry's arrival in the family? Somehow he doubted it.

"He could have taught Henry how to be a gunsmith," Matt suggested.

She bristled. "I wanted to do it. I . . . I figured it should be in my blood."

He wondered how a little girl would feel when the father who hankered after a son brought home a fatherless boy to add to the family. Matt knew well enough how the fatherless boy would feel, but he'd never before tried to put himself in the position of the child who feared being displaced, who believed her love wasn't powerful enough, that she herself wasn't wonderful enough, to assuage her parent's desire for a boy child.

"You might've been better off if your father had just left Henry in the dumpster."

"What's a dumpster?"

Matt hadn't realized that he'd voiced his thoughts

aloud. His natural inclination was to squelch Kate's curiosity with a sharp, sarcastic remark, but he couldn't bear just then to watch her lean away and treat him to one of her scornful glances. He sketched a boxy figure in the air. "I just assumed Henry'd been found in a dumpster. It's like a big garbage container."

Kate's chin dropped, and she gasped. "Matt Kincaid, you should be ashamed of yourself for even suggesting such a thing! Why, no mother would throw her baby into one of those dumpster things!"

He couldn't believe he'd strayed onto the subject. "Some would, Kate. Lots of them do, where I come from."

"Those poor babies!" Damn if tears didn't sparkle in her eyes.

"They don't remember being thrown in a dumpster."

"How do you know?"

"I just know."

She swallowed, and pressed her fingers against her lips while her eyes grew round and enormous with suspicion. Matt whirled away from her pity without confirming a thing.

"I would hate to live in a place where people tossed babies in dumpsters," Kate whispered, drawing him back to her. She cradled her rifle close to her breast in what Matt felt sure was an unconscious imitation of what Kate would do with any babies who found their way into her arms. "Folks must be meaner in big cities than they are in North Platte."

"Way meaner," Matt said shortly, although he welcomed the opportunity to change the subject. "A lot meaner than Disgusta, even. You know, you shouldn't care so much what she says about you, Kate."

"Oh, I don't." Kate's carefully careless shrug made a lie of her words and told Matt that she did care, very much. "I don't pay her any mind at all. But now she's gone and made my life a misery by insisting Henry has no business living under the same roof with me since Pa passed on. I don't think anyone else would have paid us any mind if she hadn't made such a fuss, but now she has the whole town all riled up about it."

He found himself struck anew by the differences between his own time and this more restrictive era. A woman in 1997 could pursue the career of her choosing, and she could live with anyone she wanted, male or female, related or not.

He realized, too, that 1997's freedom altered a man's role, as well. If Pinckney, Tiffany, or Heather had complained that someone dared question their lifestyle, he would've muttered a casual, "Screw 'em," and not worried about it at all.

But Kate, trying so hard to hold her head high amid the gossip, trying so hard to hold the remnants of her family together, roused an unfamiliar, thoroughly male instinct. He wanted to protect her, wanted to still the criticism and beat into submission the demands that she break up her family.

And he could do this. For the first time in his life, simply standing by someone's side would be worth more than all his money, all his power and influence.

"I guess they'll just have to un-rile themselves now, won't they, Mrs. Kincaid?" He spoke softly, shaken by the realization of how important one person could be to another.

She blinked, and cocked her head as if wondering who on earth he might be addressing, and then her color deepened when she realized what he meant. "Oh!"

"And what does the formidable Disgusta have to say about your plan to join the Wild West Show?"

"She says it's probably the best thing I could do."

"That surprises me."

"Well, Annie Oakley sort of paved the way for me, if you know what I mean. She proved that a woman can still be a lady even if she masters a man's skill and performs in front of people all over the world. Mrs. Merriweather claims that when a woman becomes famous she can get away with anything. That's why . . ."

"Why what?"

"Why I can give you a divorce once I take off with the show. It wouldn't reflect badly on you at all, Matt, because everyone would understand that a man's pride won't stand for a wife to go traipsing all over the world. And since I'd be sort of famous, I could get away with it, too."

"Would you still call yourself Kate Kincaid?" He didn't know why he asked that question, except that he still felt a strong urge to protect her. He had to put a stop to that, at once. She wasn't a real wife requiring the protection of his name, for God's sake, just one more bothersome complication in the whole series of events that had transpired since he'd found himself facing the fog through the window of the Dismal Lodge.

"I . . . well, no. Annie Oakley never took on her husband's name. Besides, I always planned to join the Wild West Show as Kate Monroe, as a tribute to my pa."

This very modern attitude should have satisfied him. Professional women often retained their maiden names, he knew. Truth to tell, he'd intended to make it part of a prenuptial agreement that his chosen bride retain *her* maiden name, hyphenated with his, to buy him entrée into the social circles he'd aimed to crack.

He'd simply never imagined that linking his name to Kate's would forge a connection so natural, so right, that it might ache like an amputation to hear it abandoned.

"I never knew your full name until just now," he said. "You'll always be Kate Kincaid in my mind."

He knew he spoke the truth. And he knew he'd think about her often when he'd returned to his own time. He'd known her for only one day, kept her within his sight for only a few hours of that day, and already he could imagine her in a thousand ways he hadn't seen. Holding him tight while her hair tumbled over them, shielding them both. Bending that graceful neck of hers to study one of Augusta Merriweather's notes for self-improvement. Her lush lips moving softly while she read to herself, while she murmured the secret word that would send him back to his own time.

"I'd better go start dinner, Kate."

"Right. But, um, what do I do?"

He didn't know. How did a person cure a phobia? He had no patience for phobias himself, wouldn't indulge them, believed his will was strong enough to overcome any fear. But he'd promised to help her, he *had* to help her.

"You stand there and watch me while I walk back to the house. That way you'll know for sure that you can't hurt me."

"And then I should try shooting again."

The word *yes* was on the tip of his tongue, but the sudden pallor of her skin hinted that the fright she'd acquired would not be dismissed so easily. "No, Kate. You just walk over to your targets and look at them for a while. Listen to the birds and cows. It's amazing how soothing they sound. Let it sink in that you're really, truly alone."

"Really, truly alone."

Her whisper stirred something to life deep in Matt's heart, something that had been hurt and abandoned so often that it had retreated far beyond the pain. "I'll wave to you from the door," he said impulsively. "In about ten minutes. We can do that a couple of times, and then you can come back to the house."

"You'll be there every time I look for you."

"Sure. I'll be right there. Every time."

She nodded.

He felt her gaze on his back all the way to the house.

The ensuing ten minutes could have been spent productively, doing things like finding oil and spices and cooking utensils. Instead, he raced around collecting the strips of paper he'd hidden. He cursed himself for neglecting to count the strips when he'd made them. He gathered a fistful, but wasn't sure that he'd found them all.

With no watch to mark time and the parlor clock too faint to hear well, he found himself counting out the seconds the way he'd learned as a boy. "One, one thousand. Two, one thousand." Six hundred seconds in ten minutes. He'd probably always known that, he'd just never thought about it before. But then being around Kate seemed to force him into looking at a lot of things in different ways.

She was watching, her slim body tense, when he popped through the door and sent her a cheery wave. She slumped, the way a person does when they find something they thought they'd lost. Then she waved back, and turned to examine the bottles lined along the rail.

He stared at the graceful picture she made until a chicken came up and pecked at his boot. He snapped out of his reverie and then tried to estimate how many seconds he'd forgotten to count off.

"My time's too valuable for this," Matt muttered in frustration. Hell, his accountants couldn't even calculate what he earned on an hourly basis. If he made hamburgers for dinner tonight, the labor factor would make a couple of sandwiches cost more than an entire McDonald's franchise. In ten minutes, his businesses generated enough cash to launch a Wild West Show of his own. But that probably wouldn't bring him half as good a feeling inside as counting off the minutes until he could rush to the door and find Kate watching for him.

"This is stupid," he said, and wondered if he'd always talked to himself in such a crotchety voice.

"One, one thousand," he began all over again. He didn't sound so bad-tempered, once he was counting. Probably because numbers felt safe, familiar. Not because each second he counted off meant he was that much closer to seeing Kate wave to him again.

11

Kate heard the sounds of Henry's home-coming: the outdoor pump handle's rusty squeak as he sloughed off the day's dust, the harsh rasp of the boot scraper shaving the mud from his feet, the heavy thud of his tread upon the stoop. The needle she plied against the ragged gash in Matt's shirt pricked her finger, adding a tiny crimson blossom to the brown stains that had resisted her best efforts with the washboard.

Matt clanged and crashed away at the stove, so absorbed with the contents of the skillets he had bubbling there that he was oblivious to Henry's arrival.

"Well, ain't this cozy," Henry commented as he walked through the door. Animosity wafted from him as surely as appetizing aromas drifted from Matt's skillets.

Some said that Henry's eyes, black and inexpressive as a lump of charcoal, proved that he possessed more than a drop of Indian blood. Others claimed his ability to wipe his face clean of all expression proved the same. Nobody could offer an explanation for Henry's wavy brown hair or ruddy complexion, and Henry himself could provide no insight to his parentage, for he'd only been about two years old when Kate's pa found him abandoned in a hollow at the base of a pine tree.

Now that she thought on it, a hollow pine tree wasn't much of an improvement over what Matt had called a "dumpster." She ought to apologize to him for calling his hometown a terrible place, but she didn't want to bring up the subject of abandoned children again. The way Matt's eyes had darkened, his firm jaw tensed, had reminded her of her pa's last days, when her father had tried pretending he wasn't suffering any pain. Kate doubted that Matt had cancer, which meant the anguish he tried to hide from her stemmed from another source.

She wondered why he knew so much about dumpsters and abandoned babies. She thought she might know the answer.

"Evening, brother dearest," Kate said to Henry.

A choking sound, quickly muffled, came from the vicinity of the stove, but when Matt whirled around, there was no evidence of laughter on his features. "Henry," he acknowledged.

"You're cooking?"

"Kate needs to have time to practice."

Kate noticed that he exhibited no embarrassment at taking on a woman's chore. Nor did he mention her failure with the rifle, or hint that she'd lost her nerve. He turned away from Henry a little and closed one eye in a quick wink that she knew her foster brother couldn't see. They shared a secret! The realization sent her heart thumping. And then he shot her a smile, warm and with a little hint of pride, the way her long-abandoned fantasies had imagined a real husband might look at her one day. It rattled her heart even more, and sent heat coursing over her skin, because she knew she didn't deserve it.

"Ain't that convenient for you, Kate." Henry yanked his chair away from the table and lowered himself into it, tilting back until the rear legs squeaked a protest.

"I appreciate Matt's help."

"I'll just bet you do." Henry let his chair thump forward. "What I meant is, it's awful convenient that he couldn't move a muscle yesterday, and now that he's married to you, he's practically juggling cast iron skillets. It makes a body wonder."

"Is that so?" Matt glanced at Kate and then he leaned against the wall. Tension seemed to emanate from him despite his casual pose. "Does it make you wonder, babe?"

Never in her life would she have imagined it would feel good to hear such a diminutive nickname applied to her. And never in her life had she felt so certain that the next words she said would be among the most important of her life. "I'm grateful," she burst out. "I think it's a miracle."

She'd earned Matt's approval. She could see it shining from him, along with something more, something softer, which he quickly masked.

"Yeah, a miracle. It's like a guardian angel sent me here," Matt said.

He crossed the room. He came up behind Kate's chair. She felt his hands curl over the tops of her shoulders and then his fingers began toying with the lace at the edge of her collar. Her pulse quickened. They shared a secret; they stood together against Henry. It

felt so good. Too good. She had to keep reminding herself that it was only temporary, she had to.

"I knew I hadn't hurt him too badly," Kate said to
Henry. The light pressure of Matt's fingers messed up
her breathing somehow, so that she sounded all
uncertain and fluttery when she meant to speak with
confidence. "I'm not surprised at all that he's up and
about so soon."

Henry's neck turned a dull red. His eyes seemed
riveted upon Matt's fingers. She couldn't help remembering that if Henry had had his way, Matt's fingers
would be stiff and cold with the permanent stillness
of death, not all warm and pliant and capable of robbing a woman of her wits. She set Matt's shirt aside,
because her fingers had gone curiously clumsy and
she didn't want to risk stabbing herself again.

Henry had been concerned that a badly repaired
plow joint wouldn't hold up to the day's work and he
might not be able to finish seeding the southernmost
field with the rye they always planted as winter ground
cover. "Did the plow make it through the day, Henry?"

"Naw." He drew a shuddering breath and tore his
gaze away from the vicinity of her throat. "I had to go
into town and let Finley reweld the joint."

Kate didn't know what an important businessman
like Matt would make of their mundane farm talk.
She knew Henry, like her pa, enjoyed having her
attention after a long day's work, and she really
should take an interest, considering it was her farm.
"You'll have to finish that field tomorrow, I guess."

"Maybe, maybe not. We're getting company tomorrow, and it could be interesting to stick around the
house." He let a rare smile tweak his lips. Perhaps it
was his smile's very rarity that twisted Henry's features until they seemed gloating and vindictive. "I ran

into Augusta Merriweather in town. She's so worried about you that she made me promise to pick her up so she can visit with you here tomorrow."

"Oh, no. Oh, my stars." Kate pressed her hand against her chest, which suddenly felt as though someone had commenced pounding on a kettle drum deep inside it. "You told her I got married? You . . . you didn't tell her everything, did you?"

"Of course I told her that you got married. I thought she'd take an apoplectic fit after I told her Buford Tarsy conducted the wedding service. She's all fired up, but then she's expecting to come charging out here to find you acting nursemaid over a sick man. I expect she's sitting at her desk right now filling an entire notebook with all the ways you messed up this time, Kate."

She might have fainted if not for Matt's grip on her shoulders. His hands felt so solid, so reassuring. Her hand reached toward his, as if she might absorb some of his strength through a touch. She meant to brush against him briefly, no more, but he caught her fingers between his and entwined them together.

It was amazing how his wordless support helped clear her thoughts. She shouldn't be angry at Henry; all he'd done was bring about a confrontation with Augusta Merriweather a little sooner than Kate had anticipated. It shouldn't upset her so. She'd married Matt partly on account of Mrs. Merriweather's disapproval of Kate's living arrangements. It'd serve the old biddy right if she had to admit that her interference had pushed Kate into marriage with a man she didn't love just so she could hold her head up when she went into town, just so she could stop the untrue gossip about her before it reached Colonel Cody's ears.

It wasn't so bad, though, being married to a man

she didn't love. At least not so far. Matt's thumb traced alongside her forefinger, sending delightful shivers coursing through her. She leaned her head back. It pressed into his firm belly. She stared up at him, up and up for what seemed forever, to see his head tilted down toward hers and little wrinkles crinkling the skin around his eyes and his remarkable golden-brown hair falling loose to frame his face.

"So I get to meet the formidable Disgusta." He spoke so softly that she was sure Henry couldn't decipher the low rumble that vibrated straight through Matt and into her. He gave a wicked chuckle, so full of devilish anticipation that she couldn't help giggling a little, too.

Henry's chair scraped along the floor, and the table quivered from the force of his hands slamming down on top of it. The harsh sounds dragged Kate out of the curious lassitude that had overtaken her.

"What's wrong, Henry?"

"I'm tempted to have my dinner and sleep out in the bunkhouse with the hands. Whatever the hell he's cooking stinks so bad it's ruining my appetite."

Kate knew Henry would stay with just a bit of coaxing—he always backed down from his threats to abandon her if she pleaded with him. But before she could cajole him out of his temper, Matt jumped right into the silence.

"Gosh darn, you do look pretty sick," he said, without a trace of sympathy. "It's the oregano that's turning your stomach. My cooking instructor always said I tended to be a little heavy-handed with spices. You'd better get down to the bunkhouse if the smell's bothering you. A man has to eat to keep up his strength, you know."

Henry stood as still as if he'd been nailed to the floor. Kate knew he didn't want to leave Matt alone with her any more than she wanted Augusta

Merriweather to visit her for tea. She couldn't bring herself to take Henry's side, though, not when Matt sounded so delighted at the prospect of Henry's leaving. She couldn't go against her husband's wishes—temporary though he might be. Besides, it felt kind of nice to let Henry suffer the consequences of his highhanded behavior for once. She hadn't realized until just now how she'd taken to bowing down in the face of his ultimatums.

"Yes, you go on, Henry," she said softly. "Maybe you'll feel better enough to take breakfast with us in the morning."

Naked pain such as she'd never seen him betray, not even when Pa had died, shafted across Henry's rough features. She stifled a cry and gripped her hands together in her lap. But she didn't look at Henry again, and didn't say anything, until the door closed behind him.

Matt's fingers slipped from her shoulders. She felt suddenly, unbearably alone, aching.

"He's used to getting his way with you, isn't he?"

"No. Actually, he wasn't like this until just recently."

Matt snorted his disbelief. "Hard to believe. Older brothers—even foster brothers—usually like to boss their sisters around."

"Oh, Henry's not older than me. I'm six years older than him, twenty-six to his twenty."

"What?" He gaped at her in disbelief. "You look like his kid sister!"

She raised a hand and touched her cheek. "It's the gun grease, I expect. You can't wear gloves when you're fixing a fine gun. I never could seem to learn how to keep my hands away from my face when I work. Pa says . . . said there's something in the grease that softens the skin."

"Isn't twenty-six a little long in the tooth to be single?" From what he remembered, people married young in the late nineteenth century.

Mortification flooded through her, silencing her when she meant to scold him for making such rude remarks about her advanced age. "I had a beau once," she said when she regained control of her tongue. "I was only sixteen, and Pa wanted us to wait until I turned eighteen before marrying."

"What happened?"

"He got killed in an Indian fight."

Matt studied her soberly. She wished she could have summoned a little grief under the circumstances. It might have bolstered her pride if Matt believed she'd remained single because of mourning the love of her life. In truth, she hadn't thought about Frank Collins for a long time. She couldn't remember how his voice sounded, and had only the haziest recollection of his face.

"I'm sorry," Matt said.

"Your sympathy's not necessary except for acknowledging the loss of a life." Kate drew a shuddering breath. "Frank and I never loved each other."

"Then why—"

"Frank's pa was after him to settle down and take over the family ranch. The Collinses have a big spread, lots of cattle, lots of money. Frank hated farming. He picked me to irritate his folks. I accepted because he promised I could keep on working with guns and it would make it easier for me in town." She felt the embarrassment heat her skin. "You don't have to come out and say it," she whispered. "I know it's a terrible thing to do, to think of marrying for spite and convenience."

"People marry for all kinds of reasons," Matt said, but he offered the observation in the polite manner of one who held little interest in the subject. And then he shifted back to his fascination with her foster brother's age as if she hadn't gone and admitted the most shameful secret of her life.

"Twenty. I've been tiptoeing around a punk that couldn't order a drink in a bar without getting carded."

"That's not true. Henry drinks all the time without playing cards." She would swear that something about Henry's young age embarrassed Matt. "Since you're not from these parts, you don't know what the weather does to folks' faces. The sun and the wind take a terrible toll. I'm very lucky that I don't have to work out in the fields like some of the women do."

"Twenty." Matt paid her no mind, just kept looking toward the door where Henry had disappeared, and now she would swear there was a hint of admiration in his regard.

"Matt?"

"Hmmm?"

"Your dinner doesn't really stink."

"I know it doesn't."

"Henry didn't mean it."

"I know."

"He really wanted to stay."

"I know that, too." He shook his head and gave a little laugh. "Twenty. Not bad. Not bad at all."

"Oh, he isn't bad!" Matt looked like he wanted to interrupt her, but Kate was so thrilled by his perception that she kept chattering. "Once he gets over these silly notions of his and you get to know the real Henry hidden inside, you'll like him."

Matt drew in a sharp, sudden breath, like someone who'd been caught at hiding things himself. "He's a lot like me," Matt mused. "Or I guess I should say he's a lot like I was, when I was his age."

It seemed impossible that Matt, golden-haired, perfect, with his cocky, confident grin, could have anything in common with homely, insecure Henry. But then, she didn't know anything about Matt, did she?

And then she remembered Matt's familiarity with dumpsters and abandoned babies. She remembered him waving to her from the kitchen door, every ten minutes on the dot, according to the watch she kept pinned on her shirtwaist. Henry would never have done anything like that. He wouldn't have suggested it in the first place, as Matt had done, and he would have called her silly if she'd asked him herself.

Her body, of all things, started tormenting her with a variety of sensations. Her shoulders still tingled from Matt's reassuring touch. Her chin trembled with the memory of how he'd tipped it up when he'd reminded her that she hadn't always belittled herself. The entire front of her, from breasts to knees, throbbed with the remembered sensation of his firm length pressed into hers, when he'd promised he'd help her get her confidence back. Her ears warmed with the memory of his breath brushing against them as he'd repeated Mrs. Merriweather's secret name. And her eyes—oh, lord, her eyes—threatened to turn all misty just thinking about Matt's sculpted, half-naked body kneeling on the bunkhouse bed.

A decent woman wouldn't dwell on such a memory. She shuttered it from her mind, knowing it couldn't be entirely erased, and redirected her thoughts to Matt's many small kindnesses. His dismay over her inability to shoot. His assumption of the cooking chores so she could practice. His bolstering her confidence when she called herself clumsy. Those things, and a dozen others. If she added all those incidents together, why, they told her more about Matt

Kincaid than she would have learned through two weeks of solid discussions.

She didn't know whether she should be pleased, or frightened, that she found herself so attuned to a man who would pass so briefly through her life.

"Dinner's ready," Matt said.

She wasn't hungry, not anymore, but there was a new emptiness inside that clamored to be filled. Maybe food would help. "That sounds good."

"You're confident Henry won't come back tonight and catch you sleeping in the other bedroom?" Matt asked as he watched Kate hang her dark-blue skirt on the door peg and gather its wine-colored twin into her arms.

She shook her head. "He's too proud. He'll be here for breakfast tomorrow, though."

"I'll make him something special."

"You don't have to bother. Henry's a plain man. He'd settle for a few bowls of oatmeal, a half-dozen or so eggs, a loaf sliced thick and toasted, a ham steak or two and maybe a dozen strips of bacon. Well, he works hard," she added with a defensive edge when Matt snorted his disbelief.

She looked so cute, ready to do battle for her foster-brother while swathed in a shapeless cotton nightgown that gathered around her neck and fell in voluminous folds to the floor. She'd braided her hair into one giant plait, and its thick length curled against her neck and dangled over her breast, with the brushy end jittering enticingly with her every breath.

Her skin glowed in the candlelight. He made a mental note to ask his laboratory chemists to check the chemical composition of gun grease when he got back to 1997, to see whether it might offer new possibilities for Kincaid Group's cosmetic line.

Kiss Me, Kate, they could call the line, if the products helped the women who used them look half as enticing as Kate.

"Brother dearest doesn't worry much about his cholesterol, does he?" he forced himself to say.

"There you go again with those words." Color flared in her cheeks, and he decided she looked even cuter when flustered.

He knew he probably sounded a like a fourth-grade bully trying to impress his prettiest classmate, but he teased her with every cholesterol-related medical term he could remember. "Triglycerides, hypertension, arteriosclerosis, . . . um . . . atherosclerosis."

"I couldn't understand that word the first time you said it. Repeating it isn't going to help."

"Arteriosclerosis and atherosclerosis are two different words."

"They sound the same to me. What's the difference?"

For all he knew, Kate might be right—they could well mean the same thing. He'd enjoyed teasing her so much that he'd forgotten his usual cautious habit of never saying anything he couldn't back up.

"It's a subtle difference, but very important," he said, striving for an explanation that would let him save face—to himself. "Sort of like looking at two similar animals and being able to tell right off the bat that one's a dog and one's a puppy."

"One thing is a lesser version of the other."

"I believe that explains it."

"Sort of the way you find yourself liking some people, and loving others."

"Maybe." He tensed, growing uncomfortable at the path this conversation was taking. He relaxed a little when she merely nodded and stared down at the skirt she held, and then she stiffened him right back up again.

"Matt . . . do you like me?"

"Well," he said through a throat gone tight, while his heart hammered in his chest and his instincts urged him to run. Without thinking, he took a step back away from her, and he could see it wounded her. "Who wouldn't like you?"

"Oh, there's lots of people who don't like me."

"I find that hard to believe."

"You'll meet one tomorrow."

"Mrs. Merriweather." He missed Kate's smile. "Disgusta," he added.

It brought him a flicker, a pale imitation of her real smile. "She provokes the worst in me."

"I have to admit that your relationship with her puzzles me, Kate. I don't understand why you're so worried about pleasing her."

"She's the second most important woman in town, next to Mrs. Cody, of course. If Mrs. Merriweather decides that I've scandalized myself beyond redemption, she'll be sure to turn Mrs. Cody against me, too, and then I'll never get a part in the Wild West Show. Folks spread a lot of nasty rumors about the way Colonel Cody acts up when he's away from North Platte, but nobody can deny that he relies on Mrs. Cody's advice."

Matt supposed Kate's concerns weren't so different from those that drove him to earn the approval of society's blue bloods. While he was considering how he might encourage Kate without making his own efforts look ridiculous, she interrupted his thoughts.

"That's why I asked if you liked me. Because I was wondering if it would be too hard on you to pretend, just for tomorrow, that you like me at least a little bit."

I do like you, Kate. More than a little bit.

She didn't seem to hear him; and then he realized that he hadn't spoken aloud. Habit, and an ingrained reflex of guarding against impulse, had held his tongue silent. He felt ashamed when she flushed with embarrassment, when she rushed to speak into the awkward silence that followed her appeal for his help.

"You see, if Mrs. Merriweather thinks we like each other, then she might accept the whole notion of us being married. She'd have to quit saying it's not right for Henry living under the same roof with me . . . with us. She couldn't continue mocking my gunsmithing work if she understands that my husband approves of it."

"Don't worry. I can make people believe anything I want them to believe." He supposed that he sounded so harsh because, while he approved of Kate's practical reasoning, it perversely annoyed him. It didn't seem fair that she was trying to push him into admitting that he liked her without doing the same herself. He found himself appealing to her, just as she had done to him. "You'd have to pretend you liked me, too."

"Oh, I wouldn't have to pretend. I like you a lot." She gave him a real smile then, as if she'd just admitted how much she enjoyed eating ice cream cones. The thought of Kate's pink tongue darting out and licking melted ice cream away from a cone roused a ferocious ache in Matt's loins.

And still he could not admit the truth to her. "I won't embarrass you, Kate. But my clothes might. I don't have anything to wear except Henry's old shirt."

"I mended yours, but you're right, it's not appropriate for afternoon tea." Her lashes fluttered low against her cheeks. "I guess you've attended a lot of fancy teas in all those big cities."

"Dozens. Hundreds, maybe." And never enjoyed a single one of them, he added to himself, but a man couldn't very well decline the invitations that came his way when his aspiration was to move comfortably within that social circle.

"The women probably wear beautiful clothes at those teas," Kate whispered, staring down at the plain dark skirt clutched in her arms.

"Nothing as pretty as your blue dress." Matt jutted his jaw at the muslin-draped garment. "Don't worry, Kate. We'll make a fine-looking couple for Mrs. Merriweather."

Kate sent him a sizzling glance from head to toe, and then blushed as furiously as if he'd given her the once over. "Oh, Matt, I can't tell you how much I appreciate this."

He could think of a hundred ways for her to show him, though. He couldn't articulate a single one without sounding like a lecher. She eased backward through the door, her braid bobbing at every step, with her eyes shining with a lesser version of the light he wanted to see burning from them when she looked his way.

And when she was halfway down the hall, and couldn't see the naked longing he knew he projected, he called out to her. "Kate, I just want you to know . . ." He swallowed. She stilled, not turning, which he regretted, because it might have silenced him. But with her standing so quietly, looking so fragile and in need of the protection only he could offer, he couldn't help blurting out what he wanted to say.

"Tomorrow," he said, "I won't be pretending."

12

"I could tell you enjoyed my cooking last night, Kate, but I didn't think it would pack weight on you so fast."

A smile tugged at Matt's lips, but since no sparkle turned his eyes into golden topaz, his good humor seemed fake to Kate. She welcomed his determinedly cheerful mood. When he revealed a hint of long-buried pain, when the agony of unhealed inner wounds blazed from him, she forgot all about her own needs and wanted nothing more than to erase that anguish from his heart.

But she couldn't afford to indulge that womanly side of herself today. Matt wanted no part of it, for one thing. And she had to keep all her wits about her if she meant to get through this ordeal with Mrs. Merriweather.

Kate didn't understand what Matt was talking about anyway with his reference to her putting on

son Wilfred is a fine lawyer. We can rely on his discretion when it comes to dissolving whatever mess Buford Tarsy created. It will take the utmost delicacy, the most brilliant maneuvering on my part, but I am sure I can resurrect your good name unsullied by this unfortunate lapse."

"She has a good name," said Matt, drawing Kate close to his side. "It's Mrs. Kincaid."

Mrs. Merriweather treated them both to the quelling glare that sent belligerent cowboys scurrying from her path. North Platte's most solid citizens quaked before Mrs. Merriweather's wrath. Kate's own knees were knocking beneath the concealing folds of her gown. She peeped up at Matt and saw the chiseled edge of his jawline holding steady.

"You," Mrs. Merriweather spat, deigning at last to acknowledge Matt's presence. "Why, just look at you. You dared call me Mrs. M.!"

"You know, I'm sorry about that. Kate did mention that you gave her permission to call you by your given name. I should have realized that the privilege extends to her husband as well . . . Augusta."

For a moment Kate feared Mrs. Merriweather's fury would send her sliding right off the horsehide sofa. Her cheeks became mottled and the topmost feather in her hat quivered as if it were still attached to a bird struggling to free itself.

"Please forgive my husband, Mrs. Merriweather," Kate put in. "He's not from around these parts. He's not used to our ways."

"You don't have to apologize for me, babe." Surprisingly, he seemed more angered by her attempt to placate Mrs. Merriweather than by the old harridan's scornful treatment of him.

"She most certainly does," Mrs. Merriweather

snapped. "She's the only one here with any notion of proper, respectful behavior."

That roused Matt's rumbling chuckle. "See that! She approves of you today, Kate."

"I do not!"

"So she did the wrong thing by apologizing for me?"

"No. I mean yes, she did that exactly right—"

"See, I told you so." Matt gave Kate a gentle squeeze. "She likes you. She really likes you."

This was terrible. Matt was making everything worse, not better. Despising herself for a coward, Kate considered running out of the room, but Henry blocked the doorway, leaning against the jamb with his arms crossed. One of his rare smiles brightened his features, but Kate could take no joy in it, for she felt certain it came at her expense. He wouldn't come to her rescue.

Matt, too, abandoned her at that moment. His arm retreated from her waist and he stepped away from her. He took several determined strides and planted himself in front of their visitor. Kate stifled a moan and slumped, even though she knew that any departure from a ramrod-stiff posture would earn a written reprimand as well as Mrs. Merriweather's verbal disapproval. Kate hadn't the strength to hold herself straight just then. With any luck, Mrs. Merriweather's full attention was so fixed upon Matt that she might not notice Kate's rounded shoulders.

"My dear lady," Matt said, addressing Mrs. Merriweather. And then he sort of tilted his head just a little to the side, and executed a bow from the waist, keeping an easy smile on his face and his eyes upon Mrs. Merriweather the whole time.

He looked so elegant and courtly that Kate did

indeed forget for a minute that he was clad in denim and patched homespun, that he'd pinned a ridiculous cluster of fall-bronzed leaves to his shoulder to cover the bloodstains on his shirt. He offered his hand to Mrs. Merriweather, who must've set the world's record for the number of swallows performed by one throat in the space of a few seconds. She tentatively touched her fingertips to Matt's as if she feared a more substantial contact might scald her.

He curled his fingers around Mrs. Merriweather's, then lifted her pudgy hand to his lips and brushed it with a gentle kiss.

If that didn't beat all! Here she was, married to the man, and he'd gone and kissed another woman before ever kissing her!

Not that she wanted Matt Kincaid's kisses. Not at all. They'd agreed that this marriage was a temporary convenience, nothing more. They slept in separate bedrooms. Kissing had no place in a marriage such as theirs.

Matt released Mrs. Merriweather's hand, and she withdrew it to her lap with a small whimper of disappointment. He rose to his full height and looked down at his toes, contrite as a schoolboy caught sticking wads of used chewing gum on the teacher's chair.

"Please forgive my enthusiastic outbursts."

Mrs. Merriweather sniffed, proving she had not yet been won over.

"Kate told me so much about you, but her descriptions pale against the reality of meeting a prime filly like you in person."

Kate gritted her teeth and flinched at Matt's barnyard comparison. Mrs. Merriweather merely shifted her feet upon the floor, and then used the added leverage to push herself farther back on the sofa, sitting straighter.

"I know your visit was prompted by concern for Kate. But the mere fact that a woman of your stature chose to call on us so soon after our wedding practically drives me speechless with amazement."

Speechless, my eye, thought Kate. She hadn't heard him blab so much in all the time she'd known him. Not that it would do him a bit of good. Mrs. Merriweather was far too sophisticated to fall for Matt's flamboyant blarney.

"And gratitude," Matt continued without missing a beat. "The good citizens of North Platte can't fail to notice the honor this visit brings upon us."

"Well." Mrs. Merriweather sniffed again, but it was a half-hearted shadow of her normally scornful dismissal. "Well."

It struck Kate then how easily Matt had taken control of the situation, how his decisive actions tended to quell their normal behavior. She and Henry stood there, mute and still as a pair of under-worked mimes. Mrs. Merriweather practically inhaled Matt's blatant flattery. She would have scolded Kate soundly if she'd ever exhibited so much blushing and simpering as flitted across the older woman's rounded and well-powdered features. All at once Kate understood why females should guard against revealing their susceptibility toward a man. Kate, for one, found Mrs. Merriweather's simpering display powerfully annoying.

"We have refreshments," Kate said.

That roused Mrs. Merriweather from her daze. "You didn't try your hand at petits fours again, did you, Kate my dear?" She and Kate shuddered as one at the mention of those tooth-cracking squares.

"Actually, Matt prepared something special for us."

"Matt?" Mrs. Merriweather's jaw dropped.

"I never met a man likes to putter around in the kitchen so much," Henry said.

"Don't be so modest, babe," Matt said, ignoring Henry's attack on his masculinity. He bestowed a proud smile upon Kate. "Kate helped me."

"Oh dear." The news obviously didn't please Mrs. Merriweather.

"Kate prepared the dough. I did the sauce and the toppings."

"So it's some sort of elaborate confection?" Mrs. Merriweather's eyes took on a distinct sparkle.

"Nah," said Matt. "It's just pizza."

"Pizza?"

"Matt says it's very popular where he comes from," Kate rushed to explain. "People enjoy pizza so much that they have it delivered to their homes in special little pouches."

"The pouches keep it warm," said Matt. "You can eat it cold, but it's better hot. That's why I figured we'd wait until we're ready to eat before I slide it into the oven. It should only take about ten minutes, and then we can enjoy some genuine wood-fired pizza."

"Well, go and fire away, young man." Mrs. Merriweather gave him a little wave of her hand.

"I'll make the tea," said Kate. When Matt's face dropped with disappointment, she asked, "What's wrong?"

"Tea with pizza?"

"Well, what would you suggest in place of tea?" asked Mrs. Merriweather.

"A cold one," he said promptly. "Beer."

Henry gave a mocking, superior-sounding snort. "Mrs. Merriweather is a lady. She don't drink beer."

"Well, actually . . ." The very tip of Mrs. Merriweather's tongue took a swipe along her lower lip. "That wagon ride was exceptionally dusty, Henry. This prolonged Indian summer weather takes a toll on a body. One or two tiny swallows of beer might not be considered improper under the circumstances."

"We have bottled beer in the springhouse," Kate offered impulsively, then regretted it at once. Mrs. Merriweather was sure to scold her for storing strong spirits on the premises. "The only reason I have some is because Pa always kept a stock of Mr. Gruber's homemade brew on hand, claiming a man couldn't afford to go riding into town every time he had to slake his thirst."

"Henry can fetch the beer for us," Mrs. Merriweather decreed.

"Let's go into the kitchen, then," said Matt. "Get along, little dogies."

Kate cringed, but Mrs. Merriweather simpered all the more. Perhaps she hadn't heard what Matt said, or understood that he meant for them to take refreshments around the kitchen table.

"All of us?" Kate asked.

"Sure, all of us."

"But . . ." Kate waved a hand, encompassing the parlor. She'd risen before dawn to shake the curtains, to dust between every carved toe in the claw-footed furniture, to pick the lint from the upholstery and carpet. She'd even wrapped a rag around her broom and swept down the dark-green walls after tackling the ever-bothersome cobwebs. Mrs. Merriweather hadn't spared a glance upon the parlor's impeccable state.

"Pizza tastes best when you eat it without utensils," Matt said. Mrs. Merriweather and Kate gasped in accord. Then that devil-spawn of a husband caught Mrs. Merriweather's hand in his and wriggled first the woman's puffy forefinger, and then her thumb. "Right from these delicate digits, Augusta. And it's a good idea to hunch forward a little when you eat it, just in case I was overzealous with the sauce. We wouldn't want anything dripping down the front of that exquisite creation you're wearing."

"Ladies don't eat with their fingers," Kate snapped. "Ladies don't hunch over when they eat, and they certainly don't dribble, considering the dainty bites they take." Good lord, she sounded shriller than Mrs. Merriweather in full voice.

"Please?" Matt murmured, running his thumb along Mrs. Merriweather's forefinger.

"Well, maybe just this once." Mrs. Merriweather batted her eyelashes. "You go fetch that beer now, Henry, and bring it to us in the kitchen."

They devoured Matt's pizza and clamored for more, until he had baked two additional pies. Matt complied eagerly with the demand, since it meant using the extra dough Kate had intended for the next day's bread. Now she'd have to make more. He couldn't wait to watch his temporary wife kneading dough again.

He'd been mesmerized by the tilt of her fine head, by the little puffs of air she expelled to blow away a troublesome tendril of hair. She'd looked edible herself, with flour dusting the crest of her cheeks and powdering her arms, with her sleeves rolled up beyond her elbows and those damned neck buttons undone.

Mrs. Merriweather sent Henry on refill runs to the springhouse between each pizza. Henry chewed on his slices with the stolid resignation of a man whose wife had packed nothing but unsalted rice cakes in his lunchbox, and he didn't imbibe at all. Matt nursed a couple of beers, surprised by and a little wary of its kick. The beer boasted a heady richness. He supposed Mr. Gruber's homemade brew was microbrewing at its best. Kate and Augusta, those erstwhile Victorian ladies, packed in pizza and beer with the gusto of a couple of linebackers carbo-loading before a big game.

The two women had withdrawn to Kate's bedroom at one point and returned red-faced and giggling, pressing their index fingers against their lips and making exaggerated shushing sounds. Augusta's abdominal dimensions had increased considerably during the interval, and her rose-colored gown strained at the seams accordingly. She'd probably had Kate help her loosen her girdle or whatever the hell it was women wore to make themselves look thinner.

"Matt," Kate said softly, "I really like pizza."

Her eyes sparkled with genuine pleasure. A good bit of her hair had fallen free of its loose upsweep, and shining tendrils had fallen to curl in tantalizing wisps against her skin. Skin which had taken on the warm rosy glow of a woman who'd just been thoroughly loved—or maybe was just a little bit tipsy. A tiny spot of sauce clung to the edge of her upper lip, begging to be kissed away. He breathed a silent prayer of thanks that they were sitting around a square table, with each person having a side to themselves with no need to touch.

Matt forced himself to look away from Kate's face, but concentrating on her hands turned out to be just as distracting. She toyed with a discarded crust—both she and Augusta had been appalled when he told them they shouldn't eat the crusts, but then they'd stacked them in neat little piles next to their plates. Watching her press the soft dough, rub her thumb over the smooth, baked surface, made his skin pulsate, craving her touch.

"Too bad I didn't have any pepperoni," he said, his voice harsh with a hunger that no food could alleviate.

"Pepperoni?" queried Augusta. "What on earth is that?"

"My husband boasts an amazing vocabulary." Kate sent him a proud smile that made him feel like he'd fought off six wolves with one hand tied behind his back.

"Yeah," Henry said with a sneer. "DOWMTAB-STA, DOWMTABSTA."

Matt caught himself jerking with each repetition of the word.

"DOWMTABSTA, DOWMTABSTA? Are you cussing in the—hic—presence of ladies, Henry Monroe?" Augusta's head wobbled a little as she fixed a glare upon Henry.

"Ask *him* if it's a cuss word." Henry's jaw jutted toward Matt. "He's the one always spouting the damned thing. And look at this. Found it wedged in the outside Sears catalog." He dug in his pocket for something, which he then slammed down in front of Kate with enough force to make both women jump.

Dread clutched Matt's gut. He'd forgotten to retrieve the slips he'd hidden in the outhouse.

Kate unfolded the slip and bent over it. Her lips moved silently, sounding out each letter. *Don't say it,* Matt prayed. *I'm not ready to go yet.* And then he gave himself a mental shake. Of course he was ready to go. He had more important matters to attend to than baking pizzas and swilling beer, better things to do than lurk around hoping Kate would start kneading dough.

And he would leave in a New York minute, if he

wasn't bound by his responsibility to restore Kate's confidence in her marksmanship. He seized on that thought with surprising relief, even while his analytical mind wondered whether it might not serve Kate just as well if he disappeared. As soon as she accepted the fact that he was permanently gone, her fear of shooting him would fade. Or maybe, knowing he'd abandoned her after promising to help her, she'd be happy to imagine his face gracing every bottle and target she shattered.

Somehow, the thought of her feelings for him hardening into hatred hurt worse than the guilt he felt over shaking her confidence.

He eased the slip from her and wadded it into a ball. "That's nothing important, Kate."

She shot him a smile of such dazzling relief that he wondered if she somehow knew what would happen once she said those words.

"I think—hic—" said Augusta, "that I shall take a look at that outside Sears catalog myself."

13

While Henry handed Augusta into the wagon, Matt and Kate stood framed by the front doorway, the very picture of proud newlyweds waving good-bye to their first official guest.

Matt judged the opening they stood in to be at least forty inches wide—plenty wide enough for two people to stand separately. But they were pretending to be happily wed, for Augusta's sake, and it seemed to him that a happily married man would curl his arm around his wife's shoulders and draw her close so they could wave good-bye as one. Together.

Kate participated in the deceptive display of affection with more enthusiasm than he'd expected. With a little sigh, she subsided against him, all warm and soft and outwardly willing. She stood angled so that the softness of her breast pressed against his ribs. Those damned ribs of his weren't doing much of a job of protecting his heart. Physically, he qualified,

not emotionally. The gentle pressure, the sensation of
Kate's soft flesh accommodating his, sent his pulse
soaring higher than any aerobic workout.

And then it raised itself another notch when Kate
rested her cheek against his chest. Her light breathing
stole through the spaces between the buttons on his
shirt, teasing his skin with the gentlest of caresses. He
ached to wrap his free arm around Kate's slim form,
enclose her in his embrace, until she stood pressed
head to toe against him. Instead, he forced himself to
put his arm to a more suitable use, which meant waving it toward Augusta with all the vigor of an ecstatic
Olympic coach urging his first-place runner across the
finish line.

Henry vaulted into the driver's seat and flicked the
reins over the horses' backs. They took off with a
lurch. Augusta clapped one hand over her hat and
used the other to maintain what appeared to be her
very precarious balance.

Matt and Kate stood locked together, watching the
wagon until it was no more than a pinpoint in the distance, until the dust stirred by its departure had
drifted back to the earth, until there was no possible
way Augusta could turn around and see that they
were still locked together. Kate made no move to
break the contact. Matt gently disengaged himself,
and found himself catching her when she swayed a little. Something within him—primal, male, potent—
gloried at the knowledge that such a casual embrace
could weaken her knees.

She trembled between his hands, and then gave a
mighty yawn.

"Good lord, I'm so tired I can barely stand
straight," she said. "I thought she'd never leave."

Disappointment shafted through him, and hard on

its heels ran desperation. He had to get away from this place, from this time. His instincts had deserted him. Misreading Kate's sleepiness for passion was bad enough; even worse was the way it hurt to realize that her snuggling, her apparent intoxication with him, were only pretense.

"She was having a good time. I thought you were, too."

"Oh, I had the very best time! Then all of a sudden, bam, my eyelids started drooping." To prove her point, she blinked up at him, slow, languid, her eyes dreamy and longing for bed.

"Beer does that to you." Matt's voice grated against his ears. He remembered long-ago days when a folding chair and rickety card table were his only furniture, and reams of scribbled pie-in-the-sky business plans cushioned his head when he couldn't force himself to stay awake another minute. Sometimes a plan would prove so promising that he'd toast it with a few beers. He'd awakened after those lonely celebrations with more beer cans than he cared to count littering the floor. Poor Kate was in store for a nasty headache and cottony mouth tomorrow morning. "You'd better get yourself straight to bed."

"And why should I take advice from a two-timing husband like you?"

"Two-timing?"

In answer, she lifted her hand, cocked at the wrist, and let it wobble in his general direction. "Planting your lips all over another woman in the presence of your wife. Tsk, tsk."

So, the chaste kiss he'd placed upon Augusta Merriweather's hand had roused a spark of jealousy. The realization should have sounded warning bells, cautioning him against letting Kate get too involved; instead, he found himself absurdly pleased that she'd noticed—and cared.

"It won't ever happen again," he promised solemnly.

She sniffed in an excellent imitation of Augusta Merriweather, except for the little giggle that was pure Kate.

"It was a harmless gesture," he protested with mock dismay.

"Show me."

Don't do this, he told himself even as he caught her hand and lifted it to his lips. *Don't do this.* Kate's skin was petal soft beneath his lips and he doubted gun grease had anything to do with its fine texture. *Don't do this.* He eased her hand over. Her palm opened for him and he kissed that, too, meaning it to be the barest brushing of lips against skin, but either she lost her balance or he lost control, he didn't know which, and he found himself wishing he could claim every inch of her body in just that fashion.

She stared up at him, wide-eyed with confusion. He muttered a curse and backed away. "Go to bed, Kate."

"Oh, I can't do that. I have to wait until Henry's asleep, so I can sneak into Pa's old room. It'll be at least an hour before he gets back from seeing Augusta home, and hours after that before he's ready to go to bed himself."

Maybe she wasn't as tipsy as he'd thought, if she remembered so many details about their ruse. And then she tittered, granting him a shred of hope that she hadn't been as troubled as he by his ill-conceived kiss.

"I'm purely surprised to find I had so much sneakiness buried in my character, Matt."

He'd never met a more generous, caring soul than Kate, whose eyes and expression revealed every one of her emotions. "You're not sneaky," he murmured.

"I'm not?" Those expressive eyes and quivering lips betrayed serious disappointment.

"Well, maybe a little bit sneaky," he said, just to make her happy. This sent such a self-satisfied tilt to her lips that he decided to take advantage of her good humor. "You really have to get to bed, Kate. Believe me, the more sleep you get now, the better you'll feel tomorrow. I'll make you a deal that should appeal to your sneaky side. You go to sleep in your own bed now, and I'll wake you once Henry's snoring."

"Then I can *sneak* into Pa's room." She pressed her fingers against her lips, but not before another giggle escaped. "But what'll you do while I'm asleep, Matt? Are you going to visit with Henry?"

"Lord, no." He didn't even try to hide the shudder that passed through him at that suggestion. The last thing he wanted to do was spend a couple of hours in Henry's company, bearing the weight of the younger man's wounded animosity undiluted by Kate's presence.

Come to think of it, he could do with a few hours' sleep himself, considering he'd spent most of the previous night tossing and turning while his mind calculated the distance between his bed and Kate's. "Maybe I'll just take a nap right along with you."

"Together?" she whispered.

Together. She was always saying that word to him, with the wistful longing of a woman who'd never found herself part of a couple, who always found herself peeking from the outside while others worked and played and did things . . . together. He understood, with the ache of one who'd always found himself on the fringes, not quite a stranger, not quite a member of a family. But Kate had had a real mother and father. He wondered what kind of life she'd led to foster such a palpable loneliness, and then dismissed his curiosity. He wouldn't be around long enough to learn such intimate details about her. And he didn't care, not at all, not really.

"I can rest in your rocking chair," he said.

"Oh." She looked away. "Okay."

She made no demands, and did not question his intentions. She simply accepted that he would sleep in her rocking chair and keep his urges under control while she slumbered in the bed right next to him. The depth of her trust staggered him; he wanted to grip her by her shoulders and shake her, and tell her that her faith in him was misplaced. How ironic. All his life he'd struggled to prove everyone wrong, and now that someone believed in him unconditionally, he doubted himself.

"It fits right into our plan, Kate. When Henry comes home and finds us locked together in the bedroom, he'll be more convinced than ever that we've consummated our marriage."

He had hoped to rouse another giggle, but had to settle for a smile. A smile of such heartbreaking disappointment that he suspected she made it merely to keep herself from crying. He told himself that it was none of his concern. Anyone who belted down a few too many brews often turned maudlin.

"That's real sneaky, Matt."

"Yeah."

She moved away from him into the hall, and began walking slowly to the bedroom. He'd done exactly right in sending her away. There was no reason why an ache should grip him somewhere in the region of his chest at the sight of her narrow form walking alone down the hallway. Soon enough he'd be walking alone himself, solitary, as he was meant to be.

Even so, he wished he had the right to experience, just for a little while, what it would feel like to walk side by side with Kate Monroe. Together.

Kate hesitated at the threshold of her room. The pleasant lightheadedness brought on by the beer had begun to dissipate the instant Matt stepped away from her. It deserted her entirely now, leaving a tingling, unspecific yearning in its wake. It suddenly seemed very foolhardy to cross that threshold, feeling as she did, knowing Matt followed a few steps behind.

He made the decision for her by coming up behind her and bumping his chest into her shoulders. The contact pushed her into the bedroom, with Matt following close on her heels.

"Sorry. I didn't realize you'd stopped walking."

"That's all right."

She didn't know if he looked at her while they exchanged their mundane remarks, because she kept her head lowered, unable to meet his gaze. Silly, silly, to have swallowed that third glass of beer. She hadn't meant to, limiting herself to the tiniest of sips. But sip after sip had produced the same results as if she'd tilted her head back and gulped down the whole glassful without stopping for breath.

Kate firmly scolded herself to stop rationalizing. She hadn't really been drunk, at least not drunk enough to account for lounging against Matt like a cat seeking a warm spot next to the woodstove. And she'd practically come right out and begged the man to kiss her hand! Which he'd done, thoroughly and with such skill that she fancied her palm still burned from the imprint of his lips, as if he'd branded her for life.

She wished she were tipsy now, if only to give her

some excuse for the racing of her heart, the inner tremors quaking through her limbs. She stole a peek at Matt, who seemed unaffected by the beer, despite drinking as much as she had. He stood in front of her rocker, staring down at its spindly arms and pouched cane seat with dismay, and she couldn't blame him. She couldn't imagine a more uncomfortable refuge for a man of his size. Why, the back of the chair would barely graze his shoulder blades, and his knees would stick out about a foot beyond the edge of the seat. He'd have no support for his head, no relaxation for his legs. The thought cheered her. Maybe he'd change his mind about this sneaky plan.

"Doesn't look too restful," she commented with false casualness.

"I've slept in worse places."

His remark jolted her. He carried himself with such elegance, moved with such grace, that she'd just assumed he'd come from a wealthy family who could afford dancing and deportment lessons, and a well-paid nanny to tuck pampered children into their feather beds and quilts each night. But pampered, well-loved children didn't grow up knowing all about abandoned babies and dumpsters.

She pondered this contradiction—yet another to go along with the others. Matt's confident outward bearing conflicted with the raw glimpses she'd caught of his inner soul. In her home, he wore denim and homespun, and yet she couldn't help believing he was more accustomed to clothing himself in white linen and fine piqué.

He was a stranger to his clothes, and she realized that he didn't quite fit anywhere else, either.

He prepared mouthwatering meals with the skill of a paid cook, and yet he'd been baffled at first by the cookstove's simple stoking and temperature control methods. He'd been delighted, though, with the hot water reservoir, even if his reaction had made no sense. "Cool," he'd said when she lifted the lid to reveal the steaming water.

He was forever digging through her silverware, looking for special knives and other utensils she'd never heard of. "I see you've been spared the Ginsu knife commercials." "Don't you have a whisk, Kate?" "I'd kill for my Cuisinart right now." He'd disbelieved her when she showed him her precious stock of cooking herbs and told her she must have more stocked away. "Where's the lemon pepper? The bay leaves? The curry powder?"

He didn't fit in her bedroom, either.

On very dark nights, she couldn't see the walls from the middle of her huge old feather bed. When she was a little girl, she'd been convinced that the room was far too big for one person, and only the certainty that her parents slept not far away stopped her from sobbing out her loneliness.

As an adult, she'd lost her fear, but still found the room wonderfully spacious. Its dimensions seemed to have shrunk since Matt stepped into it, though, almost as though the walls were as eager as she was to move closer to him. He dwarfed her furniture so that the pieces looked like long-cherished relics of childhood—which they were—but everything had been plenty big enough, until he'd come along.

He'd made the bed himself that morning, to her surprise, and stretched her mama's last quilt over everything as a bedspread. Though he'd apparently balked at putting Miss Ada back in her long-held place of honor at the middle of the pillow: he'd settled her atop the dresser with her faded skirts spread about her in perfect order.

Without Miss Ada on the bed, she and Matt would fill up that big old featherbed just fine.

Oh, lord, where had that thought sprung from? She made a little sound of distress, which distracted Matt from his glowering at the rocker.

"You should get ready for bed, Kate. Henry's not here. I'll go out into the hall while you change."

She nodded, and moved slightly away so that he wouldn't brush against her as he walked through the door.

For a moment she hesitated. She'd never undressed before with a man hovering just beyond the wall, knowing exactly what she was doing. If the situation were reversed, she'd probably be standing here imagining Matt's long, deft fingers loosening his buttons, sliding the cloth away from his skin until every sculpted, golden inch was revealed. Matt Kincaid, naked. Good lord! She vowed never to enjoy beer again, if this wanton thinking was what it led to.

She concentrated on removing her own garments and cursed Mary Margaret's desertion with every button she struggled to slip free. Then she realized she wasn't being fair to the little housemaid who had departed so tearfully, and took to cursing Mary Margaret's close-minded parents instead. And then she thought that the parents might let Mary Margaret return once they heard Kate was respectably married, and so she stopped cursing them, so as not to jinx the possibility.

She almost lapsed in that resolve when the most agile twisting of her limbs wouldn't let her free her corset ties. She'd fastened the darned thing herself— why couldn't she untie it now? Her conscience offered a ready response: maybe the knot had tightened on account of her swallowing enough pizza and beer to add two inches to her waistline.

"Are you decent?"

Matt's low voice rolled over her like warm honey. She reveled in it for a moment, and then realized she wasn't decent at all, not in thought or appearance. She stood there in the waning daylight with the bodice of her gown sagging down to her waist. She scooped up the dark blue silk and clasped it to her bosom, leaving her back bare to his sight.

"I guess I could use a little help."

Dusk was beginning to set in outside, which always threw her window into deep shadow. The window glass reflected an insubstantial Matt as he spun around the corner—thank God, he hadn't been looking at her, but must've been leaning against the wall in the hallway. She wished then that she'd thought to light a candle, for it turned her window into the next best thing to a mirror, and she could have watched him without his being aware of it. As it was, the window reflected just the haziest image of his fine features furrowed in concentration, just a tawny smudge that showed how his hair fell against his forehead as he bent his head to study the puzzle presented by her corset.

She wondered if her memory of him would fade in time, so that when she thought of him, she'd have to settle for a pale reflection of Matt's golden male splendor.

"If you could just loosen these knots, I can manage the rest," she said.

He grunted an acknowledgment, and made short work of the knots. "Why do you wear this thing?"

"All ladies wear corsets." She tried to hide her amazement. Although they'd never discussed such matters, she didn't have a single doubt that he'd undressed more than a few women. And she felt equally sure that he didn't bother with the overblown, slatternly type who disregarded corsets altogether.

"Some ladies might need them. You don't."

She supposed it was a compliment; her body certainly reacted to it as if it were one. She blushed with pleasure to think that he'd noticed her natural slimness.

"You seemed to like the way I looked in my dress when you first saw me wearing it." She remembered those golden-brown eyes riveted upon the vee at her waist.

"I like the way you look in everything you wear, Kate." His hand brushed the length of her back. "I like the way you look right now."

He spoke in the gruff tone of a man forced to make an admission against his will, and yet a pleasurable tremor coursed through her. It was easy enough to imagine how she looked from his vantage; she'd helped lace other women's corsets.

"I can finish in just a few minutes now," she said, and ended on a shuddering sigh when she felt his finger slip beneath the upper edge of her corset to slide against the skin along her shoulder blade.

"That damned corset digs into your skin."

"The marks will fade."

His finger traced her flesh again, and then his hands shifted to the lacing, his thumbs loosening each crossing, and then he was gone. She heard a soft thump from the hallway and supposed he'd slumped back against the wall.

She couldn't keep sending him in and out of the room like a butler doing his lady's bidding. She shrugged out of her gown, unbuttoned her petticoat and bustle from her corset, and let everything fall to the floor. She peeled the corset up and over her head and added that to the heap. Clad only in her low-cut combination, she fumbled in the dresser drawer for her lady's Pyjama, which was even more concealing than the flannel nightgown she'd worn the night before. For some reason, it seemed important to cover herself up. It took her two tries to get each leg into the right opening—perhaps the beer's effect hadn't dissipated as thoroughly as she'd hoped—and then she buttoned it clear up to her neck, though she usually left the two topmost buttons undone.

There. Now six yards of stout flannel covered her from ankles to neck, not to mention her wool combination. Matt Kincaid wouldn't get one glimpse of the kind of skin that invited improper strokes of the finger. But just to be safe, she gathered her discarded gown into her arms as a sort of barrier before summoning him. "You can come back in now."

He sauntered back in with the easy grace of a lion. His glance flicked over her from head to toe. "Charming," he drawled. "What is it—a jumpsuit?"

"Lady's Pyjamas are the latest thing," she said, wondering what a jumpsuit might be. "Well, in North Platte, at least."

"Always trying to catch up with New York fashion, right?"

She nodded. That explained it. He had mentioned he divided his time between New York, Chicago, and Los Angeles. Probably every woman in New York City wore something called a jumpsuit to bed. She wondered if he knew enough about them to give her some design hints, so she could introduce the fashion to North Platte.

But then, was he the sort of man who paid much mind to style? His garments certainly hadn't indicated as much. If he were truly her husband, she'd work her fingers to the bone creating garments fine enough to do justice to his good looks. And even then it wouldn't be enough, she realized, because she wanted to see more of Matt Kincaid than the polished, slick surface he presented to the world. She didn't know what gave him joy. He knew all about her hopes and dreams, and yet never gave her a hint as to what made his spirit soar.

"I don't know anything about you," she blurted out.

He grew very still. "That's not true."

"It is so true. All I know about you is your name, and that you don't have a real place to call home, and that you're some kind of businessman."

He turned his head a little, jutting his jaw skyward, as if the bare litany of what she knew about him both shamed him and demanded that he defend it. "Maybe that's all there is to know about me, Kate."

"No." His comment appalled her. Perhaps he'd meant it as a joke, but no, he met her gaze unflinchingly, without a hint of a smile. He lifted his head a notch, and a sudden bleakness overtook his features.

She busied herself with hanging her gown and tucking the muslin protective sheet over it. Too long, she was taking too long to come up with something that would wipe that anguish from his face.

She realized suddenly that she did indeed know many things about Matt Kincaid, and all of them were impossibly difficult for a straightforward woman like herself to put into words. He hadn't mocked her dreams. He'd shouldered woman's work in order to allow her time to practice, and then hadn't made fun of her when she found herself unable to shoot. He'd stood up against Henry and Augusta when they tried decimating her with their sharp wits and tongues, and he'd turned Augusta from harpy to friend in the space of a single afternoon.

"You're very good with people," she said, figuring that would be a good start.

"I'm very good at manipulating people," he corrected her. "There's a difference, Kate, and it isn't an ability most men would be proud to claim."

"Then why do you do it?"

"To get my way."

"Are you manipulating me, too?"

"Sometimes." She flinched, and pain flashed across his features, mirroring her own. "Not now," he added quietly.

"How will I know when you're doing it?"

"You probably won't. Don't trust me, Kate. Everything I do has an ulterior motive."

She wondered wildly which of the dozen kindnesses he'd shown her had been carefully calculated to manipulate her—but for what purpose? She lived a quiet life here in North Platte, and held but a single aspiration: to join the Wild West Show. They'd both agreed that their marriage was a temporary convenience, easily shed. *I need you,* she'd told him. *I need you too,* he'd admitted, offering no real explanation.

Her brain, fumbling for enlightenment, pounced upon some of the toe-curling tales that circulated whenever folks got together to gossip, tales of gunslingers trying to dodge an unsavory past, of embezzlers and thieves running away from prosecution. Such a man might welcome a temporary marriage with a sort of respectable woman in a quiet frontier town.

Try as she might, she couldn't imagine Matt filling one of those roles. Even so, it would be prudent to be wary around him.

"I can't trust you or believe anything you say."

"No, you can't."

"Has anyone ever dared trust or believe in you?"

She shocked herself with her boldness, and wished she could call back the question when he sucked in his breath as if she'd walloped him in the belly.

"No."

She wondered what it had cost him to make that admission. But before she could ask, he snatched her mama's last quilt off the bed with no care for its age or sentimental value. He cocooned himself within it like a cowboy preparing for a cold night without a campfire. Or like someone piling on an added layer of false protection to keep a curious woman from poking at secret tender spots.

"I don't care to continue this discussion," he grumbled from within the quilt.

With that, he plopped himself down in the rocker with his back facing her so that he looked like a giant version of those enchilada things Mrs. Clemson's Mexican cook had prepared the one time Kate had been invited to lunch. In under a minute, a very unconvincing snore came from the vicinity of his head.

Well, she could take a hint. Surprisingly, she felt herself smiling. She had the feeling that Mr. Matt-the-Manipulator Kincaid didn't often find himself backing off from confrontation. And then she sobered. She remembered the bleak despair in his eyes when he'd admitted nobody had ever trusted him, and that memory squelched any satisfaction she felt in forcing him to retreat from her curiosity.

She closed their door softly, enclosing within the room's space a man who had never been trusted and a woman who wished she could be the first, even though she had no business wishing such a thing. She stole over to the bed and crawled beneath the covers, pulling them clear up to her chin.

Her life would have taken an entirely different turn, she realized, if nobody had trusted or believed in her. Her pa's faith in her shooting ability had been the bedrock upon which she'd built her dream. Henry had seemed to share that faith too, until recently. She'd thrived on their belief in her until her own confidence outweighed theirs. That had troubled her, sometimes, but now she thought that perhaps it was the way it should be. There always came a time when a person had to stop depending upon the support of others and begin to rely upon herself. From Matt's sketchy comments, she gathered that he'd been forced into depending on himself far too soon, and for far too much.

The twilight deepened, making the room plenty dark enough to fall asleep. But she lay awake for a very long time, wondering how a person ever summoned the strength to go on if nobody'd ever believed in him.

She lay awake so long that she heard Henry come home. She listened to him search the house, heard him pause and sigh before her closed bedroom door, and then plod to his own room with the weary tread of an old, old man.

At the first whistling hints of Henry's snoring, she eased from the bed. Tiptoeing past Matt in the rocking chair, she froze at the door, judging the quality of Matt's breathing. He wasn't asleep, she would swear it, but he murmured no encouragement for her to stay, whispered no good night wishes. She slipped through the door, and stole into Pa's room. She settled into the bed.

Her ears attuned to the sounds coming from her room: the creak of old wood as Matt levered himself off the rocking chair, the faint clicking snicks as the abandoned chair rocked into stillness, the groan of the bed ropes as he eased himself into her bed.

Her instincts had been on target—he hadn't been asleep any more than she had. He could have asked her to stay, if he'd wanted her company. She remembered that old cat that he'd mentioned, the one that never jumped up onto his lap. He fed that cat sometimes, the way he sometimes sent a few crumbs of kindness Kate's way. A woman could learn a lot from a smart cat.

She murmured a silent prayer of thanks that she'd followed her intuition to leave the room the minute she'd heard Henry snoring. It had been easier on her pride, leaving on her own, than waiting until Matt sent her away.

14

Henry might hate his guts, but that didn't stop him from consuming the lion's share of their breakfast, Matt noted sourly. The clod sat there forking and chewing and swallowing his heart-attack-on-a-plate breakfast with the mindless efficiency of a wood chipper.

Well, Henry might as well eat everything. Kate, subdued and pale as befitted one suffering from a hangover, merely toyed with her food. Matt took a few bites, but nothing had any taste, and it didn't seem to make a dent in the emptiness that gripped him somewhere in the region of his gut.

Of course, the atmosphere didn't help. So much tension vibrated through the room that, if only he could figure out how to harness it, he might have been able to power a television set. If only he had a television set.

Now he'd done it. Now that he'd relaxed his guard

and allowed himself to remember some of what he was missing, homesickness was sure to wash through him. He expected that it would hit suddenly, with enough force to make him drop his fork. He waited. And waited a bit more, until he got distracted by the play of Kate's slender fingers tracing the rim of her coffee mug. He had no appetite for food, but developed an instant urge to substitute himself for Kate's coffee mug, so she might draw enticing patterns against his skin rather than on cold, impervious porcelain.

There would be some back in 1997 who might say that Kate wouldn't notice the difference, he'd prided himself on developing such a tough shell. Kate's gentle touch posed a serious threat to his imperviousness, like sweet springtime breezes swirling around a snowman. When snowmen melted, they left their smiles behind to mark the place where they'd been created and defeated.

Good God, he was supposed to be hungering for the future! Instead, he just felt hungry, but not for food. Perhaps thinking about television hadn't been enough to prompt homesickness—God knew he'd spent little enough time watching the crap the networks called entertainment. No wonder he caught himself staring at Kate when he should be hankering for the future. He forced himself to concentrate on compiling an inventory of the things he missed.

He missed fresh-squeezed orange juice and his Vita-Mix machine and his electric coffee grinder. Missed reading his home-delivered *Wall Street Journal* while his CD player entertained him with the sounds of Mannheim Steamroller. He missed IHOP, Dunkin' Donuts, any of the hundred and one places where he'd met for informal breakfast meetings amid the clatter of silverware, the chatter of waitresses.

Coffee grinders and waitresses. He didn't know what that said about him, that the only things he could summon some longing for were either inanimate objects or nameless hirelings who were paid to be nice to him. He found himself staring at Kate again, and realized with a start that Tiffany, Heather, and what's-her-name hadn't made his list.

"It's been a long time since you wore your hair down at the table, Kate," said Henry, providing a welcome break into Matt's thoughts.

"Oh. I suppose so." Kate raised a self-conscious hand to pat at the back of her neck, where she'd caught her hair back with a piece of ribbon. "I couldn't pin it up this morning. It was too tangled."

Henry paused with his overloaded fork lifted halfway to his mouth, and then with a muttered oath he slammed the utensil to the table, sending chunks of syrup-laden pancake flying.

Before Matt could say a word Henry pushed away from the table with so much force that his dishes slid into each other and his chair crashed to the floor. He bolted from the kitchen.

"Well, what on earth got him so riled up?" Kate continued poking at her food while her puzzled gaze watched Henry's furious progress toward the barn.

"The hair thing." Matt straightened the chair and started stacking the dishes. He eyed the chunks of pancake glued to the floor and the trickles of syrup trailing over the edge of the table. The mess could lie there until Henry cleaned it up. It'd serve the overgrown adolescent right to scrape everything clean with Kate's skin-eating lye soap.

"Henry's never paid a lick of attention to my hair."

"He probably noticed it more than you realized." Matt spoke with the authority of one who'd found himself spellbound by the play of sunlight against her hair, by the springy vitality of it curling over her shoulders. She still didn't seem to understand. "Kate, he thinks your hair got tangled from spending the night in bed with me."

"No!" Mortification oozed from her like that damned syrup spreading all over everything. "With one thing and another . . . I mean, I wasn't quite myself yesterday and I forgot to braid it before going to bed, that's all. And this morning I had to beat Henry to the kitchen before he caught me in Pa's room, and now that Mary Margaret's gone it takes a good two hours to brush out my hair by myself once it gets like this, and—"

"Kate, slow down." Matt pressed a finger against her lips. "Our plan's working. He thinks we've consummated the marriage. It's okay."

"Oh, that's right. Our plan." She continued blushing, despite his reassurances.

"Does it really take you two hours to brush out your hair?"

She nodded. "By myself, yes. When Mary Margaret worked here, she helped and it didn't take nearly so long. It tangles something fierce. I don't wear it down very often anymore."

He remembered the way her hair had whipped in the wind that first day, when she'd shot him. It suited her, to wear it waving wild and free. She never managed to get it completely under control, because a stray tendril or two always escaped its bonds to curl with shining vibrancy against her skin.

"Don't you use a conditioner?"

"A what?"

"You know, the stuff you put on after you rinse out the shampoo. It helps with detangling."

"Matt, believe me, if somebody invented a product like that, he'd be an instant millionaire and I'd be his first customer."

"I'll help you brush it."

He regretted his offer at once. But she gave him no opportunity to call it back. Instead she gazed at him with such rapturous delight that he would have gladly curried a herd of woolly mammoths, if only she would keep looking at him like that.

"Oh, would you! Would it . . . Would it be too much if I asked you to wait while I run out and wash it first? I haven't been able to wash it since the other day when you, um, arrived. The knots really do work free easier when my hair's wet. And it'll dry real quick in the sun while I practice."

Matt hadn't witnessed anyone so hellbent on washing her hair since the head cheerleader had turned him down when he dared to ask her out on a date. At least Kate wasn't turning down his offer, and she hadn't flinched at the mention of rifle practice. He supposed that was progress of a sort, and forgave himself for making his impulsive offer.

"Are you up to handling firearms this morning?"

"Why wouldn't I be?"

"I thought you might be a little . . . unsteady, after the beer."

"I only had three glasses, Matt."

"They seemed to affect you."

"No, I simply get a bit silly and tired if I drink more than two measures of any kind of spirits. My pa always said I inherited his taste for drinking but not his head for it. No matter how much I practiced, I never got any better at it."

"You've been practicing drinking beer?"

"Well, sure. It would be dangerous for a gal to go

off with the Wild West Show without learning her limits."

All of a sudden, Matt felt a sudden stab of kinship for Henry, an understanding of why the younger man sabotaged Kate at every turn. Kate and Henry both had alluded to their belief that Buffalo Bill Cody was a womanizer. A sweet innocent like Kate had no business running off with him. Practicing drinking beer in her safe, sturdy ranch house could never prepare her for the debauchery that Matt felt certain prevailed in a performing troupe.

The image of Kate's hair blowing free, which had haunted him mere moments ago, returned to taunt him with more sinister implications. Hundreds of men, thousands of men, could gape at Kate as much as they liked, watching that glorious hair stream in the breeze, staring at her fringes dancing against her firm curves, and nobody could force them to close their eyes, because they would have paid for the privilege.

Yes, he could understand Henry a little better now. If Kate truly belonged to Matt, he wouldn't let her go, either.

Too bad Kate didn't keep a couple of pigs in her barnyard, he mused. He could have used a couple of timely oinks to remind him that men of the twentieth century didn't hold such restrictive views of what women could and couldn't do.

She'd risen from her chair and reached both hands to the back of her neck while she worked her hair ribbon loose. Her posture stretched her white cotton blouse tight against her breasts. She didn't wear a bra. Maybe bras hadn't been invented yet. Too bad Big 'Un wouldn't allow Matt to screw up history a little, because he'd like to pay off whoever invented bras and tear up the patent. Kate's breasts beckoned, soft and full and unrestricted, the perfect natural shape for a man to fit his hand around.

Screw all those politically correct feminist beliefs. If Kate belonged to him, he wouldn't let her go.

But she didn't belong to him. She had a dream, which he'd jeopardized by crashing into her life, and no matter what he and Henry wanted, Kate deserved the chance to make her dream come true. He returned to the safe topic of washing hair.

"It must be difficult to rinse the shampoo out in that shallow stream."

"I wouldn't wash my hair in the stream, especially not on a fine day like this. I'll use the shower, though the water will probably be almost as cold."

"You have a *shower?*" He didn't bother hiding his incredulousness. Ever since he got here he'd been dousing himself at the stream. Its frigid water hinted that winter lurked, waiting for this glorious stint of Indian summer to dissipate.

"Well, sure. Didn't you notice the barrel hanging near the eave?"

"Oh, that barrel." He'd noticed the barrel, all right, and the phone-booth-sized stall beneath it, but had thought it some animal-related structure. "A shower," he repeated in disbelief.

"I'll do myself up real quick."

She scampered down the hallway and returned with an armful of soft cloths. Towels, he supposed. After shooting him another grateful smile, she darted through the door. And then he did his best to clean up Henry's mess, concentrating fiercely upon the unpleasant chore in a vain attempt to forget that Kate stood nearby, naked beneath a stream of water, her body glistening in the sunlight.

A shower. God knew he needed one. He'd visit

that little stall himself as soon as he could. He hoped the water would be damned cold. Maybe it would bring him to his senses.

She returned in minutes, fully dressed, and with a towel wrapped around her head. His relief at finding her well covered didn't last longer than a heartbeat. Her collar hung askew and her blouse and skirt clung in damp patches against her skin. Her skin glimmered pearly pink at the wet patches, more alluring than the images conjured by Matt's overworked imagination.

He stepped behind a chair, using it as a shield to guard her against his physical reaction to her damp, sweet-scented desirability. "Sit here while I brush," he said.

She sat down and unwound the towel, then bowed her head as he began working upon the thick, sinuous mass of her hair. He should be grateful, he realized, that she'd suggested washing her hair first, because he didn't know how he could endure handling it in its dry, supple state, with it running through his fingers like sheer silk. Wet, and redolent of lily of the valley, it was as squeaky clean as the advertisements always promised but never delivered. None of the split ends or chemical damage that Pinckney and those two other what's-their-names were forever spending a fortune to alleviate.

He lifted all Kate's hair at once when he'd untangled it, revealing the vulnerable curve of her neck, the proud line of her chin. With long strokes from her scalp to the ends of her hair, he marveled at the strength it required to keep at it and keep at it . . . And she did it herself for two hours, every time.

"It's done," he said, letting the nearly dried, sweet-smelling mass tumble over the edge of the chair as he stepped away.

She rose and whirled around to face him. She drew a tendril over her shoulder, rubbing it between her fingers. She shivered, but with delight, not fear. "I declare, Matt, nobody's ever done anything for me that felt that good."

I could do things that would make you feel even better. He bit his lip to stop the words, and while he gained control, his mind taunted him with the memories of the furs, the jewels, the luxury vacations he'd gifted women with over the years without earning such heartfelt delight.

"It was nothing," was all he said.

Kate stroked her rifle's satiny smooth stock. She had helped her pa sand it and varnish it until its sheen surpassed that of the finest walnut furniture. She'd participated in every step of its construction. No finer rifle existed, she would bet her life on it. Already she'd had not-so-casual inquiries from gentlemen in town asking if she'd given any thought to selling the four rifles Crandall Monroe had handcrafted during his lifetime.

This particular weapon had been made for her and her alone. Its weight suited her perfectly. The butt had been carved to match the ridge of her collarbone; a unique, barely perceptible dip in the stock nestled her cheek. This rifle fit her so comfortably, seemed so much a part of her, that she sometimes surprised herself by finding she'd carried it along without noticing the effort instead of putting it away. It had been a friend of sorts, the means to achieving a long-held dream—and now she couldn't lift it without wanting to fling it away.

Steeling herself, she hoisted it to her shoulder. The tremors seized her as soon as she lined up the sights, sending the barrel jittering so wildly that she was more apt to blow off one of her toes than shatter her glass bottle targets. She clamped her teeth together to stop them from rattling. If she could get just one shot off, maybe she'd break this jinx. Every ingrained safety lesson her pa had ever taught her screamed a warning, but she closed her eyes anyway and curled her fingers around the trigger. She would shoot blind. Now, she would shoot. She would. Now. Now.

Closing her eyes only made it worse. At once she was taunted by the image of Matt suddenly appearing in her sights, after she'd squeezed the trigger. Only in this nightmare of a daydream, he hadn't managed to slide down the rock fast enough to take the bullet in his shoulder, and the blood drenching his shoulder gushed from a mortal wound. With a small whimper of defeat, she opened her eyes and cradled her rifle across her arms.

"Kate? You don't have to worry about me. I'm here, by the kitchen door."

"I know." She knew Matt had come out onto the back stoop to watch her because the god-awful din had stopped. She'd never known a soul who raised such a commotion in the kitchen, and she suspected that someone who ordinarily moved with such economical grace had to go out of his way to cause so much clanging and slamming. He was trying to let her know she could shoot safely without worrying about him popping up in front of her. She made a feeble wave in Matt's direction, torn between bursting into tears over her cowardice or his kindness.

"Are you all right? You've been out there a long time."

"I'm fine. I'm just . . . easing myself back into it slowly."

"Well, okay." He didn't sound as though he believed her any more than she believed herself. "You take your time. And don't worry if you hear a lot of noise—I'm going to start something else, and I might not be as quiet."

She didn't know if the half-smile he sent her meant he was joking or telling the truth. "I just hope my stove lids and skillets can hold up under the strain," she answered.

He ducked back into the kitchen without responding. In a couple of minutes, as promised, the din recommenced at such an accelerated level that she wouldn't be surprised to find a train engine had blasted through her house with all its bells and whistles in full voice.

Matt's noisy efforts accomplished nothing. Instead of making progress, she'd gone backward. She couldn't even lift her beloved rifle, let alone try shooting it. The funny part was, she couldn't seem to summon much grief over her lost ability. The clamor coming from the kitchen beckoned more enticingly than a pipe organ calling crowds to a circus parade.

She swallowed. She tried to look on the bright side and couldn't really find one. Colonel Cody would be home any day now, and Augusta had let it slip the day before that at least two female sharpshooters had come from out of town and taken rooms at the Pacific House hotel, hoping to gain an audition with him. That information ought to worry her a whole lot more than it did.

She trudged back to the kitchen. She knew Matt wouldn't be able to hear if she merely called out that he could stop making all the noise.

She poked her head past the doorway, wincing at the noise. "M—." His name died in her throat.

He stood with his back to the door, facing the stove. He'd changed into his sleeveless shirt, but baring his arms hadn't been enough to keep him cool, for a dark vee of perspiration colored the shirt from his shoulders to the middle of his back.

He balanced on one leg. He held his other leg straight out in front of him, with the toes hooked under the oven door handle, swiveling his hip and flexing his leg to rhythmically open the door and slam it shut. She couldn't imagine the strength and muscle discipline required for such an activity, even though his position drew his britches so shockingly tight across his backside and thighs that she could see plenty of evidence of that strength, and how nicely he fit together.

She was as bad as him, staring at backsides! She shifted her attention to his upper body, and realized his strength wasn't limited to his legs. He held a cast-iron skillet in each hand and banged them together with the enthusiasm of a schoolboy clapping erasers for his favorite teacher. With each movement, the homespun stretched across his shoulders. His upper arms bulged and flexed, each muscular indentation highlighted by a light sheen of sweat. He sure was one magnificent man from behind. From the front, too, if she were honest with herself. And he was employing all that magnificent male beauty for her. It made her feel a little breathless, a little shaky, but not at all the same sort of shakiness she'd felt outside while trying to shoot.

Despite his exertions he seemed to be breathing easily—in fact, it sounded like he was counting. Under his breath, but in a way she'd never heard. "One, seven. Two, seven. Three, seven." Until he got up to the number ten, and he started, "One, eight, two, eight . . ."

"Matt?" He didn't hear her. "Matt!"

That time he heard her. With a sharp cry, he bounced at the knee and then swiveled on his stationary foot, reminding her of the ballet dancers she'd seen hopping across the stage at Lloyd's Opera House. He held the skillets high and wide apart.

"I'd sure hate to be a fly mashed between those swatters," she said, trying for a light touch over the sudden tightness of her throat.

"Jesus, Kate." He swallowed, and looked at the skillets the way she'd taken to looking at her rifle lately. Although he'd been banging them pretty good with no obvious effort, his arms shook a little when he lowered the skillets to his sides. And then he blushed, a dull, clay-colored stain rising from his throat to his face. From the way he scowled, she imagined he felt the heat in his face and was not pleased about it.

"Do you always do that?" she asked. He'd asked the same thing of her when she'd apologized for her dropping the tray; now she understood why he'd forced her to admit she hadn't been clumsy. She hated seeing Matt look so humiliated at being caught doing a kindness, acting as though he'd done something wrong.

"No, I'm normally very quiet in the kitchen."

"That's not what I mean. Do you always get embarrassed when people catch you doing nice things for them?"

He didn't answer her for a full two minutes. She bit her tongue to keep from bursting into chatter to cover the awkward silence. She suspected his lack of response might be one of those manipulative characteristics he'd mentioned, and if so, she'd be playing right into his hands by changing the subject.

"Since I've never done anything quote-unquote nice for anyone, I guess I'd have to say I'm batting a thousand. I'm not embarrassed at all."

Well, maybe he had batted those darned skillets together a thousand times—he ought to know, he'd been counting. She could refute the beginning of his statement, though, and she did.

"Matt, what you were doing with those skillets was nice. You were trying to help me."

"I'm trying to help myself."

"By helping me regain my confidence?"

"Yes, damn it, by helping you regain your confidence!"

She swayed a little, overcome with mortification. How could she have forgotten that he'd warned her never to trust or believe in him? Theirs was a temporary arrangement, meant to help him recover his strength and memory while she kept her reputation spotless until she'd had a chance to audition for Colonel Cody.

Matt's rapid recovery had turned their agreement into a decidedly one-side bargain, and everything he'd done since—doing the cooking so she could practice, helping her with her hair, deflecting Henry's ire—only increased her debt to him. She had no business growing all lead-chested and tight-throated over the reminder that he'd made a bad bargain and was eager to conclude the deal as soon as possible.

"I . . . I just came to tell you that I'm finished practicing for today. I need to spend a few hours in the gun shop."

He gave a curt nod. "I was thinking of taking a little run myself."

"Run? To where?"

"Not *away,* if that's what you're afraid of."

The pain shafted through her so quickly that she had no chance to bite her tongue, no chance to muffle the humiliating whimper that escaped her throat. Just because Matt couldn't be trusted or believed didn't mean he should doubt the motives of everyone else.

"I never thought that for an instant," she whispered. "You promised you'd stay until my audition."

"Oh, Jesus, Kate." With an angry flick of his wrists he sent the skillets clattering to the table. Then, to her astonishment, he reared back and kicked the pine baseboard. "What the hell am I doing?" he muttered.

"I believe it's called a temper tantrum," Kate said.

"I don't have a temper!" he roared.

She let an insulted, disbelieving little sniff answer for herself. Judging by the dismay flickering across Matt's features, it seemed that Mrs. Merriweather had been right in calling it one of a woman's most potent weapons.

"I'm going for a run." He stared down at his feet and shuddered as if the sight of his stout leather boots displeased him. "I need air. I need to work off some energy."

"Fine. I'll be in the gun shop."

"Fine."

"Fine."

He bolted from the house. Kate leaned in the doorway, watching him diminish in a haze of dust. From his frantic speed, you'd think the man feared she meant to grab up those skillets herself and smash something soft, like his heart, between the unforgiving cast iron.

There was no earthly reason why such a thought should cheer her. But it did.

15

The boots weighed down Matt's feet and rubbed raw the very areas his Reeboks would have cushioned in comfort. The Nebraska plains stretched flat to the eyes, but not to the feet. Low-lying grassy tufts crouched against the dirt like bad-tempered hedgehogs, snagging his toes and sending him stumbling over rocks and into depressions in the soil.

If someone were watching him from afar, he'd probably look like one of those half-starved, shambling wrecks who escaped from a third-world prison after having been beaten and tortured and humiliated past endurance. Such an escapee had every reason in the world to run, while he, Matt Kincaid, ran for his life because . . . because . . .

Because Kate had said he was nice.

Nice. He'd sat across conference tables and listened to every vile epithet hurled his way without flinching. He'd taken a perverse sort of pleasure in knowing some admired his thick skin, some envied it, some simply gave in to his demands because they knew he was impervious to insults.

His breath rasped in his ears. His heart pounded louder than those damned skillets that had brought this all about. He could see birds flitting through the sky, cows in the distance, but heard nothing except for his own breath and thrumming pulse. And then something whirled near his head. He suddenly found himself sprawled face-first in the dirt with a band of iron holding his arms clamped to his sides.

The thud jarred him back to his senses, and restored his hearing. He heard the huffing of a horse, the jingling of its tack, the groan of leather as its rider dismounted. No band of iron encircled him, but a coil of tough rope—he'd been lassoed like a runaway bull. Matt curled his legs. He could leap to his feet in an instant, once he knew which direction to face.

"Running out on her already, Kincaid?"

Matt muttered an oath when he recognized the voice. He inhaled some gritty dust in the process, but didn't consider it prudent to start spitting it out just then. "I wasn't going anywhere, Henry."

"Could have fooled me." Henry called an indecipherable command to his horse. The animal responded with a snort and shifted its position, easing the pressure on the rope.

Matt rolled, then swiveled into a sitting position while he flexed against the rope, loosening it. Henry stood looking down at him, his cowboy hat casting his face in full shadow and the rest of him not much more detailed, with the sun lighting him from behind. Matt had no intention of peering up and blinking in awe as if Henry were Clint goddamned Eastwood, so he stood and let the noose fall to the ground around his

feet. Mindful of the horse, who watched with its ears
pricked interestedly, he stepped out of the rope circle
before Henry could issue another command that
might entrap him again.

He still couldn't believe Henry was a mere twenty
years old. Kate had explained how hard work out-
doors had weathered his skin, but there was a sense
of maturity and purpose about the man that would
have led Matt to trust him, if they'd met under different circumstances.

Under *these* circumstances, with no other humans
in sight and Henry's hand resting casually atop the
butt of his pistol, Matt didn't trust him at all.

"So, where were you going?"

"Out there, a little farther." Matt waved one hand
over the plains and swiped some of the grit from his
mouth with the other. "Then back to the house. Just a
short run."

"Huh. You got so much energy to waste, why don't
you try pitching in with the chores?"

"I don't—"

"Yeah, that's right, you don't dirty your hands with
men's work." Henry's contemptuous glance raked
over Matt from head to toe. Matt didn't have to look
to know his clothes were caked with so much dust
that he might as well have spent the day wrestling
calves to the ground, or whatever it was that Henry
did all day.

Well, so what? He was sick to death of placating
Henry and skirting around the real explanations for
his behavior. Since he couldn't divulge the truth
about himself without sounding like a lunatic, he settled for putting Henry in his place. "It's not worth the
effort to try explaining things to you." He turned on
his heel and began walking back toward the ranch.

He hadn't worked off all his excess energy yet, but he'd be damned if he'd break into a run and make it seem like he was afraid.

"You don't turn your back on me!" Henry hollered.

Matt kept on walking. He heard a few grunts and then that whistling whine that had preceded his fall. The son of a bitch meant to rope him again! He ducked and sidestepped, and with a lightning-quick motion caught the flying noose at the base of its knot. The lasso dangled impotently against his arm. He turned the rope around his palm, once, twice, and then remembered that Henry had a horse on his side, and loosened one of the turns so he couldn't be entrapped in the twists. He jerked his arm, drawing the rope taut between himself and Henry.

"Don't try this again." Matt spoke the order with the emotionless calm that warned that anything less than instant obedience would be punished without mercy. CEOs from every developed country—as well as more than a few from third-world countries— dreaded facing that impassive face, that deadened tone of voice, across the negotiating table.

Henry met him, man to man, for the space of two heartbeats before looking away. He dropped the section of rope he'd been holding. Its end was still tied to the horse, but tension no longer hummed along its length.

The wind teased a cowlick from Henry's dry-as-straw brown hair. His face didn't appear quite so mature and weather-ravaged with him scowling down at his toes like a little boy who'd been caught tormenting the neighbor's dog. He slumped, but even so, the edges of his sleeves bared gangly wrists, his pants skimmed his boots a good two inches higher that they should have. He suddenly looked every inch the still-growing, twenty-year-old, inexperienced youth that he was, and Matt Kincaid felt like the worst sort of bully for venting his frustration upon him.

He reminds me of myself when I was that age, Matt had told Kate, and realized anew the truth of it. When he was Henry's age, he would never have settled for half-truths and innuendo—he'd wanted answers, whether the truth seemed palatable or not. He'd demanded to be taken seriously. He'd wriggled and wormed his way into private functions and business affairs, refusing to be ignored. Although his goals had been loftier than Henry's seemed to be, he'd fought no less tenaciously until he'd gotten what he'd wanted.

Matt quelled the little spark of kinship he felt. If he wasn't careful, he'd start clapping Henry on the shoulder and calling him "son" when Henry was the one technically old enough to be *Matt's* great-great grandfather. As hungry for affection as Henry appeared to be, he'd latch on like a leech. That was the last thing Matt needed—another emotional entanglement, when he hadn't managed to work himself free of the first one.

And who was he to say his goals were any loftier than Henry's? asked that damned little voice in his head. A ranch and a woman like Kate were damn fine goals, at least for this day and age. Maybe for any day and age. He smothered that notion, too.

"I ain't never seen anyone catch a hurled lasso like that." Since Henry's head was still firmly pointed toward his boots, the grudging compliment came out as little more than a mumble.

"I'm not like anyone you know," Matt said.

He began looping the rope, walking slowly toward Henry as he did. He'd coiled almost all of it by the time he stood two paces in front of Henry. Then he held it out, wondering if Henry would recognize it as one of the strangest peace offerings of all time. He did. Henry accepted the coil and dropped his hand to his side, lightly whapping the rope against his thigh, and it was as if that symbolic spanking lightened the tension that had held them from the beginning.

"You can't blame me for not taking to you," Henry muttered.

"No, I can't. But you have to admit that I didn't exactly ask for what happened back at that rock."

"No, I guess you didn't."

Matt supposed that was progress of a sort, absolving each other of blame. If only this were a business deal, he'd know how to pursue that tenuous line of communication, bring it around to the heart of the subject. Instead, he found himself floundering for words, wishing on one hand that he'd learned more about soothing emotional wounds than plugging holes in investment strategy, and berating himself on the other hand for getting all soft-hearted.

"I just don't know why she had to do it!" Henry burst out, denying Matt any more time to ponder the problem. "She knows I would take care of her. I'd lay down my life for her."

"She knows that."

"Then why?"

Matt couldn't, in the face of Henry's anguish, lash out that it was all his own fault for pursuing Kate's hand in marriage. He tried instead to articulate thoughts and regrets that had tormented him throughout childhood, until he'd realized there was no changing what had gone before.

"I never knew my mother, Henry. Did you?"

"I don't know." Henry kicked at the dirt. "I was

just a baby when Pa Monroe found me. Miz Monroe
was sickly and she died a couple years after they took
me in. I still remember her." A bleakness ran across
Henry's expression.

"You blamed yourself when she died," Matt said.

"It wasn't none of my doing." Henry shrugged with
false nonchalance. "I wanted her to stay with us. She
died anyway."

Just as he wanted Kate to stay, Matt suspected. He
recognized in Henry the sort of guilt only a child
could feel when a loved one is lost and they shoulder
the blame. But he couldn't very well enter into a
heart-to-heart conversation along those lines without
revealing more about himself than he cared to let
Henry know.

"Then Kate's the one who changed your diapers?"
Henry nodded. "She wiped your ass when it looked
like you'd smeared it in mustard, and cleaned the snot
off your nose and picked you up when you fell and got
a boo-boo."

Henry flushed. "So what?"

"I've known old women who look at their fifty-
year-old sons and tell me they didn't see a powerful
businessman, but a gap-toothed little toddler running
across the kitchen floor with his diaper sagging
around his knees. They say mothers always remember
their children that way."

"Yeah. So what?"

"So Kate's older than you. You were a living,
breathing baby doll for her, better than any Cabbage
Patch Kid or whatever the hell they call them these
days."

"Kate ain't my mother."

"No, but there's something inside a good woman
that lets her take in orphans and foundlings and love

them until she forgets she didn't bear that child herself. You're like a son to her, Henry. She simply can't
look at you and see the man you've become."

Matt hoped like hell that he hadn't completely
ruined Henry's psyche with his half-baked psychology. But even as he'd tried explaining things to Henry,
he'd found he based his comments on inner beliefs he
hadn't known he possessed.

"Kate doesn't need me anymore, now that you're
here."

Matt suspected that Henry had just articulated his
real fear. And again, he could sympathize with an
empathy he disliked exploring. He'd run away from
more foster homes than he could remember, but there
had been a time when a whispered, *Matt, you'll
always have a home with us,* might have kept him
from running. And another time, if only someone had
spared a minute from their familial grief to remember
him hovering around the edges long enough to say,
*We're going to need you now more than ever. Please
stay, Matt . . .*

The Monroe ranch had been Henry's home for as
long as he could remember. He'd lost first his foster
mother, then his foster father, and now feared losing
the only person in the world who cared about him.
Marrying Kate had probably seemed like the only
solution to a man who feared losing everything important.

"Kate needs you, Henry. I won't be here for very
long."

Henry's head shot up, and his eyes blazed with
fury.

"She knows," Matt went on. "We have sort of a
deal. By marrying me, Kate deflected the gossips in
town who were saying something improper was going

on between you two. I don't know if you understand how much Kate endured to let you stay on in the house with her after her father died."

Matt could tell by the belligerent set to Henry's jaw that he'd heard the gossip.

"They ain't nothing but a bunch of biddies with more time on their hands than sense."

"Maybe so, but those biddies could ruin Kate's chance at an audition if the wrong kind of gossip reaches Mrs. Cody's ears. From what I understand, Mrs. Cody's opinion carries a lot of weight with her husband."

"I reckon so."

"Once Kate gets a job with the show, I'll be leaving."

"What if she doesn't get hired?"

"I'll be leaving regardless." The calm announcement weighed like lead in Matt's gut. "She'll need you either way, Henry. If she goes traveling with the show, she'll be counting on you to keep the ranch going. If she doesn't get the job, she'll have to depend on you for moral support. It'll be a blow to her pride."

His leaving wouldn't be a blow, though, Matt added silently. She'd probably be glad to see the last of him.

"Sounds to me like you'd be leaving her in just as much trouble as she started. Maybe more."

"I won't get her pregnant, if that's what you're alluding to. And you won't give the gossips any more ammunition if you get busy right away and find another housekeeper. Find yourself a girlfriend, while you're at it. Nobody will talk about you if there's a third person in the house and if you're, um, courting another woman."

Henry stared broodingly out toward the horizon. Matt dared hope that logic would prevail. But then the younger man shook his head.

"Not a chance, Kincaid. I know what I want."

"What about what Kate wants?"

"Seems to me she won't be as picky once she's been deserted by you and rejected by Colonel Cody. Seems to me I just have to bide my time to get my way."

Sheer rage, so fine and pure that he'd never felt its equal, surged through Matt. He curled his hands into fists to keep from wrapping them around Henry's neck. And then he jammed his fists into his pockets to keep from hammering them into Henry's face. Beating Henry to a pulp might satisfy his anger, but it wouldn't solve anything. Besides, Henry didn't deserve a beating for sensing an opportunity and poising himself to take advantage of it. Matt couldn't even challenge Henry over his reluctance to let Kate go off with the show, considering how he wouldn't stand for it, either.

Big 'Un and Tarsy had screwed up royally in sending him back to this place and time. His own destiny was nowhere in sight, and his presence wasn't doing Kate a damned bit of good.

"Why did you stop me?" he asked harshly. "You thought I was running away. You should have been glad to see me go."

"Well, I've reconsidered my approach to this here situation." Henry leaned back against his horse, perfectly at ease. "I'm a changed man, Matt. I'm going to be sweet as pie to you, and all loving and understanding with Kate. I figure it's in my best interests if you hang around for a spell, so's I can fire up the rumors in town. She'll just naturally want to cry on my sympathetic shoulder once everything starts going wrong, and when I'm the only one left who cares about her."

"You bastard."

"Yep. And that's no insult, considering you ain't got no room to talk."

Matt studied his enemy. Physically, they were a match. Matt had to give himself the mental edge, considering his age and experience. But Henry knew Kate so much better than he did. That knowledge seared Matt's soul, tantalized him with a hint of how a man could happily devote the balance of his days to learning all Kate's secrets. Too bad he could not be that man.

Henry already knew how to push Kate's buttons. Worse, he knew and could command the attention of the people who held Kate's future in their hands, while Matt was nothing more than a penniless drifter with no influence over anybody. To all outward appearances, Henry would be the heavy favorite in a contest to determine the course of Kate's future.

But Matt hadn't always been wealthy and powerful. He'd stared down some of the best, and hadn't always had an arsenal of powerful weapons at his beck and call. Henry thought he held all the cards. Throwing him off balance might make him drop a few. It might be kind of fun, to get back to his roots.

"Well, since you're going to be my best buddy, you might as well walk back to the ranch with me," Matt said.

"Huh?"

Matt hid a small smile when Henry's smug smirk disappeared into confusion and then hardened into suspicion.

"You're up to something."

"Could be." Matt allowed his smile to show then. "And it could just be that I'm lonely for some guy talk."

"Guy talk?"

"You know—sports, baseball, stuff like that."

"You want to talk to me about baseball?" Henry betrayed his youth by the sudden excitement kindling in his eyes.

What Matt really wanted to do was bash a baseball bat against Henry's thick skull. But talking and walking might subdue some of the troublesome violent tendencies that had been plaguing him. Numbers. Averages. Rules. Statistics. Comfortable, safe topics to get them across that wide stretch of plain before sauntering into the barnyard.

Kate watched from the kitchen. The worried pucker between her brows vanished in a glorious smile when she saw the two of them together. She couldn't know that so much animosity sizzled between himself and Henry that the Hoover Dam power-generating station could have been rendered obsolete.

"There you are!" she said as they approached.

"You ain't my mother, Kate. You don't need to be standing on the stoop watching for me." Henry sent Matt a sidelong glance, as if to prove he'd gotten the gist of what Matt had been trying to tell him.

Kate flushed. "Um, Henry, I need to use the wagon tomorrow. I have to go into town to order some parts for Mr. Comas's pistol."

Henry stood for a long moment, glancing between Kate and Matt. He swallowed, looking decidedly nervous, but just as decidedly determined to carry out his promise to be sweet. "You let me know when you're ready and I'll harness the team. Matt can go in with you."

Kate retired first for the evening. Matt and Henry sat at the table for at least an hour in a silent, undeclared contest of wills—a fool's challenge, Matt thought, to prove which of them was more manly by staying awake the longest. Matt vowed to beat Henry at this game, and then realized that by winning he'd be the loser, because Henry would have succeeded in keeping him out of Kate's bedroom for most of the night.

He mentally tipped his hat toward the twenty-year-old son of a bitch.

"I'm going to bed," he said, after gulping down the acidic swill Kate called coffee. It tasted even worse cold than it did hot, though the company he kept might have something to do with the nasty taste in his mouth. He abandoned the cup on the table and caught the handle of the lantern to light his way to the bedroom. Henry, left in darkness, muttered a curse and then shoved away from the table. He followed at Matt's heels down the hallway, rousing the urge within Matt to simply whirl around and duke it out. One brief, telling fight would be less aggravating than this prolonged tension.

He paused with his hand on Kate's doorknob. "'Night, pardner," he murmured to Henry. "Sleep tight." He successfully fought off the urge to stick out his foot and send Henry sprawling in the dark. That would have been too juvenile.

Maybe tomorrow night.

Kate had left a single candle lit atop the dresser. It did a poor job of illuminating the room, and too fine a job of highlighting the woman who nestled against the headboard, sound asleep. She'd started out sitting up straight, Matt could tell, because her firm little bottom was still planted a good eighteen inches away from the wall. But sometime during the extra time he'd spent in a staring contest with Henry, she'd slumped until her cheek pressed into the plank headboard.

The candle cast a wavery glow over her. She'd braided her hair, except for a few loose tresses that curved over her forehead and shielded her eyes from the candlelight. The shining plait coiled over her shoulders and breasts. The tufted end quivered with each deep breath, drawing Matt's gaze toward the delightful dips and hollows formed by her slumbering body. With no effort at all, he could imagine lifting the heavy braid and rubbing it between his fingers until all the twists released and surrounded them both with the scent of lilies of the valley.

Her lashes spiked low and dark over her cheeks. Her lips curved with the hint of a smile, as though the wonderful dreams that abandoned her during the day returned during the night. Her hands sprawled open on her lap around a loose bundle of clothing—she'd obviously prepared her garments for the next day and had been sitting there waiting to bolt from the room the minute she thought the coast was clear.

If only she'd been positioned more comfortably, he would have stolen back into the hallway and bedded down in her father's old room. If only she didn't look so damned vulnerable . . . Matt's throat tightened, thinking it might frighten her if she woke in the middle of the night and found herself alone, found him missing without explanation. A wild surge of elation followed that thought. Kate might miss him! Not with the watch-checking annoyance of someone exasperated because a business meeting wasn't carrying on as scheduled, but really *miss him,* simply because he wasn't *there.*

A reality check doused that notion quickly enough. She'd miss him, all right—because she'd be afraid that Henry might catch on to the fact that they hadn't really shared a bed.

"Kate," he called softly, so he wouldn't startle her too quickly out of her sound sleep. "It's time for bed."

She stirred, and with a negative murmur, settled more fully against the headboard.

"Wake up, sleepyhead," he persisted. He set the lantern atop the dresser and stood next to the bed. He gripped her shoulder lightly, just to jostle her a little, he promised himself. His damned thumb didn't adhere to the bargain. It traced the ridge of her collarbone through the softness of much-washed cotton, and stroked against the fat rope of her braid. She was all warmth and silk and smelling of flowers, and he would be cursed for all time if he pursued his desires instead of letting her go.

His hand shook as he jammed it into his pocket.

" 'lo, Matt." She peeped somewhat shame-facedly through the wing of hair that shielded her eyes. She smothered a yawn with her hand, and then arched herself into a sitting position with a modified stretch. The motion curved her back and sent her lush breasts into prominence, tantalizing Matt with the image of what it might be like to watch Kate stretch without a full bolt of cotton covering her lithe form.

"Henry's gone to his room." His voice rasped like gravel. She smiled sleepily and stretched again.

All the strength in his legs deserted him. He dropped down on the bed as close to the footboard as he could get. Even so, his weight counterbalanced the mattress. Kate came sliding toward him. She stopped herself by planting her hands against his chest and by pure reflex his arms shot out to enfold her before she could tumble off the bed to the floor.

"I . . . I should slip out to Pa's room now," she whispered.

"No. You don't have to go. You can stay here tonight."

Her lips parted in a silent "O."

The warmth of her, the scent of her, the uncertain excitement stoking the smoky green fire in her eyes, intoxicated his senses more than vintage Dom Perignon. He knew he had to offer her a fuller explanation, but it was so damned hard to think, so difficult to form a coherent thought, with his arms wrapped around his sleep-warmed, temporary wife.

"It doesn't make sense for you to be the first one up in the morning, Kate. I'm going to wake up earlier, so I can bring in the wood and get breakfast started. You can keep your room, and I'll sleep in your father's old room until . . . well, until."

"Oh." He fancied a bit of the light had deserted her; perhaps it was only the candle guttering low, the lantern running out of oil.

But if that were the case, it shouldn't have been possible for him to see the red impression marring her cheek where it had rested against the headboard. He traced the mark with a gentle finger. She glanced away from him, and his attention followed hers. Her mirror framed their reflections. They stared back at themselves, looking for all the world as though they were locked in a loving embrace.

She disengaged herself from his arms, and after straightening, touched the red line on her cheek herself. "First my corset digging into my skin, then this," she murmured.

"Hmm?" His arms ached, missing the feel of her.

She shrugged. "Oh, nothing. It's just that the only times you ever touch me it's on account of my getting myself creased up some way or another."

"You *want* me to touch you?"

"No! Y . . . yes. I don't know."

Where was that goddamned pesky conscience

voice when he needed it? Where were all his vows and good intentions, his noble purpose in holding himself aloof to avoid getting further entangled with her? No whispers of caution let out so much as a peep when Matt caught Kate against him, when his fingers made nimble work of the ribbons at her throat and his lips found the pulse beating there.

Why didn't she resist him, remind him this wasn't part of their deal? Up and up went his lips and tongue, tracing the curve of her jawline, tasting the silk of her skin, finding lips that were wonderfully responsive and almost as demanding as his own. His hands found the splendid shape of her, the glorious in-and-out curves of a woman and the soft, full swell of her breasts already peaked with a desire that kindled his own even higher.

He lowered her to the bed. Feeling her beneath him, her taut frame curving and adjusting to embrace him ever closer, maddened him almost beyond thought. He couldn't take her like this, with his boots on and his fingers fumbling with the unfamiliar row of buttons where a zipper ought to be. With a growl of frustration he tore himself away from her to dispose of his clothes so he might love her properly.

A breeze wafted through the window, cooling some of his heat.

The dose of fresh air brought about the arrival of something worse than his conscience: Henry's reproving face took shape in Matt's mind. *You promised not to get her pregnant.*

Kate lay upon the bed, flushed from his kisses, with one arm crossed over her middle and the other lying against the quilt, palm outstretched, waiting for him to return. He ached to join her, to strip every inch of cotton from her body and celebrate each uncovered inch, to claim her again and again and make her so thoroughly his own that no other man could ever catch her eye.

"I can't do this." He'd never found words so difficult to form.

She blinked and her eyes widened with dismay, as if his words had broken a magical spell upon her.

"Oh my God." She blushed, clapped one hand over her mouth, and sat up with the other clutching the edges of her nightgown together.

"I'm sorry." It sounded inadequate. He knew she deserved a better apology, but a lifetime of refusing to admit fault meant he didn't know the right words to call upon.

"You don't have to apologize. It's all my fault."

"*Your* fault?" She couldn't have said anything to surprise him more.

"Men don't like . . . I mean, I know I'm not the sort of woman you would have chosen."

She was about to denigrate herself again. *Men don't like women like me.* He could hear it vibrate in the air as clearly as if she'd spoken the words.

"You're wrong, Kate. There's nothing I want to do more than make love to you."

"Then . . . why?"

How simple it would be to point out the risk of pregnancy. Such an admission would do nothing to ease her humiliation or erase her ridiculous belief that she wasn't desirable. And it was only half an explanation anyway. But a man who found it impossible to apologize certainly couldn't articulate all the regrets raging through him.

It gave him pause when he realized that he'd never cut anyone an inch of slack when he believed they hurt him or failed him in some way. He'd walked around passing judgment as if he were perfect in his treatment of others. He wasn't such a hotshot, if he looked at himself through Kate's eyes. He fumbled for some kind of explanation.

"If we were back . . . where I belong, Kate, we could do this without worrying about the consequences. But here, *now,* I can't protect you. As much as it costs me to turn away from you now, I have to do it, because I couldn't live with the worry of leaving you carrying my child."

"You mean people can do . . . this . . . where you come from without worrying about having a child?"

"Something like a ninety-seven percent guarantee. And it can be taken care of if you're one of the unlucky three percent. There are other things to worry about, though, where I come from. Herpes, AIDS."

"Aids—why would you worry about helping someone?"

Such innocence. Yes, lovers risked much to copulate in his rightful time, but so many mistakes could be corrected, so many precautions could be taken. If he claimed all Kate's sweet innocence, she risked everything. It gave him pause, and stole his breath to think of how the commitment inherent in lovemaking had been diminished in his own time.

"It's complicated, Kate. And I don't have to worry about AIDS, either. I've always been careful, and I've been tested."

"I . . . I didn't know you were supposed to take a test before . . ." She blushed more furiously. "I guess that must make it . . . better, if you pass the test and don't have to worry about doing things wrong, or anything."

"Better?" He gave a short laugh, recalling the

unemotional romps he'd shared with women whose faces he couldn't remember. "Let's just say that I've walked away from many opportunities where I come from, and never found it so difficult as I find walking away from you."

"You're leaving me." Such desolation. It struck at his core, and taunted him with the knowledge that this brief separation was but a weak shadow of the permanent separation that would come soon.

"It's just for the night, Kate." He wasn't certain if he sought to reassure her, or himself.

"You'll be in Pa's old room." She held herself rigid, silently imploring him for confirmation.

"In a while. First, I'm going down to the stream for a bath."

"That water's like ice at night, Matt."

"I know. I'm counting on it."

16

Kate's world had spun so topsy-turvy that she wouldn't have been surprised to find the sky turned dusty brown and the road cloud-studded blue. Instead, road and sky retained their usual colors as she drove into North Platte with Matt.

Her dream of joining the Wild West Show had been so all-consuming that it had blotted out the usual female cravings for creating a home, raising a family. Now, she couldn't help thinking about the small improvements she might make to her home to make it more comfortable for Matt. Her arms felt empty, as if they ached to be wrapped around a man's shoulders, or pined for the weight of a baby. Her womanly urges, so well subdued and slumbering, had been blasted awake and tormented her with every vibration jolting through the wagon.

She prayed that these longings were part of life's normal cycles, but it was pretty hard to convince herself of that when nothing of the sort had bothered her until Matt Kincaid arrived.

She shot a look at him just to make sure of his identity, because he was behaving as if his inner workings had gotten all switched around, too. He usually kept himself taciturn as a turtle and now on this trip into town, he couldn't seem to keep his mouth closed for more than five seconds.

It was bad enough that his constant commentary kept her from thinking through her problems. What was worse, he piled confusion upon confusion on her, before she'd ironed out the contradictions he'd already sprouted within her. Those sidelong, melting glances he kept sending her way were enough to turn any woman's head, except that each one was accompanied by some ridiculous comment that convinced her his mind was still addled from hitting his head against the boulder.

For instance, the horses' constant chuffing and snorting amazed him. "I never knew that horses made so much noise while they walked." They were making excellent time into North Platte, but he fretted over it. "Real horsepower is so slow." He squinted against the sunlight and muttered how he missed his Ray Bans, coughed from the dust and complained beneath his breath about the lack of paving, bemoaned the lack of roadside vending machines. He winced after one particularly bone-jarring lurch and remarked that he could have cracked a crown if he'd had his teeth clenched together.

His new volubility was just as confusing as Henry's new acceptance of Matt's presence. Topsy-turvy. And so she supposed it made perfect sense that Matt talked and talked when she knew in her heart that he normally weighed and rationed his every word, while she, who always chattered when nervous, found herself silent as a stump.

"Main Street, U.S.A.!" Matt practically fell from the wagon, he was gawking so hard as they rode into town. "The real deal! Disney World doesn't do it justice."

His outburst made no more sense than anything else he'd said, but Kate felt a surge of community pride. As sophisticated as Matt claimed to be, he obviously couldn't help being impressed by North Platte's modern advances. She began to feel a little more comfortable, enough to begin talking. "Every building in town has its own water supply, thanks to the new waterworks. Can you imagine, Matt, fresh water pouring from a spout whenever you want it, just by turning a handle!"

"Imagine that," he murmured.

"And we've got brick sidewalks in the business district. The law's really cracking down on folks who let their livestock run loose. Taxpayers have preference over livestock when it comes to occupying sidewalks, it says so in an ordinance. Anyone whose cow or horse gets caught eating from a grocer's bin or blocking a sidewalk, they get fined five dollars faster than they can think about it."

"I can think of a few places that would benefit from that kind of an ordinance," said Matt.

She swallowed the impulse to keep on listing North Platte's fine points. She'd never felt such an urge to brag about the town; she had, more often, shied away from visiting, the way a starving fox avoided taking shelter in a bear cave. She usually dreaded driving into town because it meant holding her head high while conducting her business, certain that the merchants and customers laughed about her amongst each other. She always lashed the horses into a frenzy to escape once her chores had been accomplished.

Today, with Matt at her side, she felt like extolling North Platte's every virtue. Anyone listening would think she wanted to convince Matt that her hometown was a place worth living in, worth abandoning three big cities for. But that was stupid. He wasn't planning to stay, and if anything changed his mind, she'd rather it be something other than the wonders of indoor plumbing.

And that was even sillier, because she knew he wasn't going to stay. He'd reminded her of his determination to leave only the night before. She studiously avoided thinking about that distressing scene on the bed, when she'd humiliated herself by admitting she wanted him to touch her.

She usually liked to tie the team near Lloyd's Opera House, where the building's tall facade cast restful shade for the horses. Today, though, all the hitching posts in front of the Opera House were occupied, which meant the Women's Civic Group was in session. She recognized some of the small buggies and blooded horses as belonging to North Platte's prominent families. Dozing men occupied some of the larger conveyances, and a few restive-looking fellows slouched against the walls, obviously waiting to drive their employers' wives back home once they'd finished their socializing.

Kate guided her team toward the nearby dry goods store instead. Matt leaped down to wrap the reins around the post while she set the wagon brake.

"Do you need help getting out of the wagon?" he asked.

It seemed safer to decline. After all, with most of

the townswomen inside the Opera House, there'd be no one to see her clamber unassisted from the driver's seat while a perfectly healthy male stood there doing nothing. On the other hand, letting that perfectly healthy male wrap his hands around her waist and hoist her through the air would only remind her of the way she'd felt the night before, when those same hands had molded themselves around curves no man had ever touched.

"I'm used to doing it myself," she said, refusing his assistance. He shrugged and ambled over to the store window. She punched her skirt into the valley between her legs and clutched the edges of her shawl as she began backing off the seat.

"Say, let me help yew, Katie."

Buford Tarsy, surprisingly strong in a wiry sort of way, plucked her from the wagon and settled her onto the ground. "I thought thet was yer wagon, Katie. Yew saved me a trip, on account of I been thinkin' o' ridin' out t' yer place. Er, I guess I oughta be callin' yew Miz Dowmtabsta now."

"It's Kincaid. My married name is Kate Kincaid."

"Oh, is that the feller's last name? He started talkin'?"

"I should have known you'd be concerned about Matt," Kate said. She gestured toward the sidewalk, where Matt stood inspecting the goods offered in the dry goods store window. "He bounced back remarkably quickly. He has a rather amazing constitution."

"Well, actually, yew 'n' me got more pressin' business—"

Bufie halted in midsentence when the Opera House door banged open and a flood of women surged into the street.

Bufie paled, and swallowed. "Er, I'll be seein' yew,

Katie. We can take care o' our other matters later." He pelted off toward Wald & Wheeler's Wild West Saloon.

The women clustered around the Opera House, chattering excitedly. "We'll simply have to round up more volunteers!" cried Marvella Quint. "We must scour the town for every suitable person and beg for assistance. This could be the best Engineers' May Ball *ever*!"

"It's all in the planning," said Mrs. Hetherington, who hailed from Boston and always assumed command over every social event. "The right volunteers assigned to the right committees. No room for error."

Several of the women had settled around their transportation, waiting to be handed aboard their buggies. Mrs. Hetherington graciously directed her driver to assist the more daring women who'd ridden in on horseback. A smaller group, who lived right in town, made their good-byes and headed down the sidewalk, walking toward Matt and Kate.

Kate stepped away from the wagon. She pulled out the shawl she'd tucked into her reticule in case it turned cool and wrapped it tightly about her shoulders. The unseasonable warmth had encouraged her to wear her old, comfortable calico gown today, minus her corset and bustle. The trip into town and back was uncomfortable enough without those confining garments, and she hated exposing her good blue dress to the dust that would hang over the roads during this lengthy dry spell.

None of the women approaching her had dressed with any consideration for the weather or their own comfort. They wore their winter's finest: heavy satins and fine wools, long sleeves, fashionable bustles, perfect little hats tipped at just the right angle to reveal elaborately coiffed hair.

"Why, if it isn't Kate Monroe!" Marvella Quint stopped.

"Marvella," Kate acknowledged with the barest tilt of her chin.

She fancied the air still rang with the force of Marvella's announcement proclaiming they must scour the town for every suitable volunteer to help with the annual Engineers' May Ball. No word of invitation passed Marvella's lips. A few of the other women with her shared sidelong glances and little smirks. One whispered something, but quickly fell silent when someone's sharp elbow prodded her corseted stomach.

Matt leaned against a porch support, his arms folded across his chest. His gaze flickered across Marvella's fashionable form, and then to Kate, and back to Marvella. Kate had watched him study a hundred objects with that exact air of feigned indifference and knew that not one single detail escaped his notice. She flushed to the roots of her hair, knowing that she had to come out the loser in this comparison.

Marvella sent Kate a curt little nod. "Good day, then."

She set off with her entourage lined up so neatly behind her that they might have taken lessons from a flock of newly hatched ducklings. Marvella's nose was so high in the air that she didn't notice Matt had stepped away from the porch support. She plowed right into his chest. The rest of her friends crashed into one another, bouncing off bustles and getting so tangled in their dragging skirts that they staggered about, spinning their arms like windmills to maintain their balance.

"Where's my good friend, Augusta?" Matt rumbled.

Marvella pressed her fingers against the bridge of

her nose, her features marred by an unladylike scowl that held more than a trace of pain. "You clumsy oaf! Why, I . . . I . . . I . . ." Her railing trailed away when she tipped her head back and looked Matt full in the face. He sent her a lazy smile.

"Knock your nose out of joint, little lady?"

Marvella gaped up at him. Then, with her hand still clamped over her nose, her gaze dropped a bit lower, to where Matt's shirt didn't close at the neck, revealing the strong column of his throat. Kate swore at herself—she'd meant to adjust that button! She supposed it wasn't his fault that the darned shirt gapped open, exposing part of his chest for all the world to see, but a decent man surely would clear his throat or do something to divert Marvella's most inappropriate fascination with his bare skin. Instead, he stood there drinking in her admiration like a lion soaking up the African sunshine. And instead of treating him with the haughty scorn she usually directed toward those clad in common workclothes, Marvella appeared to thoroughly approve of Matt's costume.

"Where's Mrs. Merriweather?" he prompted. And blast him if he didn't lean forward, crossing his arms and stretching his shirt clear to its limits!

"Mmm . . . mmm . . . mmm . . ."

Kate couldn't decide if Marvella was trying to spit out the word *missus* or if she was letting her appetite show out loud.

"Mrs. Merriweather sent her regrets to the meeting," Callie Clinton simpered. "She wasn't feeling well this morning."

"Ah. Too much celebration the other day, no doubt. Isn't that right, babe?" Matt sent Kate a sidelong smile, and reached toward her with his left hand.

She couldn't let his hand just dangle out there in

midair. She tucked hers in his to save him from embarrassing himself, and he pulled her right onto the sidewalk next to him. The cream of North Platte's female
society hovered around them in a mute semicircle.

"I'm sorry we couldn't do this your way." Matt sent
her such a despondent look that Kate wished she
knew what had him so upset. "You can understand
that we can't wait for a proper introduction now. Isn't
that right, ladies? You won't hold it against Kate for
keeping our news to herself—she was trying to do the
right thing."

Several breathy assents and an additional *mmm*
from Marvella urged him to continue.

"I know Augusta was looking forward to being the
first to present us to you as man and wife."

"Man and wife!" Marvella shrieked. She stopped
pressing the bridge of her nose and started flapping
her hands in front of her. She swiveled toward Kate,
still flapping excitedly. For a moment, it seemed to
Kate that Marvella meant to wrap her in a quick hug
of mutual feminine delight. But knowing Marvella
would never do such a thing, Kate stiffened, and sure
enough, Marvella turned away. The rest of the women
broke into excited chatter.

Matt studied Marvella's fluttering hands for a second or two and reached out and caught one with the
speed of a fisherman catching live flies for bait. He
pumped her limp hand enthusiastically. "Matt Kincaid. You already know my wife, Mrs. Matt Kincaid."

Somehow, he'd maneuvered Kate closer to him,
until her hip rested alongside his. That amazed her—
he was so much taller than she, and yet they matched
at the hips. She'd always considered her long, coltish
legs an embarrassment, but it felt kind of nice to
stand hip to hip with Matt and hear him call her Mrs.

Kincaid. His arm curved so familiarly around her waist that one would have thought he always kept it there. His fingers splayed against her belly, reminding her she wore no corset, but somehow it didn't seem so important anymore. What good, she wondered suddenly, was cinching a waist so tight that a man could span it with his hands, if the corset made you so numb that you couldn't feel his touch?

"Much as I'd enjoy passing the time of day with all you pretty ladies, I promised my bride I'd treat her to a, uh, er," his glance raked over the surrounding storefronts. "A milk shake. I promised her a milk shake, right, babe?"

"That's right, husband dearest," Kate murmured. "We'd best be going, if we mean to find one before dark."

Matt kept his arm clamped around her waist as they strolled casually away. It felt nice, with his big shoulder rubbing against hers and his strong arm curved down and around her from the back. "We're causing a scandal, walking so intimately," she whispered.

"Good," he whispered back. "Are they following us yet?"

She pretended to look into a passing window and peeped over her shoulder through the concealing wing of her hair. "They're beginning to."

"Good."

"Matt—where are we going?"

"I don't know. Wherever they sell milk shakes. You lead the way."

"Matt—what's a milk shake?"

He muttered a volley of curses that would have sent all the women shrieking for cover if they could have heard. "Not invented yet? No refrigeration, I suppose. Hell, have they even invented ice cream yet?"

"Of course we have ice cream." If she hadn't cut short her earlier enthusiasm, she would have already told him that North Platte conducted a booming business in the ice trade, carving solid blocks of the stuff from the numerous nearby lakes each January and packing it so well and so tightly into the storehouses that it lasted from one season to the next. "We can get some at the post office."

"They sell ice cream in the post office?"

"I suppose it's more like they sell postage stamps in the confectionery."

"Confectionery. Candies and syrupy flavorings, right? Do they sell milk?"

"Of course."

"Then we have the makings of a milk shake."

Kate made a face and shuddered at the notion of mixing milk with candy and syrup. "It sounds awful."

"Well, your friends wouldn't be following us if I'd announced I was taking you over to the Wild West Saloon to buy you a beer, would they?"

"Heavens, no!" The very thought of Marvella Quint entering a saloon was beyond Kate's imagination. "Why do you want them to follow us anyway?"

"You'll see," he said, looking rather smug.

The postmaster balked at Matt's request to whip milk, strawberry ice cream, and strawberry syrup together. "What if you won't pay for that slop when it's mixed?" he challenged. "I got plenty of Coca-Cola. That's a safer choice."

"You mean Buford Tarsy hasn't drained you dry?" asked Matt. "He once told me a fellow could have a wild time with a belly full of Coca-Cola."

"That Bufie does drink more than his share," the postmaster agreed, while Kate stared at Matt in speechless disbelief.

"How did you know Bufie likes Coca-Cola?" she managed to whisper. "I thought you two were strangers to one another."

Matt's friendly expression never wavered; no tell-tale red stained his skin, but Kate knew she'd caught him in something like a lie. A tiny muscle jumped along his jawline. His eyes flickered with a momentary alarm. Most people wouldn't have noticed his minuscule lapse of control. She wasn't most people, though. Somehow, she'd grown oddly attuned to him, as if every moment she'd spent with him, every touch, every kindness, every kiss, had forged tiny invisible connections binding them together. Bound to a manipulator, a man who'd promised to lie to her and smile while he did it. She supposed she ought to be grateful for the reminder, because she found herself all too willing to forget Matt's true nature.

"I suppose I must have overheard him mention it when he drove us home on our wedding night," Matt said.

Kate remembered every single word that had been said on that fateful evening and she knew Bufie hadn't wasted time talking about beverages. Even so, she nodded, pretending to accept Matt's explanation, and felt a pang of raw pain at the relief on his face. It served her right for neglecting to maintain a wary edge around him. She wouldn't let him slip past her guard so easily again.

Matt's hand reached toward his pocket, and then hovered over the opening. Kate remembered how he'd been affected by his lack of money, and despite her resolve to maintain a healthy distance between them, she couldn't stand the thought of his being embarrassed. She hurriedly withdrew her coin purse from her reticule.

"It's my treat," she told the pharmacist. "I promised to buy him anything he wanted. I suspect he's trying to call my bluff by coming up with this awful concoction, like some little bully taunting a schoolgirl with worms."

The postmaster chuckled, though he frowned his disapproval all the while as he beat the specified ingredients into a frothy pink sludge and poured it into a tall buttermilk glass.

"Two straws," Matt announced. "We're going to share."

By now Marvella and her entourage had gathered in front of the confectionery window, peering in like penniless children hungering after the sweet treats contained within. Matt guided Kate to the lone table and adjusted their chairs so that they sat side by side, facing the window.

"There's an art to drinking milk shakes," he explained, as animated as a child waiting to reveal a long-held secret. Kate wanted to slap that anticipatory grin right from his face and tell him that he wasn't fooling her with his pretend excitement, but instead she found herself leaning forward, drawn into his enthusiasm. He stuck the straws into the pink froth. The milk shake was so thick that the straws stood straight without falling against the glass. "You place your left elbow on the table, Kate. I'm going to do the same with my right. Then you reach for the straw closest to me and start drinking."

"I won't do that," Kate announced primly. "It sounds rude." Not to mention disgusting—she wasn't going to take a sip of that pink stuff.

"It's not rude. I'm going to drink from the straw on your side."

"We'll get our arms all crossed up."

"That's the idea. C'mon, Kate. Give it a shot."

It sounded like a dare, and served as a reminder that she couldn't shoot her gun anymore. She might as well aim for the pink stuff. She did as Matt instructed, but nearly sent the milk shake crashing to the floor when Matt snaked his arm under and around hers and brought his head toward the straw. The position drew her closer to him, so close she could feel his warmth wafting from his shirt, she could smell his clean, stream-washed scent.

"Look at me while you suck on the straw," he whispered.

She tried, but her gaze kept faltering beneath his. Their lips were mere inches apart. His worked with gentle pressure, drawing the thick pink froth into his mouth. Unconsciously, she copied his movements. The taste, so sweet and cold and rich, burst against her tongue. She gasped with delighted surprise. He lost his straw, too, in a wide smile.

"You have a tiny bit of milk shake on your lip," he murmured.

She touched her lip where the straw had rested, embarrassed that she hadn't managed to stay tidy with Marvella and the other women looking on. "Here?"

"No. Here." He bent ever so slightly and placed a soft kiss at the corner of her mouth. She meant to protest, but her intention died stillborn when his tongue traced her lower lip and he cupped the back of her head with one hand, drawing her closer. "God, you taste so sweet," he whispered just before claiming her lips again. He tasted of man and milk shake, a potent combination that could addict a woman for all eternity if she weren't careful, if she didn't remind herself that this was all an act, a show put on for the

benefit of the scandalized women watching through
the front window.

"Say, young feller," called the postmaster. Kate
wished she could sink straight through the floor.
She'd lose all the progress she'd made with Augusta
once Marvella carried word that the postmaster had
chastised Kate for smooching in public. But the postmaster didn't seem concerned with their outrageous
behavior. He approached them somewhat diffidently.
His bushy mustache sported a milky pink frosting.
"Would you mind if I offered this here milk shake to
my other customers?"

"Be my guest."

"Well gosh, thanks." The man grinned and slid his
hand across the table, returning the coins Kate had
given him to pay for the drink. "Don't seem right taking your money, under the circumstances. And I got a
box full of empty bottles in my storage room, Kate.
You're welcome to them."

"Why, thank you!" She smiled at him, which hardly
seemed payment enough, considering how difficult target bottles were to come by. And yet the postmaster
seemed completely satisfied. Funny, she reflected, she
hadn't realized he even knew about her sharpshooting.
Her gratitude turned to guilt when he dragged the heavy
box to their table and she realized she didn't even know
the postmaster's name to thank him more effusively.

Though she and Matt had escaped a scolding, the
interruption had shattered their passionate spell. Matt
slouched in his chair, tipping it back onto its rear legs.
"Go ahead. Finish it. But don't drink it too fast, or
you'll get a headache."

She tried to drink it. But with him watching her,
she became conscious of herself in ways she'd never
noticed before. So many minute motions accompanied

the simple act, and Matt seemed fascinated by every one of them. He made a small sound when she curled her hand around the straw. He drew a sharp breath when she lowered her head and parted her lips to take the straw into her mouth. He held his breath while she curled her tongue around the straw, and groaned when her throat worked and her cheeks flexed with the effort of drawing the thick strawberry shake through it.

For some reason, his rapt attention left her all jumpy and tingling, but not with embarrassment; all hollow and hungry, but with no appetite for milk shakes or anything else the postmaster might sell in the confectionery.

"I've had enough," she said, pushing the glass toward Matt. "You finish it."

He ignored the straws and downed several mouthfuls in quick succession, despite his warning to drink it slowly. The headache must have shown up as promised, for he winced and pressed a hand against his temple. He hoisted the bottle box to his shoulder.

"Let's get out of here."

"Thanks for the idea!" the postmaster called as they left.

"Don't thank me until you know for sure that Big 'Un won't erase the recipe from your mind," Matt muttered, still grimacing against his headache. "I don't know when milk shakes were supposed to be invented."

"What on earth are you talking about?" Kate asked.

"Nothing. It's not important."

Once he deposited the bottle box in the wagon, he kept his hands on her the whole rest of the time they spent in town. Around her waist as they walked the sidewalks, delivering the guns and pistols Kate had repaired and picking up other weapons requiring attention. Touching her lightly on the shoulder while she handed Mr. Longwell the list she'd laboriously copied from her parts catalogs so he could telegraph the orders. Holding her hand while they toured the town, while he asked her a hundred questions about the way things worked, the methods of conducting business in a town located so far away from major cities. He kept touching her until long after Marvella and her minions had abandoned their gaping, until the townsfolk started looking upon them with indulgent smiles instead of avid speculation.

He kept touching her until she got so used to the feel of his strength joined with hers that she didn't know why she'd always found it so hard to talk to the townsfolk. The postmaster wasn't the only merchant who responded to her smile and shy attempts at conversation. She'd always been so certain that they looked down on her that she'd conducted her transactions in a brisk, no-nonsense manner. She'd always been so anxious to conclude her business that she hadn't given them, or herself, a chance to show how friendly they could be.

With Matt at her side, she could hear another person chuckle without immediately assuming they were laughing at her. She could interpret the little flare of agitation on Mr. Longwell's face as the result of trying to cram too much work into too little time, rather than dismay over dealing with a woman carrying on a man's occupation. She could almost, *almost,* count it a perfect day, except for the memory of Marvella's snub in not asking Kate to volunteer to help with the Engineers' May Ball.

"I guess I'm not going to be asked to help with the Ball again this year," she said as Matt helped her into the wagon.

He studied her for a long moment. "If you want to get involved, you should have asked them."

"Me ask? You heard them say they needed volunteers."

"Yeah, and they know you heard it. They probably figured you weren't interested, or you would've said something."

She'd never considered asking. "It's humiliating enough to be excluded without having the added mortification of being turned down face to face," she said, surprising herself by making the shameful admission out loud.

"When you really want something, you have to be willing to risk everything to get it," Matt said.

"But what if you fail?"

"You might fail. You never know until you try."

"I don't know, Matt. It requires a lot of courage to take that kind of risk."

"It takes even more courage to live with yourself when you realize you've given up trying." A brief flash of something like regret flickered across his face, and then he broke into a humorless smile. She'd gotten used to the sight of that smile, because he always reverted to it when he wanted to change the subject. She wasn't ready to move onto a new topic.

"Have you ever asked straight out for something important?"

"I've always managed to get what I want."

It was a manipulator's evasive answer if she ever heard one. "You didn't answer my question—have you ever asked, when something was important to you."

"No."

"Why not?"

"I guess I've never come across anything that important," he said. "You'll learn for yourself soon enough that you won't have to ask for much."

"What do you mean?"

"You want those women to be your friends? Well, once you become famous, they'll hang onto you like leeches. They'll be bragging all over the place about how you grew up together. They'll convince themselves, and try to convince you, that they've been your best friends for years."

"But they won't really mean it, will they?" A glimmer of sadness darkened her eyes. "I'll still be the same Kate Monroe that they laughed at behind their hands."

"It doesn't matter why they accept you, Kate."

"Of course it matters." She sent him a reproachful look. "Now I know why my pa warned me that I'd have to be even more careful around people after I joined the Show than I am now."

"Well, right now, I'd say those women have to be careful around you. I think they're afraid of you."

He shocked her. "Afraid of *me?* I'm so scared around them, I can't speak two words without fearing I'll faint dead away."

He gave a short laugh. "When they look at you, they see a strong, independent woman who succeeds at a trade their own husbands can't master. They know you're following your dream. You stand up against society to protect your foster brother. You make your own fashion statement. Not to mention you snared the best-looking bachelor these parts have ever seen."

"Matt!"

His eyes twinkled with deviltry. He leaned close

and winked up at her. "I've never seen an uglier bunch of guys."

"And what makes you think *you're* so handsome?" she countered. Her heart did a reluctant flip-flop, responding to his charm even while she scolded herself for succumbing.

He dropped his voice to a conspiratorial whisper and rubbed his hand against his jawline. It sounded like sandpaper scraping against a block of solid oak. "I've been sneaking into your gun grease while you're asleep. I think it's working. Did you see the way those women were panting after me?"

"Matt!"

"Let's go home, Kate."

It gave her a warm, sweet feeling to hear him say that, to have him vault into the wagon and saw ineffectually at the reins until she took pity upon the horses and gathered the reins into her own more capable hands.

"Home," she repeated, and felt equal measures of disappointment and delight at the sense of rightness that greeted the idea. "Together."

17

Matt spotted the note as soon as they entered the kitchen. He snatched it from the table and read it in a glance.

"What is it?" asked Kate.

Matt read the terse message aloud. "Southwest fence down. Cattle loose. Could be gone a while." No salutation, no signature, but no doubt whose bold, slashing writing announced that Matt and Kate would be quite alone for a couple of days. No doubt about the barely suppressed rage that had caused the writer's pencil to dig deeper with every word, until the words in the last sentence were nearly ripped through the paper.

Henry's sweet-as-pie intentions had surely turned sour and not at all pie-like at the notion of leaving Matt and Kate to their own devices, but Matt could take no pleasure in winning this round. Henry's departure to attend ranch business proved how willing he was to put Kate's best interests ahead of his own desires. It was like a gift, a simple, no-fuss-required offering from Henry to Kate that cast Matt's coercive companionship in a very dim light.

He didn't like the feeling. He'd never doubted his superiority over other men when it came to business matters or the sort of competition that involved physical prowess, like his tang soo do studies. What was it about Kate, about this simpler and yet subtly more complicated era, that left Matt feeling like the kid who got the most toys for his birthday party, and found they all fell apart the minute he tried showing them off?

He deliberately directed his thoughts toward the more pressing concern: alone with Kate. Problem . . . or opportunity?

Too late to wish that he hadn't spent most of the day indulging himself by touching her whenever he'd wanted. Time and again he'd scolded himself for taking pleasure in the contact. It was for Kate's sake, he'd tried telling himself. He'd meant to confuse those hoity-toity females she was so desperate to impress by pretending to dote on her. He couldn't pinpoint the exact moment when he'd forgotten to pretend and began doting in earnest.

Though not a vain man, he had learned long ago that women were physically attracted to him, which meant his body was an asset. He'd honed it, kept it well groomed, took pleasure in what it brought to him. It had always behaved quite well up until now, content to settle for what his mind permitted his body to enjoy.

Today, his body felt composed of separate entities, all clamoring for satisfaction. His skin craved the silken heat of Kate's. His fingers tingled, wanting to

hold, to possess, to stroke delicate curves while sensing the surging pulse simmering within her. His eye-
sight seemed sharper with her beside him, his hearing
keener, his sense of smell pleasurably adrift on the
scent of lily of the valley and sun-warmed female. And
so he'd held her against himself, touched her whenever he'd wanted, kissed her. He'd prayed all the
while that an overdose of Kate would drive those for-
bidden cravings into oblivion, only to find himself
more firmly addicted than ever before.

Alone with Kate . . . definitely a problem.

She stood near the door, oblivious to his inner turmoil. One slender hand rested against the doorjamb.
She stared toward the horizon, rigid with worry. "I
hope he doesn't spend too much time trying to round
up those cattle."

"I thought cattle could fend for themselves." Matt
remembered old movies where John Wayne and the
boys were always going out to round up cows and
new calves in the spring.

"They can. They'd be just fine, if they'd have run
off in another direction. But since they broke through
the southwest fence, there's only Mr. Miller's horse
ranch between our land and Indian territory."

"Indians?" He could barely choke out his request
for clarification. Dread slammed into him with all the
force of Mike Tyson's best one-two combination.
"Not the same Indians who killed your old boy-
friend?"

"I expect they're related in some fashion."

"Jesus, Kate! When you told me he'd died in an
Indian fight, I thought you meant somewhere out
west."

"This is the west, Matt."

"What I mean is . . ." He didn't know what the hell

he meant, only that he kept coming across more reasons to stick around, taking care of her. "It must take a great deal of courage to live here."

"Courage? I don't know." She worried her lower lip with her teeth. "Maybe it's safer in a way to keep on fighting the same demons instead of exposing your weak spots to an unknown threat."

She spoke of battling Indians, but her wisdom struck a chord within Matt. He'd been battling the same set of demons all his life. The tough veneer that kept those old enemies at bay buckled like rusted metal in the face of Kate's gentle attack on his heart.

Until that moment, leaving her had been a hazy concept, minimized by the more pressing concerns of restoring her confidence and tricking her into saying the secret word. He'd done an admirable job of holding himself aloof, of holding his own emotions under firm rein. He wasn't worried at all about how the inevitable separation would affect him. Not at all. He wouldn't notice the slightest wrench, feel the tiniest tug. Not a thing. His concerns over the impending separation centered solely around Kate, a woman who'd comforted him, trusted him, without qualification. She'd admitted to harboring some affection for him, some attraction to him.

The trouble was, he'd envisioned Kate nurturing her wounded feelings in her safe, snug little ranch house, with a cheerful fire crackling on the hearth and her quilt tucked around her knees. He'd imagined that her most pressing concern would be to hide her reddened eyes from Henry. Once again, he'd underestimated the consequences of his jaunt through time. A heartsick woman who'd lost her ability to shoot would be particularly alone and vulnerable to the threat literally looming on the horizon.

Of course, Henry would be around to protect her. Of course he would, just like he was out in Indian territory now, defending Kate's cattle. Goddamned twenty year old out there doing man's work, risking his life, biding his time until Matt took his hollow, unaffected self back to 1997.

"If Henry's not coming home for dinner, we can probably make do with leftovers," he said. "Why don't you get a little rifle practice in before dark?"

"All right." A tremor shook through her. "Will you watch from the door, like before?"

"No." When she tilted her head with disappointment, he continued explaining. "Actually, I was thinking that we should go out to your practice rock."

"The place where I *shot* you?" She looked horrified.

"You have to confront your fear where it first began."

"Are you sure?"

He wasn't, not at all, but he had to do something to wrench her free of her phobia. He had to do something to get them out of the house, where three empty bedrooms beckoned and the ticking of the parlor clock reminded him of the inexorable dwindling of the time he had left to spend with Kate.

Alone with Kate . . . could he create an opportunity from a problem? Perhaps without Henry's glowering presence, he could help her regain her confidence. He might even coerce her into saying the secret word and sending him back to his own time before Henry ambled back to the ranch.

A sudden lurching in the vicinity of his stomach registered a protest. He couldn't leave her alone, even if she regained the ability to defend herself against attacking Indians. Only a coward would slink away, leaving her to face Henry by herself with the embarrassing admission that Matt had indeed abandoned her as Henry had foretold. The longer Matt thought about it, the more he realized that he'd have to hang around long enough to hand Kate over to Buffalo Bill so the Wild West Show could take her far away, where she'd be safe from Indians and safe from Henry.

How much longer—two days? Three? He braced himself for the frustration that the waste of time always spurred within him. It didn't strike. It seemed a lifetime ago that he'd fumed in his room at the Dismal Lodge, angered into a boil over the slow passage of minutes. Here he'd gone and consigned himself to days upon days of thumb-twiddling inactivity, and he felt oddly comfortable with his decision, as if his wandering soul welcomed the chance to rest for a while.

And he could think of a million ways to occupy that time. He could conduct interesting experiments—stretch out a curling length of Kate's hair, for example, and see if it would wrap all the way around him. Taste the soft skin of Kate's belly to compare it against the sweetness of her lips.

"We'll have to rehitch the horses, Matt."

Kate couldn't know the direction his thoughts had taken. She stared at him expectantly, not realizing that he stood there envisioning her hair binding her body to his.

"Horses." His eyes couldn't leave the curve of her lips.

"It's quite a ways to the rock."

"Rock." If that word appeared in a *Jeopardy!* square, the correct answer would be: *What is as hard as Matt Kincaid?* He shifted position to ease the throbbing in his loins and shook his head, sternly admonishing himself to get his head straight. The rock. He knew a few facts about that rock, thanks to the brochure in the Dismal Lodge. "That rock straddles the boundary between your ranch and Buffalo Bill's, right?"

"How'd you know that?"

Big mistake. Christ, he was getting careless. He'd nearly flubbed things back at the post office when he'd commented on Buford Tarsy's fondness for Coca-Cola, and now he'd betrayed knowledge about that damned rock. Strangers to North Platte wouldn't know those sorts of details. "Um, I think Henry must've mentioned it." Kate seemed unconvinced and was probably dying to ask him a hundred questions. He sought to divert her. "I have an idea—I'll pack some things together, and we'll have a picnic supper out by that rock once you've finished practicing."

"Is that some of that psychology you were talking about—you won't let me eat unless I practice?"

"No, but it's not a bad idea."

"I guess I'd better get my things together then. You're such a fine cook, Matt, that I've had the most unladylike appetite lately. I'd better take advantage of it . . ."

Her words trailed away, but Matt knew how she'd meant to finish the sentence: *I'd better take advantage of it before you leave.*

"Do you have a basket or something I can use for packing food?" he asked.

"My egg basket's in the larder." She nodded toward the small food storage area.

On his own turf, Matt could order a picnic complete with down-filled comforter, crystal and champagne, delectable treats prepared by five-star chefs, and a solicitous waiter to hover over them, tending their every whim until Matt ordered him out of sight. Leftovers packed into an egg basket, spread out on a moth-eaten blanket, certainly wouldn't compare. And yet, the first time Matt tried stuffing a stale chunk of bread into the basket, he missed the opening, because anticipation made his hands tremble.

The sky's color had deepened, as it often did in midafternoon, into a blue so intense that its beauty stole Kate's breath. The sun wasted its golden glow against grasses that already lay flattened and dry in anticipation of the winter soon to come. A breeze danced across the treeless plain, teasing bits of chaff and broken weeds into motion, swirling them around her practice rock.

The air had changed over the past few hours; though still warm and sweet-smelling, there was the hint of a chill when the wind kicked higher. It circled around the rock, rousing a faint whistling sigh, as if it meant to announce that all too soon blizzard-force winds would descend and obliterate all trace of sun and warmth from this part of Nebraska.

Matt would be gone soon, too. Kate shivered, and wondered if a person just kept on shivering uselessly, even after she accepted the fact that she might never again feel warm.

The waning sun illuminated the boulder's craggy surface: the crevices where she sometimes wedged feathers for fine target shooting; the ledges where she balanced glass bottles; a trailing streak of rusty reddish-brown, marking where she'd shot Matt and sent his blood coursing down the stone face.

The egg basket dangled from his hand. He'd worn the sleeveless shirt, so she could see how the basket's weight pulled his muscles into prominence. He tilted his head into the breeze, drawing great draughts of air, as if he couldn't get enough of it. Nor could she seem to get enough of looking at him. Even if she hadn't lost her confidence in her marksmanship, she doubted she'd be able to take a single shot with him providing such a dangerous distraction.

"The sun's in my eyes. I'll move around to the other side," she said.

"Good idea," said Matt with so much false cheerfulness that she knew he hadn't really believed her poor excuse for delaying taking her first shot.

She didn't feel any more confident from her new vantage point. The rock sat upon the plains as it always had, as it always would—a bullet-scarred monolith, a sentinel for the ages. No weeds dared grow in its shadow. No moss clung to its northern face. Its base dug into the earth, unpocked by gopher holes; she'd never seen a bird alight on it, even though there was no other natural perch within miles. Nothing at all within miles to offer shelter, except for the flattened prairie grasses.

"How did you do it?" she burst out.

"Do what?"

He'd stipulated that she must never ask questions about how he'd come to be at the rock, but standing there, trembling for fear of shooting him all over again, she felt imbued by righteous wrath to know what had robbed her of her confidence.

"I can't understand how you popped up right in front of me! There's no way you could have snuck across the plains without me seeing you. And I know you weren't simply hiding on the other side. It just came to me now, when I circled the rock. I had to do the same thing that day, too, on account of it was earlier and I wanted the sun at my back. What did you do, Matt—just drop out of the sky?"

"Something like that—but not quite that simple."

Her head snapped around. Considering his secretive nature, she hadn't really expected a meaningful answer to her question. Matt's admission that there had been something unusual about his sudden appearance rocked her to her core.

He met her gaze soberly, and she wished with all her might that she could trust the reluctant promise of honesty she read there. But a slight tic along his clenched jawline betrayed nervousness, and she knew he didn't expect her to believe what he was about to say. Well, he'd warned her never to trust him, so it shouldn't hurt so much to realize that he meant to lie to her. But it did.

He walked over to the rock and rested his hand against it. "You have a right to know what happened, even if it makes me sound like a lunatic."

"It can't be any worse than me admitting I'm still afraid to shoot, even though I know you won't be running into my line of fire."

"It's worse, Kate," he said. "Much worse."

She'd never known him to hesitate over his words the way he did now. She braced herself to hear one whopper of a lie. He stared up into the sky, unblinking, while the breeze ruffled his hair. She could almost visualize his mind at work, weighing and testing each word. She remembered him telling her how good he was at manipulating people, how she could never be sure if he was telling her the truth or lying to get his way. She felt a dull sort of surprise at his prolonged hesitation, for she would not have expected that a self-professed manipulator would find lies so difficult to form.

"The first time I saw this rock, I almost crashed into it with my car." When Kate opened her mouth to question him, he raised a hand. "An automobile. Horseless carriage. Motor buggy. I don't know what the hell you'd call it."

"I've heard of motor cars," she said, smarting a little. It disappointed her, that he'd stooped to Henry's tricks, falling back on such a blatant attempt to make her doubt her own intelligence. "If you rode in on one of those contraptions, it makes it even harder to understand how I missed your arrival."

"I didn't ride in. My, um, motor car is back where I came from. Just like this rock isn't here anymore, it's been relocated to northwestern Nebraska as part of the landscaping outside the Dismal Lodge."

"Matt, of course this rock is here. Right here." She slapped it. She considered a new possibility for his outrageous charade. "You're just acting crazy to cheer me up, aren't you?"

"No. I'm trying to tell you that I don't belong in this place or this time."

"I know that." She hesitated. "You don't fit in here, Matt. You're too . . . I don't know, you have this way about you, sort of like Colonel Cody. People notice you. They defer to you. You're sophisticated and smart, and I would have guessed you lived in a big city and worked as a businessman even if you hadn't told me."

"There's more to it than that." He drew a deep breath. "I'm from the future, Kate. I belong in the year 1997."

18

Of all the explanations Kate had imagined, of all the lies she'd expected Matt might tell, none approached the wildness of this declaration. Too bad it was too absurd to be believed, because it made a weird sort of sense. Matt Kincaid no more belonged on the rough-and-tumble Nebraska frontier than she did presiding over some fancy New York brownstone mansion.

"Oh," she said.

"'Oh?' That's it? 'Oh?'" He seemed disappointed at her lack of response.

"What do you expect me to say?"

"You could try calling me a liar." He jutted his jaw a notch; his eyes sparkled with challenge. Well, he'd just have to keep on jutting and challenging, because she wasn't going to rise to his bait. She'd just play along and let him get himself all tangled up in his ridiculous stories. Once he lost track of his absurd claims, he'd be forced into telling the truth.

Unfortunately, awaiting the truth from him meant owning up to one of her own secrets. "I want to believe you. It makes me want to cry, every time I think you might be lying to me."

He recoiled as if she'd slapped him. "You can't possibly believe me."

"I absolutely *never* expect anyone to doubt my word. Only bone-deep liars think they can pull the wool over people's eyes. Since you expect me to disbelieve you, that must mean you're telling the truth."

Matt looked a little dazed, and Kate sympathized. Her convoluted reasoning made her head spin a little, too, but she stood firm. She refused to make this easy for him. "You're no liar, Matt Kincaid."

He scowled, obviously put out with her failure to behave as expected. "You should demand some kind of proof before you believe a person who claims to have come from the future."

"And what kind of proof should I demand?" She began to rattle off a list of some of the strange things he'd said to her over the past few days. "Ginsu knife commercials. Ibuprofen. Cuisinart. Disney World. You could wave all those things in front of my face this very minute and I still wouldn't know what they were. For all I know, they were invented fifty years ago and just never caught up to us here in North Platte."

"You're too gullible, Kate."

"You're too cynical, Matt."

"You shouldn't believe just anybody—"

"I'm not considering believing just anybody. I'm considering believing in *you.*"

For a moment his composure cracked. The cold calculation that so often marked his gaze softened into something like wonderment. His lips parted, a genuine smile hovering at the edges, the flinty, glittering topaz of his eyes growing warm and golden with awestruck discovery, as if something inside him had been touched for the very first time.

Her hand trembled. She wished that she could truly have a wife's right to touch her husband whenever she wanted. She yearned to take his hand in hers and tell him, *I understand how you feel.*

When she was younger, she'd occasionally ventured into town, hoping to find acceptance among girls her age, only to find herself so tongue-tied, shy, and awkward next to their unconscious femininity that she'd stolen home and vowed never to humiliate herself again. On those occasions, her pa's booming welcome, his compliments at her skill with the delicate gun work and his proud clapping when she'd turned to the comfort of her target practice, restored her self-confidence. It didn't matter then that the only things she excelled at didn't quite fill the empty void within her, only that mastering them earned her pa's approval. Not a night passed without her getting on her knees and thanking God for giving her to a parent who had such unflagging belief in her.

From Matt's reaction to her casual statement, he'd never known the comforts of that kind of unconditional acceptance. How could a person who'd never received love learn to give it? Without an example to follow, an unloved person probably resorted to lying and conniving. An unloved person probably had no choice but to evolve into a self-proclaimed manipulator.

"Oh, Matt," she whispered.

But before she could touch him, before she could tell him that she understood, he turned away. His shoulders had gone all rigid and he crossed his arms over his chest, as if he'd become so accustomed to standing alone against the world that he could no longer permit anyone to stand next to him. Part of her grieved for the lost opportunity to touch his very soul; part of her whispered warnings to guard her heart against embracing a hard-core manipulator who meant to pass right through her life.

"Why did you come here?" she asked, hoping he might relent and tell her the truth.

"I didn't come willingly. I was forced." A shadow passed over his features. "Well, not actually forced. Tricked into it."

She almost laughed, his lie was so transparent. An iron-willed person like Matt would have found the past few days too frustrating to endure, if he'd really been tricked into traveling through time and then forced into a marriage with her. Frustration could account for his bouts of surliness, but not for those delightful interludes when he teased and joked and kissed her as if he really enjoyed spending time in her company. But he'd warned her that he had ulterior motives for everything he did, and it saddened her, to know that none of his heady flirtations meant anything to him.

"Who tricked you?"

"Buford Tarsy."

"Now *that* I find impossible to believe." She lost her enthusiasm for playing along.

"Buford Tarsy's ghostly spirit, I guess I should say. He appeared when I was at a vulnerable moment, and tricked me into saying that damned word—"

"DOWMTABSTA," she whispered, remembering how frantic he'd been about it.

He stood very still for a moment, and then whirled with so much speed that he was little more than a blur. He clapped his hand over her mouth. "Don't say it again, Kate. Don't."

She shook her head and tried to signal with her eyes that she wouldn't repeat the word. He released her, and stood looking at his hand as if it had betrayed him in some manner.

"What's wrong, Matt?"

He hesitated for a long time before speaking. "If you say that word twice in a row, I'll be sent back to 1997. I don't think I dare explain any more than that."

"Henry said it. Bufie, too." They'd both read the word off the note he'd scrawled. "So did Augusta. You didn't go anywhere."

"Yeah, well, I didn't screw up their lives the way I did yours. I'm responsible for you losing your confidence. I don't want to leave here until I set things right."

"I see." And it was becoming clearer to her. He had told her that she alone could provide the means for transporting him back to his home. No wonder he'd acted so funny when she'd offered to lend him the money for train fare. She hadn't understood then that he considered her an obligation, that his "transportation" couldn't be earned until he'd satisfied his sense of responsibility.

That didn't explain why a smart man like Matt conjured up this hare-brained story about time traveling. She'd have respected him more if he'd simply admitted that he'd trespassed onto her property and felt guilty about the results. But then he'd have to admit that staying around to help her was a nice thing to do. The last time she'd accused him of being nice, he'd bolted like a newly captured mustang spotting a hole in his corral. It'd serve him right if she called his bluff by shouting that word out loud and strong. He'd have to do some fast thinking to explain why he didn't disappear into the future.

She would have said the word and called his bluff, except just then her heart felt so heavy that she didn't have the energy to whisper, let alone shout. All this time she'd taken joy in his presence, and reveled in the heady notion that he found her attractive, at least a little bit, and he'd been acting sweet merely because he felt sorry for her. But then, she had no business letting him affect her that way. She'd known from the beginning that he held no real affection in his heart for her, that he would desert her when it suited him.

"I wonder what far-fetched story you'd have come up with if I'd read that stupid note out loud straight off," she said. She hated the way her voice trembled, so she took refuge in anger. "You can just be on your way, Matt Kincaid. You didn't mess up my life. I like it just the way it is. I don't need you. I don't."

He blinked twice in quick succession, but otherwise made no indication that her repudiation of him meant anything. "Fine," he said, clipping the word so it struck hard against the ear. "I'm going to put a bottle on that rock. You shoot it off, and I'll be on my way."

"I don't have to prove anything to you."

He ignored her, stalking off toward the rock with the bottle. Once he'd settled it on a ledge, he turned and faced her with his arms crossed over his chest. "Humor me."

"Oh, I expect you've had plenty of laughs at my expense already. I mean to enjoy the last laugh for myself." She gritted her teeth, determined to shoot her rifle and send him on his way before he could hurt her any more. He'd woven himself so tightly into the fabric of her being, that his desertion would tear a gaping hole in her heart. Well, what was one more hole? Her heart was already riddled with wounds, from the loss of her pa, from Marvella's rebuff in town, from the desertion of her skill. Sending Matt Kincaid away might just rip that troublesome heart right out of her, and then she wouldn't have to worry about getting hurt and teary-eyed over things that she couldn't change.

She drew a deep breath. He'd asked her to humor him. Very well. "Since I can't shoot with you standing so close to my target, DOWMTAB—"

"No!" he bellowed, simultaneously racing across the intervening space. He clapped his hand over her mouth, preventing her from saying the word.

A traitorous flicker of hope flared to life: *He doesn't want to leave me.* Hard on its heels came the voice of reality: *Remember—he feels obligated to stay.* In his own way, he was as bad as Henry, trying to take over her life just because he felt like he owed her something.

All at once she was fed up with being the recipient of so much guilt-inspired responsibility. She wriggled her lips against Matt's palm until he loosened his grip a little, and then she sank her teeth right into the soft web of skin curving from the base of his thumb to his forefinger.

"Ow! Jesus, Kate!" He fisted his wounded hand and brought it to his mouth. He grimaced and hopped away as if she'd kicked him in the privates for good measure. She wished she had. She licked her lips and wished she'd bitten down harder, because it didn't taste like she'd drawn any blood. She wished she had her old confidence back, because she'd have liked nothing better than to shoulder her rifle and blow him straight to kingdom come.

"Why did you stop me from saying the word?" she demanded.

He muttered something, but his answer was muffled against the hand he still held balled before his lips.

"DOWMTABSTA!" she shrieked. It took all her strength. She took a deep breath to lend extra volume for repeating the word, while something traitorous within her prayed he would stop her yet again.

He did. Sort of. He made a motion toward her, and then winced, jerking his hand behind him as if he feared she'd fall on it like a starving raccoon tackling a ripe ear of corn. "Don't say it, Kate."

"Maybe I don't want you hanging around here anymore."

"Maybe I don't want to leave."

"You don't?"

She despised the naked longing revealed by her quivering tones. He didn't seem to notice. His lips were parted, his eyes rounded, leaving him looking even more stunned than she was by his admission.

Even when he spoke, it was with the defensive edge that she'd heard in the voice of homesteaders who'd given up on their claims and sought to put the best possible light on their defeat. "I have to leave—eventually. Everything I've ever wanted is waiting for me in 1997."

She wondered what long-held dreams awaited him back in his own time. Jealousy coiled in her belly. A woman, for sure, she had no doubt about that. A beautiful, elegant, poised female who wouldn't have to beg to be included on a committee to plan a two-fiddle dance. It wasn't bad enough that she thought such a thing, but she had to torment herself even more by seeking verification.

"You have someone waiting for you back home, don't you."

"Several someones."

Oh, God, it was worse than she thought. "One in each city?"

"No, actually all three of them live in New York."

"I guess that cuts down on your travel bill some."

"It wouldn't matter. I have more money than I know what to do with."

And he probably paid out of his own pocket for those other women's milk shakes, she added to herself.

"Well, you can just go back to them," she said fiercely. "I don't need you."

"I know you don't," he agreed, which was terrible, because his calm declaration made her want to retract her words and beg him to stay. "Maybe . . . maybe *I* need *you.*"

He got that stunned look again, as if he'd been groping around with his eyes closed, convinced he was blind, and just that moment discovered it was his own fault that he couldn't see.

"Ha!" She winced at her inadequate response. Augusta Merriweather had tried so hard to drill lady-like retorts into her mind, but she'd forgotten every last one of them. Matt's raw vulnerability had emptied her head of everything except the overwhelming urge to gather him into her arms for a hug.

"You've managed to carve a little place in my heart for yourself, Kate." He studied her somberly. "I can't stand the thought of leaving you without seeing you succeed. I don't want to have to go through some dusty old history book to find out whether you became a star with the Wild West Show. I want to see it happen for myself."

He was so bound and determined to stick to that darned time-travel story that she couldn't help imagining the implications if it were true. If he had truly traveled through time, she would be long dead, her life little more than a few lines in an obscure history book, if that, when Matt Kincaid enjoyed the full fruits of his manhood more than a hundred years in the future. She imagined his lean, graceful form propped against a bookshelf while he thumbed through some crumbling old text, imagined the faint smile curving his lips as he read about Kate Monroe's exploits in the Wild West Show. Providing, of course, she proved good enough for someone to take the trouble to write about her.

And what if they printed a picture of her in that book—a photograph taken maybe in ten or fifteen years, when wrinkles defeated the gun grease and the sun and wind stole the vibrancy from her hair? Matt would be exactly as he stood before her now, so handsome and virile that she ached to press herself against him. She shuddered to think that he'd come across her looking like his grandmother, that she'd be nothing more than dust and bones by the time he found her name in a book. He'd probably show the picture to his three young, beautiful, milk-shake-sipping girlfriends so they could all enjoy a good laugh.

She wished his story were true, just so she could send him away now, this very minute, to nip thoughts like that in the bud.

Or perhaps she should indulge herself. Revel in his presence the way her heart urged her to do, and snap her fingers at the passage of time. He meant to leave her, whether he vanished into the future or just onto the next passenger train. A smart, worldly woman would accept the inevitable and grasp at the chance to pile up memories that would last her an eternity.

But she wasn't smart or worldly enough to indulge in a casual affair, not with Matt. She wanted to offer her body to Matt Kincaid because her heart already belonged to him. The realization made her eyes sting. She'd gone and fallen halfway in love with a man who didn't know how to love her back. Thank God she'd realized the precarious state of her heart before doing anything foolish! The sooner she chased him out of her life, the better.

"I'll try shooting," she said. He nodded, and stepped away so he stood at her back.

Mere minutes ago she'd been angry enough to shoot him; now, her grip faltered once more at the imagined fear that he'd accidentally materialize in front of her bullet again.

"I'm behind you, Kate."

"I know."

The rifle barrel danced uselessly. Her teeth began chattering at the same time a cold sheen of perspiration dampened her forehead.

Matt touched her waist, and then rested his hand against the swell of her hip. "Try it now," he whispered.

It helped, that light, caring touch of his. The rifle held steady. She rested her cheek against the stock and took aim over the sights. But no force on earth was strong enough to curl her finger around the trigger. "I can't do it," she moaned, letting the rifle slip away from shooting position.

"Yes you can." He stepped closer, and shifted his grip until both of his hands clasped her shoulder. "You can do it."

"I want to do it."

"You can." He drew a deep breath in the manner of someone summoning the strength to tackle an unpleasant task. And then she felt his chest bump up against her shoulders. He wrapped both arms around her waist, holding her close. "Try it now."

She felt the warmth of his breath against her crown. He stood stalwart as the rock, firm and solid behind her, lending his strength to her own. She felt his pulse coursing through him, throbbing against her skin until her own altered its pace to match his. Within the circle of his arms, she felt strong. So very strong. She blinked with surprise when she realized that without thinking she'd already nestled the rifle butt against her shoulder, that her cheek was pressed against the satiny wood, that her eye squinted the length of the barrel. Her finger, so strong, engaged the trigger with no effort at all.

The kickback pounded her back into Matt, who absorbed the impact without giving ground. The roar of gunfire deadened her ears for a moment to all but the hammering of her heart within her breast. Smoke hovered over them, enveloping them in an acrid-smelling cocoon that sealed them off from the rest of the world. The glass bottle had shattered, and the shards of glass tinkling against stone sounded sweeter than any music she'd ever heard.

Matt's triumphant shout rang out over the plains. His arms tightened around her with an exuberant hug that sent his hips pressing against her bottom.

"Again!" he cried.

He'd placed only one bottle for her. The last thing she wanted was for him to let go of her so he could set more targets. A drift of small pebbles covered a ledge. She narrowed her gaze upon one of the pebbles and shot it away so cleanly that her bullet left no scar against the rock.

"Yee *haw!*" With a blood-curdling whoop of delight, Matt shifted his grip upon her. He spun her around like a top and then lifted her high in the air. Her hair tumbled loose of its pins and whipped against his face. He didn't seem to mind its stinging, because a glorious grin lit him with delight. She clutched her rifle while her feet kicked for purchase—she'd never been suspended above solid ground in her entire adult life!

"You did it!" His grin widened, and then he lowered her until his lips brushed against hers in a congratulatory kiss, and then he hoisted her right back up again as if she weighed no more than her cast-iron skillets. "You did it, Kate. You broke the jinx."

"I did, didn't I?" she said, marveling from her great height. It suddenly seemed a wonderful thing to be held high above the ground unfettered by the drag of the earth. If only her spirit was able to soar free, instead of being weighed down by the knowledge that Matt's unique sense of honor would permit him to leave her now. She couldn't let him see how that realization shattered her.

He lowered her once more. He probably meant to give her another of those chaste, congratulatory kisses, but for some reason her body began trembling. Perhaps from the unaccustomed sensation of being held high in the air, perhaps from the relief of knowing her phobia had been conquered. But certainly not at the prospect of his leaving or from the hope that he might kiss her once more before going.

The tremors seemed to pass straight through her into Matt's arms, so that when his lips met hers, his grip was no longer as certain. His lips held hers, while his body absorbed her weight, slowly, slowly, until her feet touched the ground once more.

His hands rested at her waist, with his thumbs meeting low on her belly in an inadvertent imitation of the vee she'd caught him admiring on her best blue dress. At least six inches separated her nose from his chest.

Six inches wasn't so far. Less than a step, and she could press against him, let her senses be filled with his power, his scent.

Six inches was enough to remind her that despite their marriage vows, they were not two people united as one.

And yet Matt had said she'd claimed a small part of his heart for herself. Somehow he'd done the same to hers. Her heart would always ache, always feel empty, which made protecting it a futile effort. She felt a sudden empathy for the broken-hearted women who'd spent the past twenty years mourning the men they'd lost in the War Between the States. At least they had memories to pull out and savor when the Nebraska nights turned cold and lonely. Kate wouldn't have anything to remember, except for recalling that she'd once permitted her pride and six measly inches to loom like an impassable gulf between her and the man she loved.

A man who'd never learned how to love might not know how to reach out and gather some for himself. He might not even recognize love when it stood six inches away.

Kate knew she couldn't possibly make up for a lifetime of rejection by reaching out to Matt. She also knew she couldn't send him back to that cold, emotionless void without showing him exactly how much a woman in love was willing to risk.

When you really want something, you have to be willing to risk everything to get it, Matt had said.

Six inches. Once crossed, there would be no returning. On one hand, a chasm. On the other, less than a step.

She took it.

19

Matt's hands pressed at the base of Kate's spine, and then at the middle of her back, drawing her ever closer against him until the unyielding metal and wood of her rifle threatened to leave an indelible imprint upon their skin. She cradled it in one arm while her other hand traced the hard ridges of Matt's arm and then stroked over his shoulder and then found the warmth of his neck. The wind whipped at her hair, until tendrils of it mingled with his. She, who had ever treasured her rifles above all her possessions, longed to drop this most precious of them into the dirt so she might free both hands to hold Matt Kincaid close.

He groaned, a low rumble that vibrated from deep within to reach some answering place in her own body. In answer, she rose on her toes, wedging her hips against his in the most shockingly intimate gesture of her life. He surged hard against her, warm and throbbing and completely unlike the cold lifeless rifle that was proving to be more of an annoyance by the second.

She released her hold upon her rifle, and when it slid down her front, she kicked it away.

Matt drew back from her, just a little, and flicked a glance toward the discarded rifle. His lips were parted, and he was breathing as if he'd like to inhale her. When he bent his head toward hers again, his eyes narrowed, predatory, feral, and gleaming with silent triumph.

"Matt?" she whispered, frightened and exhilarated in equal measure by his passion.

"Stop me, Kate."

Even as he asked the impossible of her, he shifted his body the smallest measure until the space that had been occupied by the rifle melted into a searing contact that stole her breath.

She should do as he asked. There was no future for them, only great risk if she obeyed her wanton impulses. Oh, to have a shred of the control he seemed to be able to exert at will, for she knew without a doubt that she had but to step away from him, or shake her head in denial, and he would leave her untouched. Instead, her hands curved to frame his face. She traced the ridges of his cheekbones, the swell of his lips, even the surprisingly tender skin of his eyelids. Her touch made him shudder and close his eyes, clenching his teeth.

"I don't want to stop you." She whispered the shameful admission and buried her face against his chest.

He cupped her head with one hand. His heart thundered beneath her; the effort of maintaining control lent a barely perceptible tremor to his touch. "I'm a nobody here, Kate. I don't have any money or power. I can't give you anything."

She'd guessed right. A lifetime of rejection had convinced him that only outward trappings held any value. She had to show him how wrong he was.

"You can give me everything I want." Her lips moved against his neck. "I want you. Only you."

He grew so still that she feared she had somehow offended him. And then, unbelievably, the bold thrust of his manhood seemed to swell even more, until she wondered how he could contain it without exploding.

"Oh God, Kate, you don't know what you do to me," he whispered against her ear.

Nor did she know what he did to her. She only knew that she felt poised on the edge of a great discovery and she couldn't wait to learn the secret. She felt all shivery, but not from cold; all flushed, but not from heat. Her woman's instincts whispered that Matt alone could reveal the secret, Matt alone could soothe the shivers and cool the fever raging within her.

The picnic blanket beckoned, offering a soft clean cushion against the dust and tough prairie grass. They moved toward it in silent accord. How fitting, Kate thought, that their lovemaking should take place in the shadow of the very rock that marked the place where first they'd met, upon a blanket brought along to slake appetites.

Matt smoothed her hair away from her face. "You're beautiful," he whispered.

If not for the unnamed hunger raging through her, she might have been content to hear him murmur endearments to her forever, might have thrilled to the joy of simply touching him wherever and whenever she liked. But she craved more, something more.

The trail of his lips against hers only inflamed the hunger. Soon they were clinging to each other with more desperation than before. Matt's kisses deepened, shocking and delighting her with his skill. The few chaste kisses she'd allowed over the years had not hinted that men's lips were capable of rousing such impatience, such hungry demand for satisfaction. His kisses acted like a drug upon her, numbing her always-present self-consciousness until in his arms she did indeed feel truly beautiful, desirable above all women. She felt no shame when her shirtwaist opened at his touch, when he undid the ribbons of her chemise and sent her garments tumbling around her hips.

She had never in her life stood naked to the waist in full daylight, never reveled in the kiss of the wind against her skin or the sun's heat warming her breasts. She set those sensations aside, to remember later, for now she yearned for the brush of whiskered male flesh against hers, for the wet and warmth of Matt's questing tongue to find the aching, nameless places that craved his touch.

He pressed her fingers against his abdomen. The rough homespun of his shirt slid between his skin and hers, in, out, with each breath he took. Too much of a barrier between them; she made quick work of the buttons shielding his skin from her caress.

Kate knew that real ladies were delicate, pallid-skinned creatures who shivered even in the midday sun. She'd often despaired of her handshake, firm and vibrant, and the way it felt awkward and unwomanly against the limp, chilled grasp of her more delicate female acquaintances. An extra petticoat and heavy shawl were enough to keep her warm in winter, and she stole a secret pleasure in abandoning all but the most necessary underwear in summer months. And yet, when her hands stroked Matt Kincaid's bare flesh, she felt a soul-deep warmth penetrate to her very bones, a radiant heat that told her she had never in her life known true warmth until this moment.

The breeze stirred the flaps of his shirt, wafting from him a heady masculine scent combined with stream-fresh cleanliness. All men couldn't possibly smell this good, or else women would be forever ripping the buttons from their shirts in order to immerse themselves in the intoxicating essence. Or maybe destroying his buttons wouldn't be enough, for his warmth, his scent, roused all manner of unnamed cravings . . . she wanted more, so much more.

And so, it seemed, did he. She whimpered with mingled ecstasy and hunger when his hand cupped her breast, when his long, deft fingers stroked her tender flesh and teased her nipple into a swollen bud. His lips skimmed from her mouth to the sensitive spot between her brows, and then down to her neck. His skin against hers rasped pleasantly rough, all hot male skin crowned with the barest hint of whiskers.

Somehow, they ended up lying on the blanket. Somehow, her fingers worked the buttons free at his waist while he loosened the ribbons and buttons at hers. He stripped away the layers of calico and petticoat from her, eased her shoes from her feet, peeled her drawers from her legs, until she lay fully naked atop the blanket. Naked, but feeling wondrously cloaked by the desire she saw smoldering from his eyes. He kicked away his boots and shrugged free of his britches and pressed his full, hot, gloriously golden length against hers. Such strength in his limbs! Golden hair gilded his arms and legs, a fitting covering for his muscular splendor. She wanted to look toward the nest of golden hair curling at the apex of his thighs and found herself suddenly shy. She buried her face against his chest, feeling an abrasion similar to that upon his cheeks.

"You shave your chest," she whispered. "Why?" It seemed a shame to her, for she would have loved to bury her face amid a riot of soft golden curls.

"I'm sorry. It must feel rough against your skin." He did sound regretful, and tried pulling himself away from her a fraction of an inch, but she wouldn't let him.

"Why do you do it?"

Odd, how her mind behaved. Her body clamored for fulfillment, and yet she wanted even more to know everything about him, down to the smallest detail.

"Self-defense. It seems silly now."

She peeped up, and indeed noted a faint rosy blush tingeing his neck. "I don't understand."

"I practice the oriental art of tang soo do."

"I thought you were a businessman, not an artist."

He laughed, a gentle, soft sound so unlike his usual humorless snickers that she could not take offense. "I love the way you look at things, Kate. I'll tell you all about it later. But I'll just tell you that it's best to fight clean-shaven, so your enemy can't cause pain by deliberately yanking at the hair, or accidentally driving a blow that tugs at the roots."

"I wish you would let it grow." She kissed the broad, flat plane above his breast. "I wish you didn't have to worry about fighting enemies."

"Oh, God, Kate." With that he loomed over her, testing her strength with his weight, watching her through the tangle of his hair with the wary expression of one who was unsure he would be offered a welcome, but utterly unable to resist trying. Her heart melted at the sight. One so proud as he, so gloriously male, shouldn't doubt the effect he had on a woman. A woman more experienced than she would know what to do, what to say. She scarcely knew what they were about to do, only that she could not let him doubt his welcome for a heartbeat. She raised her hand and traced the ridge of his lips, the proud curve of his jaw.

"You're safe here, with me," she whispered.

"No, Kate. We're both in serious trouble."

"Then we'll just have to work our way through it. Together."

Together. The very word sent shivers coursing through her. She had never in her life felt part of another person, as if she were as essential to that person as air or water. And yet that late afternoon with Matt, she came to understand the true meaning of the word. Everything mingled: their breath, their hair, their limbs. Her arms, so slender and pale, entwined with his robustly larger ones. Her legs, too long for delicacy, seemed perfectly sized for wrapping round his hips, for stroking thigh to thigh, for caressing his bunching calves with the tender undersoles of her feet. So large a man, so strong a man, infinitely gentle one moment and all surging power the next, claiming what she so eagerly gave with such thorough possession that she knew she would have nothing left to offer any other man.

Together. Hard, heavy, he delved between her soft folds and claimed what she could give only once. She gloried in the giving, reveled in the sharp but brief tearing pain. He stifled her outcry with a deep kiss, plunging his tongue into her mouth in rhythm with the pumping of his hips. He was all firm skin and tensile strength, all hers, cradled in the curves of her arms and legs, buried deep within the most secret part of her, all hers, hers, hers.

And then, in the grip of so much togetherness, a part of her soared free. Tremors seized her, rocketing through her with tingling pleasure, and he could not, did not, try to stifle her cries any more. She clutched him, helpless to do anything but revel in the sensation flooding her. She did not know how long it lasted. Minutes. Hours. For whatever length, it was sufficient to make up for a lifetime of solitary aloneness.

When her senses returned, she found herself held in his rigid grip. He pressed against her, breathing hard into her hair, almost as if he feared moving. When she stirred, when she pressed her fingers against his furrowed brow, he opened his eyes and looked upon her with so much despair that it wiped away all lingering traces of pleasure.

"Kate, I . . ." To her horror, after speaking her name, he gave a little twist of his hips and disengaged himself from her, turning away and curling about himself while shudders racked through him.

She couldn't stand the separation. She sat up and tossed her hair behind her back, but the wind merely kicked it back to flutter around the both of them like a wild thing. She leaned over, desperate to know what had caused his withdrawal, his obvious pain. He seemed well enough. More than well, if truth be told, judging by the proud jutting of his manhood. Her body tingled at the sight, marveling that he'd managed to fit so much into her.

It must hurt, to find oneself swelling so far beyond the bounds of normal skin. Perhaps men did not emerge from this act of love as unscathed as some women hinted. The pain she'd felt might be duplicated, might even be multiplied, in his throbbing

agony. No, it couldn't be. She'd heard more whispered tales than she could recall about how easily
men ruined young ladies and waltzed off whistling a
merry tune.

"I did it wrong, didn't I? I should have taken that
test you told me about." She was miserably certain
that she'd hurt him with her long-legged thrashing.

He gave a choked sound that might have been a
laugh. "No, babe, you didn't do anything wrong. You
did it so well that I almost lost control."

"You . . . you *didn't* lose control?" Oh, how morti-
fying! To think that she'd been squirming like a wanton, mindless with delight, while he'd held himself in
control! Her throat tightened; her eyes stung with the
shame, and it only grew worse when a particularly
quick-falling tear coursed down her cheek to splash
against his hand.

"Oh, God, don't cry." With lightning quick speed,
he swiveled around until he held her hiccuping form
within the shelter of his arms. She pressed against
him and felt the probe of his flesh against hers, almost
as if those secret parts of them were magnet and steel.
If she shifted her hips by the merest degree, he would
slip right back inside of her, she just knew it. Which
served to prove that he wasn't the only one boasting
control, for she held herself still despite wanting nothing more than to have Matt bury himself inside her
yet again.

As if well aware of the danger, Matt altered his
position. "This is the way it has to be, Kate. If I . . . if
I let myself do exactly as I want, the risk to you is too
great. You could get pregnant."

Oh, God, she hadn't even given that a single
thought. She was as dim-witted as the sweet child
Mrs. Hetherington had borne when she was well into

her forties. Happy and eager but heartbreakingly stupid when it came to protecting herself. Of course she could end up pregnant—and then what would happen to her dreams of joining the Wild West Show? She couldn't imagine Colonel Cody hiring a sharpshooter with a bulging belly. The crowds would cringe at the sight, would whisper about her behind their hands.

And Matt could have said nothing better to remind her of the temporary nature of their arrangement. He was a gentleman. He wouldn't be so concerned about getting her pregnant if he meant to stay around, meant to make a real marriage of this sham.

Her own flagrant desires had propelled him into this act when he'd urged caution and restraint at every pause. *Stop me,* he'd begged. Mrs. Merriweather had told her time and again that a gentleman would only go so far as a lady permitted. She hadn't understood, and now she could see why Mrs. Merriweather had been too mortified to explain.

The sun hovered low on the horizon. The breeze turned sharp, and coupled with Matt's withdrawal, it left her shivering and bereft.

"Put on some clothes." He snatched his own from the dirt and began taking long strides away from her.

"Where are you going?"

"I have to find a stream."

He sought, then, to wash away all traces of what they'd done. The realization weighed like lead in her belly. "It's cold, Matt. You'd be best off to heat some water in the kitchen."

"I want it cold, Kate. Preferably slivered with ice."

Slowly, she began gathering her own garments, tugging them in place without dispelling her inner chill in the least. He had stopped about thirty paces away and stared back at her over his shoulder. An hour or so ago, she might have read that expression in his eyes as hunger, as a silent cry to be asked to stay. She knew better now than to trust her interpretation. She couldn't believe how naive she'd been to think he might need something only she could offer. Most likely, he couldn't wait to get back to his three New York sweethearts.

She forced herself to look away from him, even though she wanted desperately to feast her eyes upon that long sweep of male splendor, to marvel at every bulge and indentation and remember *I touched him there.* Instead, she concentrated on dressing, on wiping the dust from her discarded rifle, on launching herself into the wagon. He stood still as stone, watching her, making no move to help her. No effort to stop her.

Very well. She slapped the reins lightly against the horses' backs and clucked her tongue. Obediently, they pitted their weight against the harness. The wagon wheels creaked.

"Kate."

She hauled back so hard on the reins that the horses snorted in surprise. A soaring somewhere in the region of her heart stifled the pang of guilt she felt at so mistreating the patient animals.

"Will you ride back with me, Matt?"

"God, no. It would be better if we both pretended this never happened. We can't get that close to each other, ever again."

Kate flushed, realizing how seriously she'd erred in trying to bridge the gap between them. She'd let herself get all moony and lovestruck, imagining that Matt Kincaid might need her, that he might love her if she took the first step.

Pretend it never happened. Pretend she still possessed her maidenhead. Pretend her pride hadn't been shredded. Pretend she hadn't finally discovered the one thing she wanted more than anything in her entire life, that she'd risked everything to go after it, and she'd failed.

She'd show him. He wasn't the only one who knew how to erect a wall of indifference. She'd been hiding behind one for most of her life and should have known better than to try venturing away from its protection.

Maybe she wouldn't have to rebuild it all the way, though. Maybe just high enough to shield her from Matt, but not so solid that she'd sever the tenuous connections she'd made in town that day.

"I'll see you at home," she said, lifting the reins.

"Kate, I just want to tell you . . ." he drew a deep, husky breath. "I'm sorry. It won't happen again."

"You're right about that."

She clucked at the horses and gave them their heads, trusting them to take her home. She wouldn't be much use guiding them, not with all the tears blurring her eyes.

20

"You're not concentrating," Matt said.

"I've been following your so-called training program for days now, and I haven't missed once," Kate countered.

Ever since they'd made love, they hadn't spoken more than ten words that weren't related to practicing for the Wild West Show. Kate had withdrawn, exactly as Matt had hoped she would. The victory left him feeling hollow. You would think he'd lost his best friend, except he'd never had a best friend and wouldn't know how it felt to lose one.

He only knew that Kate never smiled anymore, or blurted out little tidbits about herself. She never touched him, with those light, fluttering strokes. Matt felt empty and lonely all the time, even though Kate was seldom out of his sight. They never spoke about what had happened between them, but Matt could think of nothing else.

Kate apparently had plenty of things to occupy her mind. While he stood there feeling lost and bereft, she busied herself with reloading the spent rifles and pistols spread out on a quilt. She hummed a little tune while she worked. She hummed that same melody each night while she stitched away at a new dress, the one she meant to wear for her audition. She'd confessed that she considered the expensive material a bargain, considering how much wear she'd get out of that dress once the Wild West Show went touring.

Her preoccupation with her upcoming audition, her planning for a future that did not include him, should have cheered Matt. This was exactly what he'd wanted, for her to continue on as if he'd never interrupted her life. What struck him as odd was how it seemed *he* was so reluctant to let go. How his mind turned into an empty void whenever he tried to envision the future that awaited him. He kept wanting, instead, to share Kate's excitement, like a tag-along kid who offers to be water boy so he can feel like he's part of the baseball team.

Kate had grudgingly consented to allow Matt to become her shooting coach, but it soon became apparent that the program he developed didn't begin to test her abilities. She'd easily picked off all the bottles and large shards of glass he balanced along her practice rock's ledges, and vaporized the feathers he stuffed into crevices. She'd rolled her eyes when he tacked a paper filled with smiley faces on the side of the dilapidated shed, and proceeded to shoot out the eyes and bullet-holed the smiles in each grinning circle.

"Nobody who's seen Annie Oakley perform would be impressed by any of this," she'd complained.

"What's so great about Annie Oakley?"

She gasped, and stared open-mouthed at him for a

moment as if he'd insulted Mother Theresa. And then she told him all about Annie Oakley, and he realized that he'd seriously underestimated the skill level required to become a star with the Wild West Show.

"She can shoot backward, for one thing. Like this." Kate twirled about until her back faced away from him. Using a hand-held mirror to study the shed wall behind her, she rested the rifle barrel atop her shoulder and shot a perfect smiley face into the decaying wood.

Annie Oakley could pulverize two clay pigeons in one pull; Matt insisted Kate learn how to massacre three. Annie Oakley could shatter six glass balls tossed into the air at one time, using three separate pistols to get the job done. So could Kate. Annie Oakley could run into the arena, tumble to the ground, roll over, and still hit a target dead center without pausing to aim. Annie Oakley could ride at a full gallop and pick off glass balls thrown toward her from any direction like some frontier version of a Patriot missile demolishing incoming SCUDs. "I can do that," said Kate.

Matt's heart lodged in his throat when Kate came charging toward him on horseback, with nothing but her long legs gripping her mare. She couldn't hold on with her hands because she had to aim the rifle; she couldn't guide the horse because her eyes were narrowed on the targets he threw for her. One slip on Kate's part, one stumble on the horse's part, and Kate would go tumbling to the ground. She never fell. She never missed.

If he could manage somehow to bring Kate and Annie Oakley into the future with him, the two demure women could give Rambo and Robocop a run for their money.

Kate's skill awed him, and yet there was something curiously flat about her exhibition. Matt had been entertained by the best of the twentieth century's top athletes, actors, musicians. A certain aura surrounded great talent—he wouldn't call it cockiness, exactly, but an inbred confidence that came from knowing you are the best at what you do. They expressed a joy in exercising a talent others could only dream of possessing: hockey stars high-fiving after skating circles around opponents to score impossible goals, stage actors trembling and bowing after repeated curtain calls, opera singers closing their eyes to savor the sound of their magical voices winging toward the heavens.

Kate exhibited no cockiness, no joy. She drilled her targets with the unemotional efficiency of an assembly line robot boring holes through sheet metal.

"Accuracy isn't enough," Matt said. "You have to bring some passion into the act."

She flushed, and damned if he didn't feel his own skin heating up as well. He'd been doing a lot of fruitless smoldering lately.

Each night, she retired to her bedroom, and he to her father's old room. Henry's stayed empty, silently mocking Matt with the knowledge that no one was around to stop him and Kate from making love—only Matt's newly awakened sense of honor, which had picked a damned inconvenient time to appear.

The nights loomed long, with only the muffled ticking of the parlor clock breaking the silence, counting off each minute that passed, wasted. He lay awake night after night, listening to that inexorable ticking. His sleep-deprived brain conjured hazy hallucinations of his taking one footstep in time with each tick, each tock. The analytical portion of his mind calculated that at that tick-tock pace it would take him less than a minute to cross the space between his room and Kate's.

Kate appeared for breakfast each morning primly coiffed and attired, looking well rested and ready to tackle a full day's practice. Matt bashed the skillets and whipped the breakfast eggs into a runny froth in a futile attempt to forget how she'd looked with her unbound hair providing the only cover for her sun-gilded skin.

He sometimes caught her gaze resting upon him, troubled and disappointed. He didn't care to explore the reasons, consoling himself with the knowledge that it couldn't stem from their lovemaking; she'd been a virgin, and far too inexperienced to fake the rippling orgasms and sheer ecstasy that had left her trembling in his arms.

You have to bring some passion to the act, he'd said to her just moments ago. He'd never known a woman so honestly passionate, so deeply sensual. That intensity should extend to her shooting as well. Perhaps it had, until he'd come along and forced her to guard herself against her emotions. Maintaining a calm, polite exterior tended to smother a person's warm impulses. He recognized the barriers. He'd erected enough of them himself to know how impenetrable they could become.

He wouldn't permit her to lose her soft, sweet glow. He had to do something, anything, to reignite Kate's inner flame. He knew one surefire method: hurt her until she fought back. It had always spurred him on to prove everyone wrong.

"You're not nearly as good as Annie Oakley," he spat.

His barb found its mark. She stifled a gasp. Her

hand tightened around the rifle bore until her knuckles ridged and whitened. She stared at him, wide-eyed and disillusioned. He'd earned that look from many others, when they'd ignored his warnings about the true meanness of his nature, and learned too late that he did indeed strike like a viper.

"You might as well give up," he added in a light, conversational tone that did not betray the inner anguish he felt at deliberately destroying Kate's opinion of him. "Even if Colonel Cody is foolish enough to hire you, the crowd will drive you from the ring with its boos and catcalls. You might bankrupt the show if they all ask for their money back."

"How dare you!" Matt could tell she'd meant to shriek at him, but she managed little more than a pain-roughened rasp between lips gone rigid with outrage.

"I dare everything," he shot back.

"That's a lie. You don't know what it means to take a real risk."

She was right. He kept fighting the old, safe demons instead of exposing his weak spots to a new challenger. He deliberately diverted her into another direction.

"I put my life on hold to help you, and this sorry display is the thanks I get."

"Oh, that's right. I forgot you can't return to the future until you rehabilitate little old me. Well, if anyone should get a refund, it's me. I can earn my spot in the Wild West Show without your help."

That's why he loved her, Matt thought. Knock her down and she bounced right back up. Tell her she wasn't good enough, and she kept pounding at the door until she gained entrance . . .

Wait a minute . . . he *loved* her?

The knowledge settled over him like a healing balm. He loved Kate. He loved the way she'd held onto her feisty spirit without sacrificing her loving, trusting nature. He loved the way she refused to let others' opinions alter her goals. He hadn't managed nearly so well in his own life. He had some nerve thinking she needed his help. He was the one in need. He needed Kate. She promised welcome, and love, and in her arms he would always revel in the sense of coming home.

But the woman standing in front of him at that moment was in a fine fury, her eyes smoldering with smoky fire. She glowed from within, but with outrage, not with welcome. He'd brought about that change on purpose and didn't know how to mend the breach. After a lifetime of holding everyone at arm's length, he didn't have a clue how to get close.

"I didn't exactly get an instruction manual loaded with pointers on how to deal with all this," Matt murmured.

"Well, neither did I get one telling what to do if a woman finds herself married to a lunatic who claims he belongs in the future!"

An eerie stillness descended; it seemed as though a shutter was dropping in front of him, shielding him from the threat of this small woman who struck at his heart. His lips twisted into the familiar, comfortable lines of arrogant scorn, and then he recognized what was happening. He instinctively sought the comfort of this frozen numbness whenever he felt threatened. But numbness never cured pain, it only masked it. Maybe it was time for him to start rooting out the source.

Wishing to change didn't make it automatically happen. He ventured toward it in a roundabout way.

"It's different for you," he said. "You're not the one taken out of your natural element."

"Is that so? Then why am I so catawamptiously frazzled?"

"Cat a *what?*"

"Ha! I finally stumped *you* with one of those five-dollar words."

She quivered all over with barely suppressed satisfaction, like an inexperienced stand-up comedian trying to not laugh at her own joke. She looked so pleased to have stumped him that he decided his ego could bear it if he, just once, retreated from his know-it-all stance. "I'm confused, Kate," he said, and wondered if she understood the full nature of his inner turmoil.

To his astonishment, tears swamped her brimming excitement, and her posture softened. It startled him, that his willingness to leave himself open for rejection would in turn batter down some of Kate's defenses.

"Oh, Matt, you confuse me way more than I confuse you. Ever since you came, I feel like I'm being tugged in four different directions. I can't concentrate with you around all the time."

Something wild and male surged through him, silently roaring its satisfaction. He destroyed Kate's concentration! It wouldn't rank high on a scale of world-class accomplishments, but it left him feeling more gratified than anything he could remember.

"You can't let the people watching you disturb you. You must have gotten used to your father and Henry watching you while you practiced."

"Not really. My pa didn't often have time to coach me, and Henry never cared much about my shooting."

"I thought your father worked very closely with you."

"He kept an accounting when I reported each day's hits and misses. He told me I had to develop a strong work ethic on my own, because nobody outside of him and me would care two hoots about my talent. He said he was too easy on me, that I had to learn to be tougher than my worst critic on myself." She stiffened, as if she expected him to disparage her father's behavior. "He did the best he could. Besides, he had to spend a lot of time with Henry out on the range."

"I thought he worked with you in the gunsmith shop."

"He did, sometimes. But he said it was important that I learn to handle the work on my own."

It sounded as though Crandall Monroe had given his daughter good, sound advice, but the verbal picture Kate painted differed so drastically from the Norman Rockwell image in his head that Matt had to lean against the rock to regain his equilibrium. She'd never said much about her relationship with her father, only that she'd learned gunsmithing from him and he took pride in her shooting ability. Matt's determination to hold himself aloof, to avoid caring about her, had let him imagine a storybook childhood, with a doting father indulging his daughter's every whim.

He'd gotten the impression that Kate's pa had hovered over Kate like the proverbial stage parent. Instead, he'd been off riding the range with Henry while his little girl, who knew her pa really hankered after a son, toiled alone in the gun shop, and practiced for hour upon solitary hour, hoping to accumulate a hit-and-miss average that would earn her father's approval.

And yet Kate defended her father, ferociously, claiming he'd done the best he could. Matt couldn't understand the depth of her love. Maybe he couldn't understand her father's brand of love, either. It wasn't like he was an expert on the subject. Maybe he'd been so busy running from imagined slights that he'd never learned to recognize love in its many forms.

"I'm sorry I said you're not as good as Annie Oakley."

"Then why did you say it?"

"To shock you into doing your best. You're every bit as good as Annie Oakley. Maybe better."

She peered up at him through the tangle of her lashes, looking so grateful that it stabbed his heart, and then she glanced away. Her reaction to his faint praise told him how seldom she'd been complimented for her skill.

He reached for her, but she was staring down at the quilt, her fingers picking stray bits of chaff from the cloth.

"Thank you," she whispered. "It'll make it easier to go on, knowing that you believe in me."

Matt jammed his hands in his pocket. She hadn't seen him reach toward her. She didn't realize that he hoped to hold her close while her dream propelled her away.

He was just as bad as Henry.

He hadn't given a thought to that twenty-year-old pain in the ass for days, and now it seemed that thinking about him conjured him up, for an incoming horse and rider were headed their way amid a cloud of dust.

"Henry!" Kate swiveled and tented her hand over her eyes to peer across the plain. Her shoulders slumped. "Oh. It's just Bufie Tarsy."

"Howdy do," Tarsy called as he pulled his horse to a halt. "Got some news fer yew, Kate. The colonel's on the train that'll pull in here on election day."

Matt's throat turned tight. Tarsy's arrival suddenly struck him as an omen. He wanted, he needed, more time with Kate. But hearing the old man announce Buffalo Bill's imminent arrival meant there might not be any more time. "How long until election day?" Matt demanded.

"November 6. Day after t'morrer." Tarsy stared at him quizzically. "Yew sound powerful anxious t' vote, Matt."

"I'm not registered," he muttered.

"Oh. How 'bout yew, Katie?"

"I . . . I . . ." Shudders coursed through her slim frame. "Good lord, Bufie, I'm so nervous about my audition that I don't think I can remember who's running for office."

"I kin help yew there. Writ me a list here in my new diary."

Tarsy pulled a slim leather-bound booklet from inside his jacket. Matt had seen that diary before—the older, scarred, and well-thumbed version that had gotten him into this mess back at the Dismal Lodge. Yet another sign that matters were coming to a close.

"You don't have a title burned into the leather yet," he said.

"Well, hell, I jist bought it t'day!" Bufie drew his head back a bit warily. "But fancy yew pickin' up on thet. I'm intendin' t' git it published, which means I got t' give it a ketchy title. Wrote one down on the first page. Have a look 'n' tell me what yew think."

He pushed the diary toward Matt. His hands trembled as he accepted it, and the shivering accomplished the job of opening the diary. He looked over the words scrawled inside. *Buford Tarsy: Diary of a Man That Spited Them All.*

"It's *who,* not *that.*" Matt said.

"Huh?"

"Diary of a man *who* spited them all. You want to employ the correct English usage, Bufie. You have to get it right." Good lord, he was babbling, and he couldn't seem to stop. "It's very very important for you to get all the words right."

"I guess them publishers put a lot o' store in titles."

"I don't think they do."

"Then why fret over one word?"

"Because . . . well, because someone in the future might try to mix up the first letters of each word to make new words, and they wouldn't come up with the correct combination if the title wasn't right."

"Now, why would anyone want t' do somethin' as foolish as thet?"

"People just might like to do it."

"Huh." Tarsy squinted at him in disbelief, and then his eyes widened. "Say. Since ye're so good with words 'n' English usage 'n' such, mebbe yew kin help me figger out my new carte de visite. I'm orderin' new ones t' advertise the weddin' business I started after doin' such a good job o' hitchin' yew 'n' Kate. The photographer offered me a special deal if I git two sets."

"You must be one of his best customers, Bufie," Kate said.

The old man smiled modestly. "I thought it'd be smart t' have a carte showin' I'm a writer now, too, but I cain't seem t' figger out the right way t' say it. *Buford Tarsy, Diary-er* sorter sounds like I spend all my time in the outhouse, if yew git my drift."

"Diarist," Matt said. "*Buford Tarsy, Diarist.*"

"Now thet sounds right classy. Say, mebbe he'd give you two a special deal, too. Matt, yer carte could say *Matt Kincaid, Wordsmith.* 'N' yew, Katie—*Kate Kincaid, Wild West Show Star.*"

Kate blushed, managing to look desirable, pleased, and filled with trepidation all at the same time. "I couldn't do that, Bufie. What if I don't get the job?"

"You'll get the job," said Matt.

"But what if . . ."

"No what-ifs, Kate. You'll get the job."

She narrowed her eyes with suspicion, and he knew he should compliment her for remembering his warning that she could never trust or believe in anything he said.

"I believe in you, Kate. I do."

The grim line of her lips wobbled and then burst into a smile of such shining radiance that he wanted to bask in her glow forever. He wanted to tell her, with Bufie as his witness, that he loved her. But he couldn't do that. She wouldn't believe him. He'd trained her to suspect that everything he did or said held an ulterior motive. He was well and truly caught in a trap of his own devising.

He backed away from her, alarmed by the sudden racketing of his heart, by the way his breath seemed strangled in his chest.

"Matt?"

"Kate, I . . ." He swallowed before blurting out his secret.

It was time for another reality check.

The prairie sparkled from where sunlight played against shattered glass, evidence of Kate's restored confidence in her marksmanship. Matt had accomplished what he'd set out to do. His usefulness was at an end. He should ask her to say the secret word and send him away. Kate clung to relics that had outlived their original purpose. He couldn't bear becoming one more useless memento that she didn't have the heart to discard.

She would forget all about him, Bufie's ghost had said. Big 'Un would wipe the memory of him right out of her mind. The thought left him feeling sick when he realized how easily that could be accomplished. He'd done nothing in this time or place to make his mark. Nothing except fall in love.

That could be changed. He could thwart Big 'Un in this one respect, by making such an indelible impression upon her heart that Kate would never be able to forget him. She wanted the Wild West Show. He would give her the Wild West Show, hand it to her on a platter.

"I'm going for a run," he said. "A long one." And then he took to his heels.

21

"Look at him go." Bufie stared admiringly after Matt. "I ain't seen a body run thet fast since last year's Fourth o' July pie race. Where's he headed?"

"Nowhere. He'll be back in a couple of hours." Kate hoped she sounded confident. She also hoped she didn't sound rude. But Bufie's arrival just when it seemed she and Matt might breach the chasm between them had left her feeling awfully upset with the old fellow.

Her heart still felt heavy with the words left unsaid, and it thudded with an ominous fear that she'd left it too long to tell him how much she loved him, how much she needed him. There had been a wildness in Matt, almost a terror, that she yearned to soothe.

"Yew sure he's comin' back?" Bufie echoed her trepidation.

"Oh, yes. He runs for miles every day."

"Why?"

"To stay in practice, I suppose. He's some kind of

artist and always has to defend himself against rough people who want to attack him and pull his chest hairs."

"Why would they do thet?"

"He says he practices oriental art, and you know some folks don't cotton to the Chinese."

"Huh. I wouldn't o' guessed it. He don't look like the type t' run away from a challenge."

"He doesn't." She had no proof to back up her claim, only a woman's intuitive knowledge. Cowards never mastered that arrogant tightening of the jaw that Matt Kincaid wore as naturally as other men wore smiles. Cowards slunk and minimized their strength. Matt didn't strut his physical power, but he never flinched from using it. Never hesitated to share it, either. He'd lent it to her so many times. A woman could get used to having someone like Matt around to lean on. But someone like Matt didn't care for clinging females. Someone like Matt polished himself so smooth that nothing could get a grip on him.

"You know, Katie, a man don't have t' leave town if he wants t' run away. I oughta know." Bufie flushed redder than fire-baked bricks and dug the toe of one boot into the dirt. "I'm a pure-tee takin'-t'-my-heels sorter coward, 'cept I don't never go anywheres far."

"You're no coward, Bufie."

"Am so."

Kate wished she could just collapse in a heap on the dirt. She was desperately in need of some reassurance herself, and now she had to summon a cajoling smile and strengthening words for Bufie. "You're no coward," she repeated. "You're . . . you're a reverend, among other things. I saw it written on your carte with my own eyes."

"Yew kin git anythin' yew want writ on them cartes." Bufie sent her a weak imitation of Matt's jaw-tightening. "I could order one says, *Buford Tarsy, Millionaire,* but thet ain't gonna make me a millionaire."

"Well, then, why do you keep ordering so many?"

"'Cause I'm a coward. I ain't got the guts t' stick t' one trade. I figger if I mess up one, I'll always have another trade t' turn to."

"That's not cowardly. That's smart."

"Oh yeah? Look at yew, Katie. Yew got yer heart set on joinin' the Wild West Show. Ye're goin' after it heart and soul. I'd give anything if I had one goal thet meant so much t' me."

Heart and soul. Strange words to associate with joining the Wild West Show. Her heart and soul belonged to Matt.

"Oh, Bufie, I used to dream about the Wild West Show every minute of the day. I haven't done that for a while now."

"Yew got other things on yer mind now."

She gave a quick, embarrassed nod, praying he couldn't divine the nature of the things on her mind. "You're a reverend, Bufie. Maybe you could give me some good advice."

Bufie's shoulders straightened, and a pleased smile lit his features. "I have t' admit thet I've formed a thought or two on yer plight, Katie."

"Please don't tell me you believe Mrs. Merriweather."

"Huh?"

"She's convinced that my pa encouraged me because he really wanted to join the Wild West Show himself, and he could enjoy the thrill of it through me."

"Well, now, thet Augusta Merriweather's a smart woman, but she's all wet on thet theory."

"Really?" Kate breathed. From the way her heart started pounding, she realized she'd secretly nurtured doubts about her pa's motives, too.

"Yer pa was right worried about yer future, Katie. Farmin's hard, especially on wimmin. Crandall knew thet once he passed on, yew'd be at Henry's mercy. I don't think he figgered Henry would turn romantical on yew. I think yer pa was more afraid thet Henry'd bring his own woman onto the place and sorter force yew out o' yer own home. If yew got yerself a job with Colonel Cody, yew'd have the money t' give Henry the boot, or yew could go off 'n' say 'good riddance.' Yer pa liked the notion thet yew could sorter set yer own course without dependin' on anyone else."

A sense of rightness settled over Kate. For the briefest of moments, she imagined her father's spirit held her close. "It's up to me," she whispered. "It's always been up to me. I always had the power to choose my own way."

"Yew got an audition with the colonel comin' up, Kate."

"I know. I'm going to do it, too. I'm going to perform for him and earn my spot in the Wild West Show."

"And then what'll yew choose?"

"I don't know." Maybe it would be a good thing to run away with the Wild West Show. Away from Henry, away from her gunsmithing work, away from the town where the women never accepted her as one of their own.

But perhaps she wasn't being fair. Her pa had never forced her to learn gunsmithing, she'd wanted to do it, to be close to him. Matt had opened her eyes to the way she held other women at arm's length.

"Yer pa done the best he could by yew," Bufie said. "It ain't easy fer a man t' raise a little girl without a woman around. He jist loved yer ma so much thet he never could bring himself to marry agin."

"I know."

Sometimes when she'd returned from North Platte,

silent from knowing she hadn't fit in, her pa had been the one who cried because he hadn't known how to teach her the proper airs and graces.

Her poor pa, apologizing for failing to fill all the roles it took two parents to handle. She wasn't so different. She'd been trying to force herself into becoming what she thought people wanted her to be, instead of seeking out the one role that would make her happy.

She didn't feel, in her heart, like a gunsmith, like a sharpshooter, like a social belle. She felt like Kate Kincaid. Matt's wife. A perfect fit. She stared toward the horizon, where Matt's churning figure was little more than a pinpoint in the center of a dust cloud.

Bufie's attention followed her own. "Durn," he said. "I wisht I'd a known he was an artist. D' yew think he'd draw a Chinese picture in my diary? I promise I won't attack him or try t' pull his chest hairs."

"He might. He helped you fix the title, didn't he?"

"Yep he did. Thet reminds me—I'd best rip out the old version so's I don't git confused." Bufie carefully tore the page from the diary. "Yew want t' use this paper fer kindlin', Katie?"

"Thanks, Bufie." Scrap paper was a rare commodity on the frontier. She stuffed the paper in her pocket.

"Well, then." Bufie cleared his throat and shifted his weight from one hip to another. "Well."

"You didn't come all the way out here just to tell me the colonel's going to be here in a couple of days, did you?"

"Well, now thet yew mention it, Katie, there is a little piece o' unfinished business between us. Seems t' me there's the matter o' two jugs o' corn due me."

She'd completely forgotten to pay Bufie for conducting the wedding. Henry had been outraged, she remembered, believing the cost entirely too steep. But the wedding had given her all these days with Matt. Since then, she'd gotten tougher, in a way, but more understanding, too. She'd taken a few blows to her pride, but felt more confident than ever. She'd fallen in love, and even if that love wasn't returned, she would have memories to savor over the years. Bufie's fee was a bargain.

"I could give you the money to buy two jugs at Wald and Wheeler's. But I think my pa would've liked for me to give you two of the bottles from his private store."

"Yer pa was known fer bein' a good judge o' corn," Bufie said.

"He was a good judge of character, too," Kate said, "considering who he picked for his friends."

The parlor clock chimed three times, announcing that the afternoon was half over. Shadows loomed from the corners. The windows revealed a dull gray sky. Kate lit the kitchen lantern against the gloom, feeling sad as she did so. Burning expensive kerosene this early in the day meant winter had arrived. No more sun-drenched days stolen from time.

Matt would be home at any minute to begin preparing supper. He might already be at the stream, sluicing ice water through his hair. *A man doesn't have to leave town if he wants to run away,* Bufie had said.

Matt's behavior over the past few days was proof of that. He ran himself to exhaustion, until he was so physically depleted that he could barely lift a glass of water to his lips. Almost as though he believed that draining himself of normal male strength allowed another kind of strength to develop, so that he could endure night after silent night in her presence. He'd grown so distant since making love to her that she sometimes wondered whether she'd imagined the whole thing. She sometimes wondered if a real man occupied this space with her, or if it was a ghost of the real Matt Kincaid.

But she didn't know the real Matt Kincaid. She didn't know anything about him.

She knew he'd be exhausted when he came through that door, though, and his lips would be almost blue from the long soaking he took in the frigid stream. She decided to stoke the fire in the cookstove. As she walked toward the stove, something rustled in her pocket. The paper Bufie had given her to use as kindling. Perfect.

She balled the paper in her fist and lifted the stove lid with her other hand when a niggling thought at the back of her mind made her stop.

Something about Bufie's diary had sent Matt into a mild panic. He'd acted and talked crazy, about people in the future wanting to make words out of the first letters from the title of Bufie's diary.

She replaced the stove lid.

She bent over the kitchen table and smoothed Bufie's paper until she could read the words. *Buford Tarsy: Diary of a Man That Spited Them All.* No. Matt had advised Bufie to correct the word *that* to *who*. She found a pencil and carefully crossed out *that* and wrote *who* as neatly as she could right above it. Then she copied the first letter of every word in a straight line across the bottom of the page.

And then she ran into her bedroom, and opened her underwear drawer, and removed the small slip of paper that she'd found tucked between her chemises a couple of days ago. It was exactly like the slip that Henry had found hidden in the outside Sears catalogue. DOWMTABSTA, DOWMTABSTA, was written on

the paper. Matt's secret word, the word he'd claimed
sent him traveling through time.

She returned to the kitchen and compared the letters in Matt's secret word to the letters she'd copied
from Bufie's title. They matched, if you mixed them
up a little. To make sure, she drew shaky lines con-
necting the letters from one set to the other. They
paired exactly, now that Matt had helped Bufie correct *that* to *who*.

She lowered herself into a chair, trembling so
badly that she doubted she could stand.

So, she scolded herself, what of it? What did it
mean that Matt Kincaid somehow knew how to make
up a secret word out of the first letters of the title of
Buford Tarsy's diary? Anybody could do the same.

But Matt couldn't possibly have known that Bufie
meant to buy a diary, and that he'd meant to burn a
title into the leather cover. *It's very very important to
get the words exactly right,* he'd warned Bufie, with
the zeal of someone whose fate rides on the truth.

What if . . . what if it were true, and that word
really did send Matt back and forth through time?

She started shaking.

Suppose, just suppose, she permitted herself to
believe it for a little while. Five minutes, no more.
Why would the Almighty send someone like Matt to
her? She didn't need five minutes to figure that out.
Matt Kincaid had taught her that she was strong.
He'd opened her heart to the light.

But surely the Almighty wouldn't have so inconve-
nienced Matt merely to help Kate discover what was
truly in her heart. Matt hadn't gained a thing by traveling backward in time.

Or had he?

He was a wounded man, who'd built so many

defenses around his emotions that recognizing his own innate goodness had startled him. He was a man without a real home, and she was a woman with room in her heart.

They needed each other. It was only an accident of time that had found her born in one century and him in another. An accident that had been fixed by sending Matt to where he belonged—in her arms.

When you really want something, you have to risk everything by going after it. Again and again, if need be.

She would ask him to stay. She would let him know she believed in him, that she wanted him, that she loved him. She heard a boot scrape against the stoop outside and jolted to her feet, her heart hammering with all the fullness she felt. She couldn't wait for him to open the door so she could fling herself into his arms and tell him how she'd finally found the one thing that she wanted above all else. She wanted him.

The door swung open.

"Howdy, Kate," said Henry.

After reassuring herself that Henry hadn't been hurt by the Indians, she sat with him for hours, pretending interest in his accounting of the cattle rescue. The parlor clock ticked off each passing second, mocking her for thinking Matt might want her the way she wanted him. While he'd been working with single-minded purpose toward restoring her confidence in her marksmanship, she'd been indulging in flights of fancy. He always managed to get what he wanted, he'd told her. She'd been waiting to hear a commitment from a man who'd never wanted anything badly enough to ask for it.

Matt never came home.

22

Colonel Cody's country home lay within hailing distance of North Platte, but just to make sure folks could find him without any trouble, he'd painted "Scout's Rest Ranch" in four-foot-tall letters across the southern slope of his barn roof. Those who traveled by train joked they didn't have to open their newspapers until well out of North Platte, because the tracks passed within a mile and a half of Cody's place, and his barn roof provided plenty of reading material.

Kate seldom had the chance to see the tall words for herself, because she usually approached the Cody spread from the northwest, where her practice rock marked the boundary her ranch shared with Buffalo Bill's.

Today, riding toward her audition, she welcomed her private approach. Over the past few years, the residents of North Platte had just about worn a path between town and Scout's Rest. When the imposing dwelling house was still under construction, entire families had made the long drive across the valley to watch it being built. But nothing could equal the bustle and excitement that surrounded Scout's Rest on the days when the colonel conducted auditions for the Wild West Show.

Kate had joined the crowd herself on many such days, cheering herself hoarse for the bronc busters who valiantly tried to master horses that had been specially schooled to unload their human cargo. The colonel claimed a good bucking horse was the rarest talent of all, hard to find, harder to hire. Kate glanced down at the audition schedule that had been delivered to her the day before. It proved the colonel's contention. Only three broncs were scheduled auditions. On the other hand, there were four female sharpshooters listed besides herself.

Considering her status as a hometown girl, the colonel had offered Kate the option of performing first or last. She'd asked to be scheduled for last. Going last sometimes lent the contestant an advantage. Kate hadn't considered it from that angle. She was more concerned with staying home until the last possible minute, hoping Matt might return.

Despite his promise to stay with her until the audition, he'd never returned from his run. Kate had cried herself to sleep each night and endured Henry's smug glances each day. She'd dragged herself through the motions of living, dutifully practicing her act. Sometimes she'd blinked to find she'd demolished an entire row of bottles without consciously aiming and shooting, like she'd done it in her sleep. Come to think of it, she could look back on her whole life in the same way. Up until a few days ago, it was all a big, boring blur. *No passion, no passion.*

Well, what good had passion done her? She'd

indulged in it with Matt, for a few glorious hours, and all it did was make the rest of her life seem pointless and dull. No wonder Mrs. Merriweather had served her so many lectures on the dangers of submitting to a man's lusts. All it did was stir up wild cravings that could never be assuaged, now that the passion had been spent. Better to spend one's life mired in boredom than with this great aching void dragging against your heart. Sooner or later the heart would be bound to falter, and there would be nothing to kick it back into gear.

Sounds that seldom crossed the prairie intruded upon her thoughts: childish squeals of delight, the furious trumpeting of a hard-used horse, roars of approval sliding into disappointed groans. Her absent-mindedness must have struck again, because she was almost to Colonel Cody's front door and scarcely remembered five minutes of the trip from her house.

Not only that, but she must have somehow turned her horse around to approach Scout's Rest from the south instead of the northwest, because if she squinted, she could see words stretching across the barn roof. The realization gave her a brief flicker of alarm. A sharpshooter shouldn't have to squint to read four-foot-tall words. She blinked to clear her eyes and then peered toward the barn roof again.

Good luck, Kate! read the message.

She blinked again. The message didn't change. Someone had sewn a trio of bedsheets together and painted the greeting in runny brown letters the exact color of molasses onto those sheets and then tacked the whole business to the roof.

"She's here!" shouted a familiar voice. Mrs. Hetherington?

"Well, it's about time." Mrs. Merriweather stepped from the barn's shadow and checked the timepiece pinned to her breast. "You cut it quite close, Kate my dear. Another five minutes and you would have been unfashionably late."

Kate could do nothing but gape speechlessly as Marvella Quint, Callie Clinton, and Mrs. Longwell joined the two older women. Mrs. Merriweather pulled a large white bundle from her reticule and handed one end to Mrs. Hetherington. They stretched it out between them, revealing a banner made up of basted-together bedsheets with more molasses-colored words painted onto the muslin: *Let's Go, Kate Monroe!*

"Fall in behind us, Kate my dear," Mrs. Merriweather ordered. And then she and the other women hoisted the banner to waist height and began stepping as smartly as a band of suffragists toward the crowd surging at the front of Colonel Cody's mansion. Kate's mare followed right along, as if sucked into the female tide of determination. Kate couldn't fault the mare for she was incapable of providing any guidance at the moment.

She felt like crying and laughing all at once, so touched by this unexpected show of support that she didn't know how to act. Marvella Quint peeped over her shoulder and shot Kate a tentative smile, one that Kate might have considered mocking a few days ago but now reminded her of what Matt had said, that maybe Marvella was just as afraid of Kate as she was of Marvella. She answered with a trembling smile of her own, which broadened Marvella's. Maybe, maybe they could be friends.

The crowd took notice of their miniature parade. Heads swiveled, necks craned, the way they always did when she rode into town. She wondered if they'd always smiled at her as they did now. She'd been so busy ducking her head and avoiding their eyes that she'd just never noticed.

"Ain't this a pisser!" Bufie Tarsy chortled as he puffed alongside her mare.

"I . . . I don't understand how all this came about," Kate said.

"Yew like the sayin' on them sheets, Katie? Matt put me in charge o' thinkin' up a ketchy slogan, seein' as I'm a writer 'n' all. O' course, he had t' help me some, seein' as it was my first slogan."

"Matt helped you write 'Let's go, Kate *Monroe*?'" she whispered.

"He ain't let up fer the past three days. Says he's runnin' a watchamacallit, a public ree-lations campaign. I been thinkin' o' gettin' int' thet line o' business myself. It's sorter fun, thinkin' up ketchy slogans 'n' jawin' with folks. Wonder if thet photographer'd give me another deal on a set o' cartes. Miz Longwell came up with the idee t' write the words with molasses, on account o' the sheets could be washed out after. Miz Merriweather accused her o' tryin' t' drum up business fer her husband's general store, but Matt pointed out thet usin' molasses made more sense than paintin' yer name on sheets that folks'd have t' sleep on later. Them wimmin quit jawin' the minute Matt started talkin' about beds 'n' suchlike. Thet Matt sure has a way with the ladies."

"Matt?" she said again, while her eyes raked the crowd, anxious for a glimpse of him.

"Cain't talk t' yew no more. Got work t' do." Bufie stumbled to a halt, and cupped his hands around his mouth. "Let's go, Kate Monroe!" he bellowed.

Mrs. Merriweather's back straightened and she cried out the slogan too. Mrs. Hetherington added her Bostonian-accented version on the next round, and soon half the crowd was chanting Kate's name, urging her on to success.

Kate's joy at hearing that Matt hadn't completely abandoned her fled at learning he had approved the saying using the name Kate *Monroe*. What had happened to change his mind after the day he'd sworn she would always be Kate Kincaid in his heart?

She forcibly pushed the heartache roused by that memory out of her mind and concentrated on the cheering townsfolk. Their support, their approval, swirled around her like invisible hands propping her upright as she pulled up her mare in front of Colonel W. J. Cody.

Grown women simpered and blushed like schoolgirls beneath Will Cody's attention. He was handsomer than a man had a right to be, with a perfectly groomed mustache and goatee that enhanced his good looks. He stood tall and lean with whipcord strength, topped by a headful of the thickest, best-behaved hair that ever crowned a man's head. He could place fifty performers in the arena alongside himself and still dominate the show. His booming, melodious voice held audiences spellbound. He turned a private-sized version of his charm upon Kate.

"Looks like you brought along a passel of your own fans, Missie," said the colonel.

Four sour-faced women, cradling rifles in their arms, glared at Kate from across the yard. Her competition. One stuck out her tongue and made a hideous face at her. Not so long ago, so much overt hostility would have sent Kate's confidence crumbling, would have sparked the urge to turn tail and run back to the safety of the ranch.

But the crowd pressed close, and the colonel's warm gaze rested upon her with approval. He'd called her "Missie," which everyone knew was his pet name for Annie Oakley. It would take more than a few hostile glares and one stuck-out tongue and face-pulling to swamp the confidence bubbling to life within her. Kate tilted her chin skyward just a notch.

Funny, how that tiny show of pride changed her perspective so that she caught sight of Matt Kincaid lounging against Colonel Cody's front porch rail.

Bufie had said something about Matt working around the clock for three days arranging this welcome for her. Dark smudges under his eyes seemed to back up Bufie's claim. Matt's shirt hung a little loosely upon him, and his belt appeared to be cinched a bit tighter at the waist, as if some of his magnificent physique had melted away during the past few days.

Emotions warred in her breast. Now that he stood practically in front of her, she could admit to having harbored fears about his safety. He hadn't been massacred by Indians, or gunned down by thieving drifters, or poisoned to death by rattlesnakes. He hadn't disappeared. But hard on those heart-stopping fears followed a woman's outrage over being deserted without explanation. How could he have run off like that, unarmed, penniless, without even a sack lunch, as if risking death and starvation were better alternatives than staying with her and helping see her through this audition as he'd promised?

She wished for some of his skill at peering into a person's soul. His face, so handsome that Colonel Cody receded into insignificance alongside him, revealed no clues as to what was going on in Matt's mind. His topaz gaze met hers, as unreadable as it had been on that first day when she'd thought a clunk against her practice rock had wiped all the warmth from his expression. She knew better now.

If there had been a glimmer of apology in his eyes, some little smile showing that he'd arranged all this to make things up to her, she could have forgiven his desertion. Instead, he watched her for the space of another heartbeat, and then flicked his unemotional gaze over the crowd, weighing and judging the results of his public relations campaign with the same detachment as he'd studied the furniture in her parlor.

Matt the manipulator. He'd orchestrated this gala welcome for his own purposes. *Don't forget that everything I do has an ulterior motive,* he'd warned her. The sane, sensible part of her mind worked frantically to discover how Matt might profit from doing all this for her. The silly, in-love part of her whispered no, maybe he loved her too. Maybe a man who found it hard to express his emotions might require a hundred voices to say the things he couldn't.

At that moment, Louisa Cody approached her husband and tucked a proprietary hand into the crook of his elbow.

"Lou." The colonel acknowledged his wife with a barely stifled sigh and a distinct slumping of his shoulders.

The Codys' standing in the community didn't stop people from gossiping about the sorry state of their marriage. They'd nearly divorced a while back, and some whispered that it was for the sake of Mrs. Cody's pride that the colonel stopped the proceedings. They remained married, but spent months estranged from one another. Mrs. Cody spent far more time in her North Platte townhouse than she did at Scout's Rest ranch, and seldom accompanied her husband on his far-flung travels. The colonel always came home to her; Louisa always welcomed him. But there was no joy evident in their reunions, no passion in the disinterested glances they turned upon one another in the course of public appearances.

No passion. No passion.

Kate's marriage wasn't so different from theirs, she supposed. It was worse, if truth be told. The Codys had married for love and watched that love disintegrate over the years until only responsibility and pridefulness kept them together.

Kate and Matt hadn't married for love, and they'd stopped talking to each other, at least in any meaningful way, after only a few days. Matt felt a responsibility toward her, and he would consider it absolved once she gained this job with the Wild West Show.

Now she understood his ulterior motive. He couldn't wait to be rid of her. He hadn't believed in her enough to trust her to win the Wild West Show job on her own. This public relations campaign had been organized to impress Colonel Cody, to buy Matt Kincaid's ticket out of Kate's life.

She could hold him at her side, she realized with a flash of intuition. All she had to do was prevent the word DOWMTABSTA from ever crossing her lips. She could pretend a collapse of her confidence, throw the audition so that Colonel Cody wouldn't even hire her to curry his horse. Matt might stay with her then. But he'd turn into a version of Colonel Cody, escaping from the wife he'd never loved by traveling across country on business and, if he ever returned, sighing and slumping at Kate's wifely touch. His rare smile would disappear entirely. Folks would whisper about their sham marriage; brazen hussies might feel justified in approaching Kate's handsome husband, the way loose women were said to surround Colonel Cody the minute he lit out of North Platte.

"Let's go, Kate Monroe!" piped up a small child from behind her. A chorus of children took up the chant.

Kate's heart swelled, the way tender flesh often did after sustaining a bruising blow, and yet there was something bittersweet in the pain. Matt couldn't have whipped up so much enthusiasm if the people of North Platte didn't like her at least a little bit. Their faces turned toward her, shining with hometown pride, smiling their encouragement. They believed in her. She believed in herself. She would not let any of them down.

"Colonel and Mrs. Cody." She dismounted from her mare and dropped into the neat little curtsy she'd been practicing ever since reading about the way Annie Oakley had charmed the Queen of England with her refined manners. Louisa Cody's lips pursed with approval. The colonel beamed at her.

She despised herself for looking, but she couldn't help sneaking a glance toward Matt. He leaned against the porch rail in the same position as before, with his arms crossed over his chest, his face as blank and cold as a corpse's. Well, that expression suited him, and proved he was as dead inside as he'd always claimed to be.

No passion. No passion. Perhaps a person totally devoid of passion didn't recognize it when he saw it. Matt had certainly failed to realize that she ached for him, that she'd been willing to spend the rest of her life loving him. She'd show him passion.

She gave the two best performances of her life. The first was her sharpshooting exhibition, which the colonel's stagehands swore beat Annie Oakley's hands down. And second was the successful hiding of her anguish when she bowed again and again before the wildly cheering crowd, keeping a smile pasted on her face when she couldn't keep herself from looking toward the porch and found it empty.

Matt Kincaid had left before seeing her triumph.

*   *   *

Matt propped his back against Kate's practice rock, and sat there cursing his stupidity.

He'd been walloped by the depth of his love for her the minute he'd caught sight of her sitting her horse so bravely, all but overwhelmed by the raucous reception he'd arranged for her.

Those three days he'd spent away from her had practically shredded whatever sanity he'd ever claimed. He'd had to stop himself more times than he could count from racing across the prairie just to fill himself with the sight of her, the scent of her. Each agonizing moment spent away from her probably wiped out an hour from the other end of his life.

The self-imposed separation served a dual purpose—it kept him away from her until he could prove how much he believed in her. And it had taught him the folly of trying to leave her. He'd barely endured this three-day absence. He could never survive the ultimate separation of leaving her behind while he returned to the future.

But his own stupidity had condemned him to that living hell. Soon after Kate's audition began, a man had nudged him in the side and said, "Say, your wife's really something." Matt had been so caught up in Kate's dazzling display that he'd grinned in agreement.

He'd gotten the first hint of the seriousness of his mistake when several others sought him out with similar remarks. His pride in her hadn't wavered, but another emotion had sprung up alongside it, something so alien to his nature that it had taken him a while to recognize it. Jealousy. He wanted to punch those leering, awestruck men right in the nose. He wanted to leap up onto the roof of Cody's house and scream at the crowd to stop cheering and hollering when the mood shifted from good-natured support to the sort of screaming frenzy that usually marked rock concerts.

He didn't really want to dampen their enthusiasm. Kate deserved every bit of it and more. The problem was that every man, woman and child who'd ever spurned her suddenly wanted to clasp Kate Monroe to their bosom.

He wanted to clasp her to his bosom, too. He'd wanted to do that from the start. But he'd left it too long. His declaration of love might have meant something to her before the world recognized how wonderful she was, before she brought the entire town to its knees. Now, he'd have to stand in line behind every starstruck guy in the Territory who'd suddenly developed a burning passion for her. She would think him no better than those other fair-weather admirers who sought to bask in her reflected glory, the type of person her father had warned her against.

Rather like he had always hoped to be accepted into society after marrying some WASP princess. How could he have been so stupid? He leaned his head against the rock, and then lifted it and thunked it backward. It hardly hurt at all, which just went to prove how thick-headed he was. It went right along with the thick skin, the impervious heart, that he'd spent all his life developing.

A shadow fell over him. Matt stared up and found Henry blocking the sun in an encore performance of his Clint Eastwood impersonation.

"Go to hell," Matt muttered tiredly.

"I guess that's an invite to take the seat next to you." Henry sprawled in the dirt alongside Matt.

"You're right, this is hell. Lousy seat, lousy weather, worse company."

"She got the job."

Matt nodded. There was no way a savvy showman like Cody would let a crowd-pleaser like Kate escape his clutches.

"You going to let her go?" Henry asked.

"I have to."

"I guess you do." Henry slanted a look at him. "Seeing as you love her and all."

Matt couldn't help laughing, though the sound held more desperation than humor. How in the hell had Henry realized something Matt could scarcely believe himself? "I've done nothing but insult her, bully her, antagonize her and hurt her. How do you know I love her?"

"I heard what you did, organizing the whole town to come out for her. I saw the way you looked at her, like you didn't know how you're going to live without her, and yet you did everything you could to help her get away. Made me think."

"Stop the presses."

Henry ignored the sarcasm. "I have to let her go, too. I don't love Kate the same way you do."

"I'm glad you finally realized that."

"Yeah. Well, it's a hard thing to admit. It's going to be harder still to wave good-bye when she takes off with the show."

"You'll see her again," said Matt, swallowing hard to subdue the pain that rose at knowing he would see her only once more. "She'll come back to North Platte when the show season ends, just like the colonel."

"Are you really going to leave?" asked Henry.

"I can't stay. Not now."

"I'll bet the colonel would let you travel along with Kate, if you asked."

If you asked . . .

He'd never asked Kate if she wanted him to stay. She'd grown from girl into woman waiting for others to invite her into their lives. They were two of a kind in that respect. Matt flinched at the memory of his lecturing her on the subject. He'd told her she had to be willing to risk everything to get what she wanted. Too bad he hadn't listened to his own advice.

"I'm an idiot," he muttered.

"Yeah," Henry agreed.

Kate, I love you. It had seemed impossible to squeeze those four little words through his throat, for fear that she might reject him. *I want to stay.* He'd shielded his heart behind a tough, impervious barrier. Unfortunately, he'd forgotten the cardinal rule of construction. Every barrier served two purposes—to wall things out, and trap things within. He'd sealed away all possibility of having Kate, and yet buried inside him was the tiny spark that she had kindled to life. It would burn endlessly, until it consumed him from the inside out.

All that effort to protect his heart, to no avail. He'd finally found the one thing worth risking everything for, and he'd blown his chance. Somehow, he had to regain his detachment. He had to face her once more and remind her that she must speak the words to send him away.

Matt stood and brushed the dirt from his jeans. "I'm going to go home so I can congratulate her. I'd appreciate it if you gave us a little time to ourselves."

"I guess I can sleep in the bunkhouse."

"Suit yourself. I won't be spending the night at the ranch house, either."

23

The temperature plunged as soon as the sun sank below the horizon. The wind kicked up at once, too, as if it had been waiting for the cover of darkness before revealing itself as the entity responsible for stealing all the warmth. As the frigid air settled over the prairie, fog formed near the ground, sending thick fingers swirling skyward, until Kate could barely see the house when she rode into the barnyard.

She bedded her mare for the night, forking extra straw onto the floor and an extra measure of oats into the feed bucket. Food and comfort meant more to a horse than a fervent thank you whispered into its ear, but Kate thanked her mare anyway, and rubbed her soft nose before heading for the house.

Golden light glowed from the kitchen window, diffused and blurred by the fog, providing a beacon guiding her home. Her feet dragged as she approached. She shivered in the damp, cold dark, wishing that winter might have delayed for one more day, granting her one more lingering, gentle twilight. But Indian summer, that rare and precious interlude that thwarted time, had fled. Winter, and reality, were here to stay.

She closed the kitchen door behind her, and pressed a hand to her heart when she saw Matt sitting at the kitchen table.

"I didn't expect to see you again," she said.

"I couldn't leave." Matt stared down at his hands.

Her heart thrilled to his words, and then reality doused her joy. It wasn't love, or desire, or a change of heart that held him here. A secret word held him prisoner, and she alone could free him by saying it.

He couldn't come right out and ask her to say it, according to the rules. It seemed he couldn't ask her for anything.

"I'll say the word now." She whispered, but her voice echoed in this kitchen that had so recently resounded with banging skillets and clanging oven doors. The familiar tick-tock from the parlor sounded louder, too, as if mocking her with the insidiousness of time. She'd been given so little of it to share with Matt. "Do you have everything you need?"

"No." His fingers curled, as if the kitchen's air held something he sought to capture and take to the future with him. He shuddered, and then lifted his head toward her. With a quick toss of his head, he shook his hair away from his face. His hair had grown shaggier since that day she'd found him, less well groomed, more inviting. A real wife, or a woman who knew she was loved, would have a fine time running her fingers through that hair, smoothing it behind his ears, and then tracing the whiskery edge of his strong chin.

"The colonel offered me a part in his show." Kate

clasped her hands together to stop them from reaching toward him.

"I know. When do you leave?"

"Sometime in the spring. The colonel usually opens the season around Memorial Day."

"That's a long time from now."

"I know." She didn't understand how she could speak so normally, as if her heart weren't breaking. "The time will pass quickly. I'll be busy helping the other ladies with the plans for the Engineers' May Ball."

"So they finally wised up and asked you."

They hadn't. The women had clustered about her, congratulating her, marveling at her skill. She'd impulsively asked them if she could help with the Ball and they'd pounced on her offer with such enthusiasm that she'd gotten all warm and teary-eyed. "A lot of things changed after my audition," she said.

He nodded. "You deserve it. You were magnificent."

"I didn't think you saw my performance."

"I watched from the edge of the crowd and slipped away just before you finished."

She bit her lip to keep from crying out. Matt, hovering at the edges while she'd yearned so desperately to have him close. She understood with the pain of one who'd spent her life on the outside looking in; she regretted it with the newfound knowledge of one who understood that some of the blame had to be self-directed.

"I couldn't have done it without your help," she said.

Joy blazed across his features for the space of a heartbeat, only to be replaced by a scowl. "Don't patronize me, Kate. I'm the one who almost destroyed your ability to shoot, remember?"

"You're the one who taught me how to put passion into the act."

He flinched. She pressed on. "I didn't know anything about passion until I found you."

He made an inarticulate sound and pushed himself away from the table. He stormed from his seat and began pacing the kitchen like a circus lion testing the boundaries of its cage.

"There are some things I'd like you to remember."

"You've given me plenty to remember."

"Listen to me, Kate. This is important." He stalked across the kitchen so deliberately that she thought he might be counting each step. "Buffalo Bill thinks he's a shrewd businessman. He's not. He's a showman. You make sure he pays you on time every week."

"This kitchen measures fifteen feet by fifteen feet," Kate said. "You don't need to pace it off."

"Listen to me. I don't know about income taxes in this time period. You might not have to worry about them. But it's never too early to prepare for retirement."

"Retirement? Goodness, Matt, I don't expect to spend more than two years with the Wild West Show. Annie Oakley only lasted a couple of years, and you're talking like you expect me to spend all my days shooting glass balls on Colonel Cody's behalf."

"That's a natural assumption."

"Only if the person making the assumptions lacks an imagination. I can think of plenty of interesting things to do with my life. Lots of ways to have fun."

"You can?" For a moment, she thought he meant to ask her what a woman in love might consider a fun way to pass her time. But instead, he plunged back into his pacing. "Get yourself financially stabilized just in case Cody folds early. Find yourself an honest stockbroker. Buy shares in Coca-Cola, Edison, and Bell. If they're not available now, they will be. Oh, Eastman, too, and Westinghouse and Carnegie Steel. And when the hell did J. D. Rockefeller found the Standard Oil Company? You can't lose with oil."

"Matt—"

"I'd better write those companies' names down for you in case Big 'Un wipes them out of your memory. Talk about insider trading."

"Matt—"

He waved her into silence as he began rummaging through the drawer. He found a pencil, which he stuck behind his ear, and started lifting skillets and peering underneath them. "I can never find paper in this house when I need it."

She tiptoed up to him and practically shrieked in his ear. "Matt! What on earth are you trying to do?"

He turned bleak eyes upon her. "I want you to remember me, Kate."

"And you think I'll remember you if you write other people's names on paper?"

"I don't have anything else to give you."

"Don't you remember that you told me I would always claim a little piece of your heart? That's what I want."

He carefully made his expression go blank.

She felt something inside herself shatter, as if she'd battered it once too often against his defenses. She had to admit defeat. Ignoring the ache in her heart, she forced herself to speak of sending him away.

"Should you be sitting down when I say the secret word?"

"I don't know."

"Will you disappear like this?" she snapped her fingers. "Or just sort of fade away by morning, like that fog outside?"

"It's foggy? That figures."

"When you get back to your own time, will you be paralyzed like you were when you got here?"

"I don't know." He shuddered. "I probably won't notice if I am, because I'll feel so numb."

"You will?" she whispered.

Her heart began a joyous dance, and she thought she must surely be the most foolish woman in the world, if hearing a man admit to feeling numb sounded like encouragement to her.

When you really want something, you have to risk everything to get it. It required a great deal of courage to take that kind of risk. It would take even more courage to live with herself later, knowing she'd given up too easily.

He was, after all, a hard-headed, stubborn, typical man. Maybe it hadn't sunk in on him the first time she'd tried.

"Matt, I know you don't want to hear this, but I have to thank you."

"You're right. I don't want your gratitude."

"Well, you're going to get it anyway. I don't think the colonel would have been so partial to me if it wasn't for your public relations campaign."

He shrugged her compliment away. "It wasn't any big deal. I told you that Cody's a showman. He responds to hoopla."

"It was quite a sight, watching Mrs. Merriweather and all those other woman marching around and hollering 'Let's go, Kate Monroe!'"

"I'll never forget it." A small smile tugged at his lips.

"That's too bad. I figured out some wording that

would've made that slogan much better. Maybe I ought to consider going into the public relations business with Bufie."

He quirked his brow at her. "Go ahead."

"When you're in the year 1997, and you think back on this time, you'll realize my version would have been more effective."

"How so?"

"My idea of a catchy slogan would be something like, "Matt could have stayed . . . with Kate Kincaid."

"Kate . . ."

"Matt . . ."

She swallowed hard and wrapped her arms around herself, because she wanted to keep on talking and wanted to fling herself into his arms. She couldn't, even though her heart urged her on. One person, no matter how deep her love, could not forge a strong marriage. Matt would have to help. He would have to risk something, too.

"I love you, Kate."

She was praying so hard that she wasn't sure at first whether those precious words were figments of her imagination, or whether she actually heard them. Her eyes were a little misty, too, which made it hard to see if his lips moved.

"I love you." He said it again, and this time there was no mistaking what she heard.

She hurled herself into his embrace.

"I have to ask you something. Henry thought Colonel Cody might let me tag along with you, and I was wondering if—"

"You don't have to ask. Don't you know how much I want you to stay? But what about . . . what about the future? All those women waiting for you? Your businesses?"

"None of that's important. It's only important that you believe me."

"Oh, Matt, I've always believed you, even when you told me I shouldn't. That's why I'm so worried about your houses in all those big cities . . ."

"Kate, they're nothing but houses. Here, with you, I've found a home."

"*We* found a home," she whispered. "Together."

"Together." His fingers traced her lips as if he loved feeling the word as well as hearing it. "Now, will you let me finish my question?"

"Ask away."

"Will you marry me, Kate? Really, truly marry me?"

"I do!"

He chuckled, a low rumble that started deep in his belly and soon boomed around the room. She'd never heard such a happy sound.

"You know something, Mrs. Kincaid? You have a real way with words."

24

Blast from the Past?
by Edna Winay Woodrick
for *USA Today*

NORTH PLATTE, Nebraska. The continuing investigation into the mysterious disappearance of business *wunderkind* Matt Kincaid took a bizarre twist today.

During a press conference called by the prestigious North Platte law firm, Monroe, Merriweather & Quint, spokesperson Tarsy Monroe presented documents allegedly deposited in their office for safekeeping by Matt Kincaid himself.

The handwritten documents detail Kincaid's instructions for the ongoing operation of Kincaid Group holdings, as well as a radical redistribution of his financial empire's earnings. A handful of charities stand to receive a hefty percentage of Kincaid Group's annual profits.

Exhaustive testing confirms that the handwriting and a full set of fingerprints affixed to the documents belong to Matt Kincaid. However, experts are at a loss to explain how the fingerprints and Kincaid's instructions came to be written in ink that has not been manufactured since the late 1800s. The paper also dates to before the turn of the century.

Tarsy Monroe's notarization of Kincaid's signature is written in modern ink.

"Mr. Kincaid and I used different pens," Monroe explained.

When asked how long the astonishing documents had been in their possession, attorney Monroe quipped, "What do you want me to say—that Matt Kincaid handed his instructions to my great-grandfather back in Buffalo Bill's heyday?"

Amid laughter, Monroe would admit no more than his firm has stored Kincaid's papers for "a while." Monroe refused to divulge when Kincaid actually deposited the documents, claiming attorney-client privilege. "Mr. Kincaid does not intend to come forth to defend his position or reveal his whereabouts. He understood that some might question the validity of these documents and so he instructed us to order the necessary authentication tests before revealing their existence. He specified that the documents be released today."

The date marks the one-year anniversary of Kincaid's disappearance. Kincaid, 32, vanished shortly after checking into a motel room, abandoning his personal effects and private airplane. Full-scale air and ground searches failed to unearth any clues, nor has Kincaid made any effort prior to the surfacing of these documents to get in touch with friends or business associates.

"There's no doubt that Matt Kincaid wrote those documents," stated a puzzled Kincaid Group manager, who asked to remain anonymous for security reasons. "The papers contain sensitive financial and product information known only to Mr. Kincaid and his most trusted officials. They also contain key phrases developed by Mr. Kincaid himself—code messages, if you will—that prove his authorship beyond a doubt. Mr. Kincaid understood that a man in his position could be targeted by kidnappers, terrorists, or worse, and he developed certain precautions to thwart anyone who sought to profit from terrorism. These coded phrases indicate that Mr. Kincaid does not expect to return to us, but we can act upon his instructions knowing that we are carrying out his true wishes, and not something that he was forced into writing."

FBI investigators admit to being stymied by today's revelations. "No individuals benefit from carrying out Kincaid's instructions. The charities named as beneficiaries are small, poorly funded, and have no connection to one another. We have no suspects, no leads to pursue, nothing to indicate that Matt Kincaid met with foul play. Frankly, a ransom demand would have given us something to go on. As it is, it sounds like Matt Kincaid simply got tired of what he was doing and decided to become one of the world's largest benefactors."

Those closest to the enigmatic tycoon were heartened by the documents. "Those papers were not written under duress," said Leola Marquette, 57, Kincaid's private secretary. "A lot of thought and planning went into preparing them. I know Mr. Kincaid's style well enough to tell he was happy when he wrote those instructions, very happy."

Marquette declined to speculate on the reason why Kincaid might direct such enormous sums of money toward charities devoted to orphans and abandoned children. The generous bequests contradict Kincaid's hard-nosed, miserly reputation.

Marquette defended her absent employer. "Matt Kincaid keeps his distance, so most people don't realize he's a good man."

"Independent" and "unpredictable" are other traits often associated with Kincaid, she pointed out, which could offer an unconventional solution to his disappearance.

"I hope he rode off into the sunset with a beautiful woman who loves him, and they're living happily ever after."